moment to moment

D'Artagnan Bloodhawke

iUniverse LLC
Bloomington

moment to moment

iUniverse books may be ordered through booksellers or by contacting:

iUniverse LLC
1663 Liberty Drive
Bloomington, IN 47403
www.iuniverse.com
1-800-Authors (1-800-288-4677)

ISBN: 978-1-4917-2137-7 (sc)
ISBN: 978-1-4917-2138-4 (e)

Library of Congress Control Number: 2014901182

Printed in the United States of America.

iUniverse rev. date: 02/04/2014

"NOTHING IS SACRED TO THIS GUY;
HE HAS NO OFF SWITCH . . ."

"Here, at last, is one weirded-out dude who can finally
put the world in perspective. This guy is beyond
the next level; there is no level for this guy."

D'Artagnan Bloodhawke

*****

"I PROMISE YOU'LL NEVER READ
ANYTHING LIKE THIS AGAIN . . ."

"Overwhelmed by the brilliance of the man. The
world will never see the likes of an author of this
caliber for the next five generations."

D'Artagnan Bloodhawke

*****

To the memory of Happy Eyes, for the years that have gone:
You were, and are, the spirit that drives me.

Acknowledgments

TO ALL OF MY ENEMIES; not in any specific order, or according to any possible ranking that might be imposed such as in Hell.

To the screaming, foul-mouthed, high school football coaches who lose site of the fact that they are supposed to be a role model, there to teach a sport, not to win the Super Bowl; you have all met, at least, one of those, I'm sure.

To former bosses that knew it all, despite the fact that they had reached their highest rung on the "Peter Principle" ladder when they reached the third grade. They may have been my supervisors, but they were never my superiors.

To the family institution; whoever said blood was thicker than water had no idea what they were talking about; some of my dearest, truest friends were closer to me than my dysfunctional family could ever have been.

To an assortment of vulgar people (and we've all been prey to them) such as former co-workers who stabbed me in the back; to friends who betrayed me; to all of those "diverse minorities"—that that we hear so much about these days—who showed me that prejudice, bigotry and racism aren't just offenses confined to the Anglo-Saxon race; to those "affirmative action" demigods—who by virtue of their race—denied me (because of my race) a job, and/or a rightfully earned promotion, and who—by their race—took various benefits away from me, benefits they neither earned nor deserved; to the ex-wife, the ultimate betrayal; and generally, to all those who threw additional, unnecessary obstacles in my path for me to overcome. You didn't make it easy; you made me work even harder to get what I earned, but you taught me that I had to strive even harder to make something of myself.

A lot of you were merely ignorant people; some of you were downright despicable and mean individuals; some of you were the stepchildren of Satan; a lot of you were just rude, ignorant souls lost on this earth, wandering aimlessly while trying to drag others down with you. But, whatever you were—if it wasn't for you—I'm sure I wouldn't have had to personally set the bar a lot higher, than I would normally have had to, in order to make it in this world.

Some of you I would like to single out for special attention, as you seem to have gone above and beyond to make my like the ultimate nightmare.

To a father, who was a bully with a short fuse and a gigantic temper, which he could never seem to control; a miserable wretch of a disappointment; a failure of a man who hated the world and found fault with everything in it. Some people bring sunshine into everything they do and to everyone they meet; some just bring pain. He deserves special attention for failing me, my mother and—I am sure—just about every other human being he ever had any contact with. Despite his cruelty and numerous shortcomings, he always thought of himself as a devoted Christian destined for heaven. I just hope there is a God, so that when this frayed, fallow wasteland of a human being meets Saint Peter at those pearly gates, he'll be in for one hell of a surprise. I only wish I could be there to see that. As Clint Eastwood was fond of saying: That would . . . "make my day."

I'd also like to thank organized religion for turning out such a religious zealot as my father. Without these obsessive-compulsive superstitious ritualistic organizations, I am confident the world would have been a happier place and certainly more Christian. We would have definitely fought fewer wars in the name of God (since each particular religion is more than capable of inspiring murder in the name of their own particular "true Savior") and killed, tortured and maimed less people.

Thanks to religion, I now fully understand what hypocrisy, child abuse, pedophiles, charlatans, and "spreading the word of God for profit" truly mean.

I also know that no one religion is any different from another on this planet; they all, individually, profess to "know" God and what

He truly wants us to do to attain salvation. When science proves their doctrines incorrect and false, they simply ignore the scientific data and deny the truth; telling us instead that we should believe in our "faith," not science, to get us through the day. After all, they "know" God (better than science) and what *He* truly really wants us to do to attain salvation. Personally, I believe that if Jesus ever returned to Earth, which I find to be highly unlikely, (Why would He want to come back to this place . . . EVER?), the first thing He would do is torch the Vatican.

And, not to be forgotten, I would like to give a special shout-out to *the* government (notice how I didn't say *my* government). This is not the government I was raised to believe was the greatest in the world, nor does it remotely resemble anything close to what the Constitution and the founding fathers had in mind; rather, it's an endless supply of amoral, lying, thieving, bureaucratic politicians (who I consider one step below child molesters) who defecate in this cesspool of—what they call—a democracy. This institution of the wealthy taxes one to death; steals from the people; spies on its citizens with satellites in the sky; monitors its populace with drones (and believes it has the right to kill fellow Americans, without any due process, if it deems such necessary, for national security); that pries into the lives of its residents with hidden cameras, unauthorized wiretaps and bugs; the Almighty Union that makes it more profitable for generation after generation of the useless, shiftless and lazy to sit back and collect welfare, get aid packages, free lunches and free phones, rather than work to obtain those goods and services; the officialdom that sends children off to meaningless wars to die in the name of patriotism (even animals don't eat their young like our leadership does), so that powerful politicians, corporate heads (of oil companies and banks), and war profiteers can fill their coffers as a result of their deaths; Uncle Sam who allows a living fetus to be thrown in a garbage can, to die alone, in the name of Pro-Choice (nice Uncle, huh?); Washington, D.C., a place that believes that we, the people, exist to support the government. We have become a country without morals—no boundaries, no limits—where anything goes. Thank you, Big Brother, for teaching me to always be on my guard against you, to never trust you—no matter what you say—regarding anything.

All of you prepared me for the cold-hearted, ruthless world out there and I owe you a deep, heart-felt thank you; for, without you, I would never have appreciated the truly wonderful people that did come into my world. Sometimes, it's good to have enemies because, sometimes, a wise man can learn more from his enemies than from his friends. Therefore, I say unto all of my enemies: *"Go forth and multiply,"* but not in those exact words.

You might ask: Why did this guy rant on for a couple of pages like this? I have a philosophy: Anything worth doing is worth overdoing; there is no moderation in life when it comes to satisfying one's appetites. If you're gonna love, love the best that you can. If you're gonna hate, hate the best that you can; and believe me folks, I'm trying—real hard—to do my best here. I don't know about you, but I feel a whole lot better now.

IN ADDITION to my enemies, I'd also like to dedicate this book to those indispensible people—I met along the way—that made life a true joy to go through and, without whom, it would have been a disastrous childhood: my mom, the nurse when I was younger and the peacemaker when I got older; the mother who tried—valiantly—to maintain some semblance of order in a dysfunctional family; a banker, for loans that never needed repaying; a confessor and best friend, who listened to my aspirations and dreams; and lastly, the teacher, who taught me most everything when I was growing up. The only thing she forgot to teach me was how to live without her.

A thanks to my grandmother, who had more than her share of hardships yet, stoically braved them all without the whisper of a complaint.

To my Uncle John, who was a father figure, mentor, and best buddy in my youth and throughout my life until his passing; he made all the difference. I learned so much from him, more than I could ever re-pay . . .

Last, but surely not least, some of the finest friends that one could possibly meet on the way from the cradle to grave. They say that if a man is lucky enough to count on one hand the number of true friends he has after a lifetime on this earth, he is extremely blessed. I consider myself extra lucky to have had more than that as such steady and true friends.

Originally, I had intended to individually list here (by name) some of the people that I have met, along the way, that have made a difference in my life. Then, I realized that:

1) it would be a longer list (much to my delight) than I had originally anticipated

2) I might—unknowingly and unintentionally—omit someone, thus offending a true friend and inadvertently putting myself on his or her enemies list

3) some of my friends may not wish to be grouped together in the same list with my other friends, and

4) I do not have that big of an ego, nor do I want to be so pretentious as to assume that just because I considered certain people to be friends of mine that ergo, I must have been a friend to them; they just might prefer not be recognized by me and, indeed, might very well wish to disassociate and distance themselves from me. Thus, by listing them as a friend of mine might be more of a burden for them to carry around than the compliment it was intended to be.

Therefore, for those reasons, I have decided to omit any such list.

My sincerest regrets to those of you who think I may have forgotten you, due to a sheer oversight on my part, but you know who you are and how much I truly appreciate you. Thank you in every way.

D'Artagnan Bloodhawke
Author's Website: www.DarBloodhawke.com

Author's Note

This is Volume II (the Abridged Version) of ***moment to moment***: a collection of moments, from the profound to the preposterous, inspired by a collection of curious characters, from the innate to the bizarre, and how each lives out the moments in their lives.

In this high-tech, complex, extremely materialistic world, individuals try to plan their futures like a series of pre-ordained steps that, if followed correctly, will lead to a better-than-alright subsistence for them. They seem to be caught-up in how great their existence will become once they attain their goal, whatever it may be that is success to them; be it a thriving marriage, a lucrative job, wonderful children, a magnificent home on the ocean, or a fancy foreign sports car. They forget to figure in the more sinister factors that affect their agendas.

Life is full of surprises to upset one's dreams: alcoholism; drug addiction; the death—at the age of four from leukemia—of that special, and possibly only, child you wanted so badly; the loss of that marriage; that car; that house; that career; and, possibly, your own death which you never figured on. Everyone else dies but not you; not before you get to have your dream come true.

As the masses trek through their years along their paths to fulfillment or what they feel is fulfillment, they miss out on the days of their lives. They forget to watch that special kid of theirs grow up. Or, they don't enjoy their career because of all of the self-imposed stress they put upon themselves.

As John Lennon once said: "Life is what happens to you while you're busy making other plans"; and look what happened to him while he was living large. Or, how about James Dean (bet he thought he would live forever), Marilyn Monroe, J.F.K. or Robert Kennedy.

My point being, having an agenda is fine, but try living life in the moment sometime. Like they say in tennis: Live in the moment, watch the ball, concentrate on what you are doing now, not how you missed that match point three shots before, or what you're gonna do to your opponent on the next shot. It's this shot you're in now that counts.

Life is made up of chapters, like in a book; it is a summary of moments. You are born in Chapter One and get to live a chapter for each year. Some of us, the unlucky ones, never get past Chapter One. Some of the luckier ones make it to Chapter Eighty, or Ninety. It would be nice to get in as many chapters as you can before you exit this world, but it is also about how the book ends. You don't want the last chapter to end with . . . "He died along, one rainy night, in front of the TV with the remote in his hands—without any friends or relatives nearby—and his dogs chewed his feet off from hunger; they never discovered his body until a year later." No one, for a year, even thought to concern himself or herself about how, or where you were. You want that last chapter to have the happiest conclusion as possible, taking into account the occasion.

Life is an odyssey through the unknown, towards the unknown; it consists of moments lived: some special; some not so special; sad ones; happy ones; some embarrassing; some to be truly proud of; some fully lived; some you wished you could live over, lived better or never lived at all.

The past is gone, over; you are never going to get it back. The future's not here and is uncertain at best; you're not sure how much of it you'll even get to enjoy, if any. That just leaves what's left—the now, the moment. Those moments are your life; enjoy living them as you go from moment to moment.

Contents

"To be buried in lava and not turn a hair,
it is then a man shows what stuff he is made of."

From *Malone Dies*
by
Samuel Beckett

*****

One Summer Night

It all started one summer night when Buzz—a.k.a. the Buzzard—Foonut shot the little missus, Bobbi Sue. Oh, he didn't kill her outright, though he might have been trying to; he just sort of nicked her in the left arm. Winged her, to use a pun. It kind of makes you wonder though: *What would drive a man to wanta murder his wife*? But, I wouldn't know; I'm not a "modern man," according to the ex-wife. I'm old-fashioned.

I grew up in an age when boys had peashooters and girls had cooties. We amused ourselves with Lincoln logs and Erector sets. It only cost five cents for a pack of baseball cards, and a pink slab of stale gum came with it. Milk was delivered to your house in glass bottles with cardboard stoppers. War was a card game. It took five minutes for your TV set to warm-up so we could watch Howdy Dowdy and Buffalo Bob and be part of the Peanut Gallery. We talked over party lines, listened to 45-RPM records by Elvis, used metal ice cube trays with levers on them, and stored them in the ICE BOX. Nobody had a purebred dog, but we had roller-skate keys, tinker toys, slingshots and played with popguns that shot real corks. We motored to the drive-in's in a Studebaker and watched the picture shows; and you got two of 'em, along with cartoons, newsreels, and a travelogue—usually one with pretty girls water skiing at Florida's Cypress Gardens, while holding a flag in one hand and one of her legs in the air. And,

1

when we weren't busy doing all that, we drank powered Kool-Aid with granulated sugar and chewed on Bazooka bubblegum. Hot damn!, what a great childhood we had.

Today, kids drink beer and smoke pot (or worse) while watching porn over their satellite TV's. They have every electronic gismo in the universe like cell phones that can dial-up anyone in the world. These mobile devices store memos, notes, books, photos, play games, movies, hold every recorded song since the beginning of time, have a calculator, plus a global positioning device that can track a person to within one foot of their real-time location . . . anywhere in the cosmos. It can tell you the weather in Bombay, how the stock market is doing, connect you to the Internet to surf the web for world news, find statistical information about your favorite teams in any sport, checks your e-mail, and it doubles as a camera that takes both still pictures and video . . . all in living color. It has maps that can tell you where the nearest gas station, restaurant, hotel, amusement park, escort service, sex shoppe, or coke dealer is—along with directions on how to get there. It can be waved over any barcode device—in any store, in any country—to complete any credit card purchase. All this in a phone that is flatter than a flapjack and fits into the palm of your hand. And we haven't even begun to talk about iPads, Xboxes, synthesizers, frequency translators, clock oscillators, crystals, video games, portable signal generators, OCXO's, VCXO's, TCXO's, VCTCXO's, or DRO's. God!, I haven't any idea what all of those initials even stand for.

As for women today: they hang out in crews (like gangsters working for a mob syndicate) at fancy coffee shops—where a cup of Joe cost five dollar a pop—to discuss their hapless, hopeless husbands, or who's having the latest affair. Or else, they gather together, at the local salon, and—while they're having their nails manicured, their toes pedicured, their hairs waxed, their backs massaged, their asses and abs buffed—they all pitch a bitch about how their pathetic, incompetent husbands couldn't find their G-Spot, even with the aid of one of those super-duper, butt-kicking, massive spotlights that producers use at Hollywood premieres. Some of these turbo-bitches with teeth even go so far as to suggest that their spouses must not only be morons, but gay morons to boot, since he can never seem to find that "little man in the boat." And, they are all—all of them—are still . . . still waiting—just waiting—for that elusive "Big O."

As for me? I just wonder what all these women are bringing to this party. But, what would I know? Nothing, according to the ex-wife. I'm "old-fashioned" . . . remember? I guess I must be, for men today, are almost as bad as some of these women.

Men wear their daughter's placentas around their necks, can't drink wine because it makes them too sensitive, and carry a vial of their girlfriend's blood, around their necks, to get in touch with their feminine side.

And what about me? The wife divorced me, so **NOW!**, I'm the "modern man" all right: lonely, depressed, by myself, insensitive to women, and I openly participate in debates with my fellow man as to whether or not women have a soul.

I'm Officer Corky Smidlap of the Manatee Springs PD, but most people just refer to me as "the Cork." I was summoned to the scene of this here "happening" to take the reports, along with my partner, Bucko Johnson, but we just call him . . . "Junior." I guess I had better start at the beginning, that's usually the best place to start . . . at the beginning.

This all happened in Manatee Springs: it's a small town, in the middle of Florida, right above Lake Okeechobee, next to Coconut Gardens. Most of the people here live in *manufactured homes*; they don't call 'em mobile homes any more—gives off the wrong impression, it does. People always poke fun at those kinda folks—trailer trash and all that. I'm sure you know what I mean. Manufactured home sounds so much more refined when you say it: "I live in a . . . *manufactured home!*" See what I mean?

Well, anyway, this all happened in one of those trashy trailer parks with one of those heavenly sounding names, this one being Paradise Cove: it sat right smack on Hagfish Bay and consisted exclusively of retirees: fifty-five years of age and older—no children.

It all started one summer night in mid-September. The Foonuts, who lived at Thirteen Lower Whacker Drive, were watching the weatherman on Channel Six with their bloodhound, Old Blue, when—surprise! surprise!—he told them (the weatherman, not the bloodhound) "to *expect* sum sorta *unexpected* cold snap durin' the night." The temperature was going to dip down into the low sixties.

This, in and of itself, wasn't interesting news; it's just that Bobbi Sue had recently bought herself a few of those Clivia miniatas—is how you say it, I think. It's one of those variegated houseplants that grow them orange flowers with yella throats on 'em. I'm sure you know what I mean, if you're interested in that sorta thing. Real pretty, is what they are, but super sensitive to the cold . . . and cost a pretty penny too! She had several of them, outside on the porch of her manufactured home, just getting the fresh air. However, when she heard that news report, about the cold snap, she got to speculating as to whether or not she should fetch 'em inside.

"So's, whatcha think?" wondered Bobbi Sue.

"Bout what?" replied her husband, as he continued to watch the news and simultaneously read the newspaper.

"Bout what? 'Bout what the weatherman's bin talkin' 'bout, and what we been discussin' here fer the past five minutes. That's 'bout what!'"

The Buzzard peered over the sports page. He had this one milky eye that was pointed all wrong: it looked out of his head at an odd angle and made him appear as if he had something real important working on his mind. "Well, run it by me one more time."

"'Bout my Clivia miniatas, is "'bout what.'"

"What about 'em?"

"My back teeth! Fer land's sake, Buzz, are ya payin' attention ta me or not?"

"Course I am, Peaches." Bobbi Sue was a Georgia transplant. The Buzzard nicknamed her his Georgia Peach, but most of the time he just called her Peaches. "It's about your . . . Clivia mini-sumthin', or other. Well, what'd Doc Procter say?"

"What in the world has the Doc gotta do with this?"

"Well, ya went ta see him, didn't ya?"

"'Bout what?"

"Now who ain't payin' attention?" replied Buzz with a smirk on his face, as if he had her by the short hairs now.

"You! That's who. Why in the world would I go see Doctor Procter about my Clivia miniatas?"

There and then, the man peering over the sports page knew he had just stepped into a big wiz of a cow turd. His mother hadn't raised a completely foolish son. In actuality, he had no idea what she was talking about. Marriage to him was like a bike race: sometimes you're out in front, but most of the time you're just trying to catch up. So, he just continued to smirk, hoping he could bluff his way through this prattling-on of hers.

"Should I bring in my potted plants or not?"

A light bulb went on inside Foonut's head. "Of course, of course. Didn't I jest say ta bring 'em in. Weren't ya listenin' ta me?"

Exasperated, Bobbi Sue dragged herself up from her chair in the living room. "Alright, already. I'll go and fetch 'em in."

"Meanwhile, I'm gonna take me a shower," shot back Buzz, as he sauntered down the hallway.

Several minutes later, Bobbi Sue returned. She lugged in one Clivia miniata, went outside, then lugged in another. As she re-seated herself in front of the TV, she spotted one of those little, green, garden, grass snakes scoot under her couch; it must have been hidden in one of the potted plants and once it warmed up, it came slithering out and under the sofa.

Most people don't know a lot of things in life. Most people don't know that there are more chickens than people in the world; that peanuts are one of the ingredients of dynamite; that tigers have striped skin, not just striped fur; that women blink nearly twice as much as men; that it's impossible to sneeze with your eyes open; that butterflies taste with their feet; that babies are born without kneecaps—they don't appear until the child's between two to six years of age. And most people, including the Georgia Peach, have no idea if snakes—whether they're big or little—are poisonous or not; they just assume ALL snakes are venomous.

"Dadgummit! I am surely headed straight fer damnation. God Almighty Sweet Jesus, protect me! fer I am doomed now. It's the Devil hisself!" she screamed, at the top of her lungs, like some cat caught in the fan belt of a car. She jumped on top of a lounge chair and started to recite the Act of Contrition. "Oh my God, I am heart-ly sorry fer havin' offended Thee, and I detest all my sins, because I dread the loss of Heaven and the pains of—"

It was about here that the Buzzard came charging into the living room in flip-flops with a towel wrapped around his waist. "What in tunderation is goin' on in here?" he demanded to know.

"It's the Devil; it's Satan; it's Lucifer."

"They're all here? Where?"

"Under the couch. Quick, look!"

The Buzzard got down on his hands and knees and surreptitiously peeked under the sofa. It was just about that time that Old Blue came up behind him—sniffing—and cold-nosed him under the towel on his most private of parts. Buzz thought he'd been snake-bit. Oh, I forgot to include on that "What most people don't know" list—that I just mentioned before—that most people don't know that *a jiffy* is an actual measure of time; it's exactly 1/100th of a second and that's exactly how long—*a jiffy*—it took for the Buzzard's sphincter muscle to tighten up to the size of a pinhead. Then he fainted . . . dead away.

Peaches thought he'd had a heart attack, what with the suddenness of his seizure, and dialed 911.

Being the small town that this is, with everybody knowing everyone else and where everyone else lives, the Emergency Medical Technicians—Stubby Butterbolt and Hans Glicker (a fifth generation German)—were there within minutes.

"Ah, we've been fighting again, have we, Mrs. Foonut?" said the German, as he surveyed the scene within the mobile home.

Immediately defensive, Bobbi Sue retorted with: "No, we ain't been fightin' again, Hans Glicker. It jest so happens that Mr. Foonut, here, had a heart attack, is all."

"Oh, is that all. I thought it might be somethin' serious. Like he might need a kidney transplant, or somethin'," interjected Stubby, as he proceeded to help Hans load the Buzzard onto the stretcher.

"On three," said Hans, followed by: "One, two, and . . . *a three.*" It was on "*a three*" that Stubby saw the little, green, garden grass snake and—straight away—dropped his end of the gurney. If Buzz Foonut didn't have to go to the hospital before, he most certainly had to now, for Buzz Foonut had two broken ankles.

After profusely apologizing, Stubby slammed the ambulance doors closed, flipped on the emergency lights, and off they went to the Manatee Springs General Hospital.

The Georgia Peach still had the same problem, though: What to do with that little, green, garden, grass snake in her manufactured home. Improvising, she ran next door to her neighbor, Tony Pipatoni a.k.a. the Pip.

"Now, where did you last see this thing?" he wanted to know, as he strutted into their living room with his macho swagger—a sort of Italian thing—dressed in shorts with Palm tree on them and a wife-beater undershirt; Tony was known as the Sultan of Slick.

"Right there," she said, pointing under the couch.

"No problemo," said the Pip as he rolled up a newspaper, got on all fours, and began poking around under the sofa. Little did the Pip know that that little, green, garden grass snake was gonna turn into one BIG *problemo*. "I'm an old country boy at heart."

"I thought you all was from the Bronx."

"I was. But, it was the upper Bronx, where it's more wilder and untamed."

"Oh."

"Well, it looks safe now. This must be some sort of trick snake, but they know when they're up against a hard case like me," said Tony as he stuck out his chest, then smiled with teeth that were all white and square, like those of a baby shark.

Feeling relaxed, Bobbi Sue sat down on the couch with a sigh of relief. She stretched out, her hand dangling down between the sofa cushions where—surprise! surprise!—she suddenly felt the reptile, wiggling around.

That did it. **That!,** sent her over the edge. She screamed, then fainted—just like her husband had done—and the reptile slinked back under the couch. Tony Pipatoni thought she had a heart attack and dialed 911.

"Two heart attacks . . . in one day! From the same address. Impossible!" exclaimed the dispatcher.

The Pip knelt down, realized that Bobbi Sue had only blacked out, so he tried to revive her by administering CPR. It was right about here that his wife—another New York retread named Bad Betty (appropriately named for her uncontrollable jealous streak)—walked by, on her way home from the market. She was dressed in a pair of Daisy Dukes, pony boots, and a red and orange Hawaiian shirt made out of faux fur with exploding volcanoes on it, like she was the opening act for Don Ho. Daisy Dukes on a sixty-five year-old woman with stringy, bleached-blond hair, wearing heavy make-up, made her look like a Kabuki hooker. She dressed that way because her fantasy in life had always been to become a pole dancer down at the Tingle

Tangle Club, probably inspired from her many-a-youthful night spent in a seaman's bar. I'm sure you know the type; I'm talking here about the psycho bitch from Hell with a butt as big as a weather balloon, who has skin like leather—similar to that of a Galapagos turtle—and thinks she's hotter than a Swedish meatball and smells like a French whore. It's enough to make your toes cool.

And dumb? Oh yeah. She's the type who can't figure out how to do long division and doesn't have the sense God gave a turkey. The only chance her husband had of living a contented retirement was if he took her to Monkey Jungle and prayed that a baboon would kidnap her and make her his queen.

Anyway, she saw her husband in the doorway of the mobile home, lying prone over their neighbor—his mouth to her mouth—in what she assumed to be an extremely passionate embrace. Well, she swelled up like a toad with Mad Cow disease, rushed the trailer—elbows a-pumpin'—like something out of a Japanese monster flick and proceeded to bash her husband over the head with a bag of canned goods. **DING DONG!,** like he was a human piñata, she lacerated his scalp and knocked him unconscious. Then—seeing all the damage she'd inflicted—Bad Betty, having a change of heart and temperament, decided to dial 911 in an effort to show the compassionate side of her nature, just in case she needed to plea for mercy if manslaughter charges were ever brought against her by the State.

"Another . . . HEART ATTACK?!" the dispatcher wanted to know.

"What heart attack ya talkin' 'bout?" inquired the distraught neighbor.

The two Emergency Medical Technicians, Stubby Butterbolt and Hans Glicker, got this call too. They barged back into the trailer, irritated to say the least, and woke the Georgia Peach up from her slumber.

Stubby looked at Tony's wound: "This is gonna need sum stitches," then turned to Bobbi Sue: "Hey, this ain't no taxi service we're runnin' here, you know."

The Georgia Peach managed to get herself upright, saw Bad Betty bent over her husband, but still dazed and thinking he'd been snake-bit too, went into the kitchen, returned with a bottle of whiskey and began pouring it down the Pip's throat.

By now—what with all the commotion taking place in the trailer park: sirens blaring away, ambulances coming and going, and people screaming and hollering—the police were summoned. That's where I came in. Remember me? I'm "the Cork": Officer Corky Smidlap of the Manatee Springs P.D. I arrived, along with my partner, Bucko Johnson, but we just call him, "Junior."

Anyway, when I first got there, the place reeked of hootch and I thought to myself—what with all the blood—that this was some kind of drunken brawl between neighbors; what with Mr. Pipatoni unconscious and gushing people juice all over the floor; Bad Betty picking up the remains from a broken bag of canned goods that were sprawled about the floor; and Mrs. Foonut having this big knot—'bout the size of a cow's bladder—on the back of her head.

"I'm taking you all down to the station house and let the captain on duty sort through this mess," was my first reaction.

"Let me explain," said Bad Betty.

"Please do," I said.

"I'm Mrs. Betty Pipatoni and that there on that stretcher is my husband, my Tony, but we all just refer to him as the Pip."

"How quaint."

"Actually, if you really want to know—for the record—he calls me Hot Pants and I call him the Big Babalooha."

"Well, Hot Pants, what went on here? *For the record.*"

"Well, I was on my way home from the market; I do my shopping there every Friday night. And I looked in here, as I'm scooting by, and I sees my husband—the one being attended to by Stubby and Hans there—and naturally, I just assumed, when I saw my husband—the Big Babalooha—the one hemorrhaging on the stretcher over there, passed out, and smelling of hard liquor—that he was up to no good—

"Naturally."

"—because he was kneeling over Bobbi Sue there and was a tonguing her, like a wild dog in heat, he was. Or, what I thought, at the time, was tonguing her. Course he wasn't passed out then.

"But, I come to find out now that he was just giving her CPR. I'm still a little suspicious though, as this CPR business sounds like something a man would think up when he was caught red-handed by his wife being up to no good."

"Of course. That's the first thing a man would . . . *think up* . . . as an excuse. I know I would, automatically, think that up," I replied.

"Men, sometimes, can fool the stripes off a Zebra," she said. Then, looking towards heaven, she made the sign of the cross and, as if pleading with God, said: "I just wish, God, before I die, if you could please just answer me this one question. Why is it, God, that you gave man both a penis and a brain, but only enough blood to run one at a time?" Then, seeing all the blood flowing profusely from her husband's head wound, she began to snivel. "I just hope I didn't kill him, is all."

This just keeps getting better and better, I thought to myself. Shaking my head, I turned towards Mrs. Foonut, "Now, how'd you get that big knot on your head there, Mrs. Foonut?"

"Jest call me Bobbi Sue, everybody else does, except my husband; he calls me Peaches," then she turned and glared at Mrs. Pipatoni, "which is a little more dignified than . . . Hot Pants, as far as pet names go."

"Well, Bobbi Sue, what happened here?"

"I hate ta put a lid on a great party like this, but we gotta be goin', Officer," interrupted Stubby. "This guy needs sum serious medical attention. I ain't seen nutin' this bad since old man Flucker—that weirdo on the other side of town with those gigantic carbuncles—got puffer poisonin' from all them puffer fish he ett last month. When we finally got ta his place, out on Clownfish Sound, he opens the door—naked—with an axe in one hand and a bottle of Jack Daniels in the other.

"This guy here, now, he needs sum antibodics and he may be concussed, which means we might havta do a brain scandal on him." With that, EVAC departed with the unconscious Big Babalooha, along with the sobbing Hot Pants.

"Well, Bobbi Sue, what happened here?" I repeated

"Well, it all started when I was watchin' the weatherman on Channel 6. He seys 'to *expect* sum sorta *unexpected* cold snap durin' the night,' is what he said."

A pause.

"So . . ."

"So, I asked Buzz if I should bring in my new Clivia miniatas and he seys I should go see Doc Procter."

"Doc Procter? What in the world has the Doc got to do with this?"

"Thems my very words ta him, exactly!"

"To who? Doc Procter?"

"No, my husband. I seys ta him: 'What in the world has Doc Procter gotta do with this?'"

"Well . . ."

"Well, he jest wasn't payin' attention is all. Soon as he realized what I was a talkin' 'bout, he seys: 'Of course, of course.'"

"Of course . . . meaning what?"

"Of course, meaning: I should bring in my Clivia miniatas."

"Of course."

A long pause.

"So . . ."

"So . . . I did."

"And . . ."

"And . . . that's when I spotted one of them little, green, garden grass snakes—that musta been hidden in one of them potted plants—slither out and scoot under my couch."

A much longer pause.

"And . . ."

"And . . . that's when this long nightmare began."

This was like pulling teeth with your fingers, I thought. But, before I could go any further with my interrogation—about the little, green, garden grass snake that Bobby Sue was talking about—it crawled out from under the sofa. And, before I could say anything, Bobby Sue screamed and my partner slapped leather; Bucko Johnson drew and fired faster than my ex-wife and her shyster lawyer could calculate how much back alimony I owed *them*. Too bad Junior's aim wasn't as good as his draw; he missed the reptile and hit the leg on the coffee table, next to the couch. The table fell on its side, sending the lamp—that was on it—pitching into the drapes, which imploded the bulb within the lamp, which—in turn—set the curtains on fire.

Officer Bucko Johnson to the rescue . . . again; he tried to beat out the flames—with his nightstick, of all things—but only managed to smash through the window behind the curtains. Then, he tumbled through the opening—where the window used to be—and onto

Old Blue, who was stretched out in the yard, trying to escape all the mayhem inside.

The bloodhound was startled out of his sleep, for Junior was big. Actually, Junior was fat, not big. Well, maybe he was more like . . . big and fat. To put it bluntly, his shorts were the size of the cover I put over my car at night; he was literally one corndog away from a heart transplant.

Anyway, Old Blue jumped up, so he wouldn't get trampled on and ran into the street, howling; an oncoming car swerved to avoid hitting him and plowed into our squad car, which instantaneously ignited, turned into a roaring inferno, and promptly burned to the ground—tires and all. It was like watching some fiery train wreck in slow motion.

Meanwhile, inside, the fire from the drapes spread onto the wall and the entire manufactured home quickly became unrecognizable as a habitat.

The neighbors immediately dialed 911 and the Manatee Springs Fire Department was dispatched. The firefighters were Johnny-on-the-Spot. So quick, in fact, were they to the scene, that they started raising the ladder on the fire engine when they were halfway down the street. The hook-and-ladder tore out the overhead electrical lines, which knocked out the power to Coconut Gardens and disconnected all the phone service within a twenty-block radius of Paradise Cove.

It was about this time that the two Emergency Medical Technicians, Stubby Butterbolt and Hans Glicker, returned . . . with Mr. Foonut. They were at the hospital when they got the call for another EVAC. Guess where? It was also, about that time, that Mr. Foonut was being released. They figured, *Why not? We're goin' that way, anyhow.*

As Buzz stumbled out of the ambulance on his new set of crutches, and tried to amble around his front yard on his two broken ankles—both in casts as big as snowshoes (he was only too happy to have two broken ankles, instead of being snake-bit on the head of his privates, as he originally thought)—his face went slack and turned the color of meringue. All the hairs on his head stood out; they looked like something you scoured out pans with. As he stood there in a general state of anomie—micturating in a pair of hospital pajamas while gritting his teeth down to the knubs, as if he had some kind of a rodent inside him trying to get out, and his breath smelling like hot garbage—he had this distant look on his face like the Creator had allowed him an inside glimpse into another world, like maybe the seventh circle of Hell. You know, that distant look people get when they swallow a peanut that they can't quite seem to cough up. Either that, or he was straining real hard to remember some secret formula for plastic barf. The only other alternative being that he had some sort of deformed bug up his ass. With that one milky eye, he gave off a real intense, fixed stare like nothing was gonna work . . . ever again.

Old Buzz had lost his capacity to speak, and lapsed into aphasia; you would have needed a marching band just to get him to blink. He looked like clotted milk. This was definitely not a "Eureka!" moment. You could almost see his brain sizzling, like spit on a griddle, as he tried to control the lepers in his head. He was wound up tighter than a crab's ass and didn't need any sharp surprises about now; a fall would have broken him like glass. I'm sure you know what I mean. He was more than a little dinged-up; he couldn't have counted the number of legs on a three-legged cat. All that was needed now was for someone to come along and hose him down like some old circus animal. **THIS!** was Buzz Foonut, the "modern man."

The Georgia Peach ran up to him, clutching one of her Clivia miniatas. The Buzzard looked around the neighborhood, at the disaster, at his burnt-to-the-ground manufactured home, at Peaches clutching that ridiculous plant to her breast, and he thought ta himself: *All this because of a potted plant.*

And then . . . it began to rain.

Buzz looked down into the hot ashes of, what used to be, his home. He just stared and stared, for the longest time, as if he'd just found an ear. Buried in the embers was the .22 semi-automatic he always kept on the nightstand in his bedroom, or what was left of his bedroom. He very gingerly bent down—like a man whose joints had turned to glue and had a roll of quarters up his ass—and slowly picked up the handgun. Just then, he saw that same, little, green, garden, grass snake meander out from under the rubble and scurry towards the high grass. And—without even a thought being given or taken—he turned and yelled: **"HOO-YA!"** in this hellish high-pitched squeal, like his nuts were caught in his fly, and fired at the reptile (or, at least, that's what he claimed he was firing at, afterwards), missing the serpent and nicking Bobbi Sue in her left arm. And that, my friends, is how it came to pass that Buzz Foonut shot the little missus one summer night in Manatee Springs.

I know what you're all probably wondering, *How is old Foonut doing these days?* Well, not to worry. He's doing just fine up there at the Barnacle Bay Sanitarium for the Mentally Insane. I'm not much for all that psychobabble bullshit they talk up there, but from what I hear, he has some sort of "situational disorder" involving a spastic colon that limits his social skills. And, he needs to be helmeted at all times, as they consider him a danger to himself. Whenever someone comes up behind him, he has a tendency to jump like he's spring-loaded. He ain't good for much, nowadays; could never hold a job again, unless it was guessing people's weight at a carnival, or braiding ropes, maybe. That, or working with a rake and birdseed . . . somewhere out in Nebraska. Most days, he just quietly toddles around the grounds, singing softly to himself: *"You gave me nuts, now that's all I am."* I'm not one to psychoanalyze him, but he certainly seems to be a good subject for a professional.

And me? I will never forget that look of surprise on Buzz Foonut's face, as he stood there that summer night in all that rubble—up to his knees—in what used to be his home, clutching that .22 semi-automatic, all charred—the wooden grips singed and still smoking. His last remark, as we led him away to our demolished squad car, was: "Hey! It still works!"

Well, actually, that wasn't his last remark. As we were filling out the paperwork afterwards—amidst the Buzzard's periodic, but rather intense giggling—I did overhear Buzz mumbling to himself in the back of our police cruiser, in a rather loud tone of voice, over and over again: **"UN-F---ING-BE-LIEVE-ABLE!"**

"Life is not a spectacle or a feast; it is a predicament."
George Santayana
1863-1952
Spanish-born American philosopher

*****

"Success is simply a matter of luck. Ask any failure."
Earl Wilson

*****

"I wouldn't be caught dead marrying a woman
old enough to be my wife."
Tony Curtis

*****

"I'm a freak. Touch Me!"
Hot Topic sticker

*****

Gee-Me Gumshoe, Private Dick

I was guzzling down my sixth cup of coffee, as I tore into my third pack of Lucky Strikes. It was 9:05 in the morning and I was recovering from the aftermath of a late night, over-the-top, soirée of binge drinking at the *Pig & Swig Liquor Lounge*, where I go to drink . . . when I'm not drinking at home. I'd only been open for five minutes. I sleep in the back room of my office; it saves on rent money and other frivolous spending. I also like to sleep in the back room because it keeps me near my work and on the job. I'm always "On-The-Job," as they say in the biz. See that sign on the door, the one below that big eye with all the bulging veins in it: *Gee-Me Gumshoe, P.D.* Well, that's me.

Actually, my name isn't P.D. P.D. is what I am. I'm a Private Dick. Gee-Me Gumshoe is who I am. Gee-Me Gumshoe, Private Dick. That's me! That's what's printed on my calling cards, along with that snapshot of a bloodshot eye.

As you can probably tell, I like to live well. I normally spend about fifty percent of my money on drinking, gambling, and whoring around; the other fifty percent I just blow. But, business has been off lately, so I don't have all that much extra money to blow. But, I try to look on the brighter side of life; things could be worse. I could be married; man, I'm not getting' sucked down that rabbit hole ever again.

I felt lucky today. I hadn't had a case in six months; I was due. I hadn't had a date in five years; I was due. I hadn't had sex in . . . in like . . . in like . . . I think Noah had just completed the ark was the last time. I was seriously over-due in that department. Like I was saying, "I felt lucky today."

It wasn't a second after I'd got done telling myself how lucky I felt than in walked this blond, gasping for air. She was horror on a high scale: young and sexy . . . with big breasts. She was my kind of woman. Well, to tell you the truth, any kind of woman is my kind of woman. Don't get me wrong, I'm not one of those swine that is just interested in cheap, meaningless, salty sex like some of those fanatical, chauvinistic, sexist porkers down at the *Pig & Swig Liquor Lounge*. They were like taxidermists; they'd mount anything. Come to think of it, I'm not all that sure that I'm not one of those mooks down at that rum-dum, guzzlery that I frequent; difference is I'm not all that fanatical about it. No more of the old me. I used to ask the gals if they wanted to "make five dollars *the hard way.*" But, I learned that didn't pan out very well as an icebreaker; they thought I was looking at them as some kind of a cheap whore who could suck the nails out of a board. So, now I am much more respectful of women—respectful of their feelings, that is. I always ask them their personal preferences before I *force* myself on them. Usually, I start the conversation with one of my favorite lines: "What particular sex acts won't you do, not even with a gun to your head?" Then, I'd hit them up with my best follow-up question: "How would you like to go over to my place, strip down to your panties and bra, and roll around in hot mud?" See, I have respect for women; I respect their feelings. I'll give you an example of just how hard I try not to hurt the feelings of any woman I date. I usually try to go to bed with two of them at the same time; that way, when I fall asleep, they have each other to talk to. Now, if that's not thinking about their feelings, then I don't know what is. Did I mention she had big breasts?

Some guys claim that women use sex to get men to do what they want. Personally, I say go ahead, use me for all I'm worth. Don't give it a second thought, all you women out there, use every little bit of me up. Use me up, so I'm no good for anything else in life. Use me up 'till I'm too weak to chew gum, or get out of bed to go to the can.

Women say that men use sex to get what they want too. I don't believe that for a minute. How in the world could men possibly use sex to get what they want? Sex is what they want!

The blond in my office, gasping for air, looked every bit the mystery lady. The kind of gal that could convince a guy to drink paint straight out of the can. You could tell, just by lookin' at her, that she'd had beaucoup plastic surgery; if she'd stood next to a radiator, she'd have melted. She was fulminator mercury stacked atop a pair of four-inch heels with legs up to her neck. Long legs are good; did I mention how I like my women double-jointed. Peroxide hair piled high on her head; thick, pancake make-up with scarlet rouge painted all over her face like a circus clown; all of this was poured into a tight, black evening dress—down to the floor—with colored bananas and cherries all over it, slits up both sides and a zipper in the back with the front cut down to her navel. She should be required to get some sort of permit to wear a dress like that. This was the kind of dame you had to keep a bucket of water next to, in case she should suddenly ignite.

She had that cheap look all right, like she'd been banged more than the dinner bell on the Ponderosa. You know the type of dame I'm talkin' 'bout: What vulgar people might call the town pump, dressed up as the Whore of Babylon. She was my type, all right: HOT! This sick, slick bitch was hotter than a whorehouse on nickel night. I made up my mind, right there and then, that I just might have to change the batteries in my smoke alarm—before this day was over—because this babe was just that hot.

She flashed me a smile. Wow! I was in love. And what teeth! She had a full, round mouth of the most gorgeous, whitest, biggest teeth I'd ever seen, outside of this camel I'd seen once in Washington State, at a country fair, just outside of Whiskey Dick Mountain. My brain, or what was left of it, was working overtime. What teeth! I wanted to grab hold of her—right then and there—and count each one of them with my tongue.

Yeah, it was gonna be my lucky day, all right; I could just feel it in my bones. Good thing I had my lucky t-shirt on; the one that said: "I Am that Man from Nantucket; the one your mother warned you about"; that always seemed to strike just the right tone with the ladies.

By now, I was chokin' on my own saliva and nearly swallowed my tongue; I thought about putting a block of wood between my teeth, but my mind was racing faster than Man o' War on a muddy track. I began to struggle with myself like a man caught on barbed wire. Uh, oh. I was beginning to picture her now with a whip in her hand. Then . . . I couldn't feel my feet! This barracuda could make *any* party go! Man, if I could only get this freak mama in my Man Cave, what she could do to me. I'd need a helper monkey when she got done with me.

Easy boy, settle down!, I told myself as I tried to get up, but this bad back prevented me from rising any farther than an inch off the cushion on my rocking chair. Oh, did I mention I had piles and a very—very small—amount of anal leakage?

"How'd I get a bad back?" you wonder.

I fell off a bar stool, in my early twenties, during a fraternity hazing. At least, that's what I tell people. It's a lot easier than trying to explain the gory details about the car accident.

"Car accident?"

Yeah well, I went over a cliff—in my convertible, after a weekend bender—while singing, to my drunken date, at the top of my lungs:

"BABY FACE, I'D LOVE TO SHOVE IT IN YOUR, BABY FACE,

IT'S SO MUCH CLEANER THAN THAT OTHER PLACE, BABY FACE,

YOU GOT MY BALLS A JUMPIN', KEEP THOSE OLE JAWS A PUMPIN'.

OH! . . . OH!! . . . OH!!! BABY FACE . . ."

Oh, Oh, Oh was right . . . until I hit that patch of sand, with those little, tiny-winey pebbles in it; that sorta, kinda, did me in—big time.

After five surgeries, I had lost my strength and spirit to do the horizontal hu-ha, if you get my drift.

Well, enough of this trip down memory lane. Besides, my psychiatrist said I had to learn to forget about the past. "Don't dwell on it," he said. "You don't want the general populous thinking you're an odd turd, do you?" With that said, back to my mystery lady.

She was holding one of my business cards. My cards were very plain: just my name, address and phone number on them. No picture of me. I didn't want the women, that come in here, to be able to pick me out of a line-up.

I gave her the *Glad Eye*. She couldn't escape now; the babe magnet had her in his headlights.

"Mr. Dick?" she inquired.

"Yes. I mean, No." I just love these dumb-blonde types, the dumber the better.

"You're not Give-Me Dick."

Wow! Wow-wee! That did it! My temperature was rising; it was close to the zootch mark. I took out my THINGS NOT TO DO ANYMORE list from my back pocket and quickly ran my finger down it: Don't do Jell-O shots; don't do Karaoke after Jell-O shots; don't drink champagne from your best friend's wife's shoe; don't drink champagne from your own shoe. Nope, she wasn't on the list of Not-To-Do's. Did I mention it was a very short list? And, I already told you how I felt lucky today.

"No," I replied, "I'm not 'Give-Me Dick.'"

She started to leave. I saw my rent money clickety-clackin' out the door, along with my first date in five years. "On second thought, yes. Yes, I am," I quickly added, so as not to lose a potential client.

"You just said you weren't Mr. Dick. Either you are, or you aren't. Which is it?"

"My name's not Dick, it's Gumshoe. And it's not Give-Me, it's Gee-Me. I'm Gee-Me Gumshoe, Private Dick."

She looked at my card, then at me, then at the veiny eye on my office door, trying to figure this out as if it were Einstein's Theory of Relativity; she shrugged her shoulders (I like an athletic woman), then plopped down in the chair next to my desk. "Well," she muttered, "I guess you'll do." Did I mention how I like decisive women?

The lady in black pulled out a cigarette case from her bejeweled purse, open it, and put a long, trim Virginia Slim between her choppers. Her lipstick was so thick it immediately left a queen-size imprint on the lung duster. "Match me," she commanded as she snapped her fingers which, I might add, is pretty nifty trick with gloves on.

"Excuse me?" was all I could muster-up; I was dumbfounded and still focusing on the intense, bright red lipstick impression wrapped around her cig.

She pointed to the tip of her coffin nail and repeated: "Match me."

Catching on (My mother didn't raise a complete fool); I fumbled for the Zippo in my desk. Then, this very dark thought passed in front of my brain. *Hey, wait a minute*, I though. *This broad's had so much surgery to her tits that if I light a match next to her, she just might go up like the Hindenburg.* I was so nervous—thinking about the impending detonation that just might take place in my office, at any moment—that I completely forgot about the lit butt dangling from my own lips; forgot about it until the ashes fell on my hand and burnt me. I banged my potato grabber trying to get it out of the desk, that's when she took the smoke outta my kisser and lit her cancer stick off it.

"Thanks, Bub" was her reply as she tossed my lit cigarette into the trashcan. I poured the remainder of my coffee after it; Smokey the Bear would've been proud of me. "I didn't catch your name," I inquired.

"Huda Kookalova." She punctuated her name with a smile. "My *close* (a pause and another smile) friends call me, "Puffer." With that, she tilted her body back in her chair and blew enormous smoke rings into the air like Popeye, the Sailor Man.

"Puffer, huh?" was all I could lamely reply; then, I blurted out: "My frat brothers at Greasy Rock nicknamed me Road Dog, right before they kicked me out."

She stopped puffing. "Let me ask you something, Road Dog."

"Fire away, Puffer."

"How'd you get your real name, the one on the door over there?"

"Actually, my first name is Jimmy. I dated this cupcake from Paris for ten years. She had the most intriguing accent; instead of callin' me Jimmy, she'd say: 'Gee-Me.' It wasn't until after she dumped me that I found out she wasn't a Frenchy at all; rather, she spoke with a lisp. But, I'd gotten so attached to her pronunciation of my name that I went before a judge and had it legally changed from Jimmy to Gee-Me." I figured I wouldn't bring up the fact that, technically, my real name wasn't even Jimmy Gumshoe; that would only complicate things much more.

My real, real name was Erazmo Throckmorton . . . the Third. It must be obvious to you now, as to exactly why, I changed my monocle to Jimmy Gumshoe, then to Gee-Me: my folks totally hated me, and I can prove that in a court of law. My parent's names were John and Jane Smith; yet—despite the simplicity of their names—they went to extraordinary lengths, when christening me, by giving me a completely different last name. Maybe they were trying to distance themselves from them, as they could see, even at that early of an age (only several minutes old), that I was destined to be trouble. Personally, I'd like to know, which one of them, came up with the idea of "the Third."

"It took you ten years to figure out she wasn't French? Why didn't you just ask her?"

She had me there. I looked at her sheepishly. Huda continued. "I never knew a person who had a hyphen in the middle of their first name."

"It gives it more of a European flair, don't you think?"

Kookalova had a deeply concerned look on her face. "Why'd you become a Private Dick?"

"With a last name of Gumshoe, what else could I do for a livin'?"

"Plenty!"

She had me again.

"Well, you didn't climb up fifteen flights of stairs (that should explain why [the pigeons, the chumps, the crackpots,] my clientele are so out of breath when they finally get to me, and why I ain't had any in six months) to talk about my name. What can I do for you, Doll Face?"

"Speaking of all those stairs, when did the elevator take a dump?"

"'Bout twelve years ago."

"Isn't that a fire hazard?"

"You're tellin' me! Hey, with my emphysema, it takes me about an hour and a half to get up them stairs in the morning, even with a cane." I fired up another Lucky. I saw her give my gimp stick a surprised look; I figured I'd cut her off at the pass. "Trick knee," I confessed. "Got it playin' Powder-Puff Football. So, what's your beef, Girlie?"

"Excuse me?"

I decided to give her my best, apple-butter bafflegab covered in flapdoodle, along with a simultaneous and prolonged *Glad Eye*. "You know, let's get to the Sixty-Four Thousand Dollar Question." I was met with a blank stare. "You know: What' the skinny? You in some serious Jell-O or what? Give Gee-Me the bad news.

"You behind the eight ball, boxed in, over a barrel, or in a bind? You in a fix, a jam, on the lam, or in a hole? Usually, my advice to clients, who tell me they're in a hole, is to stop digging.

"So, you in a pickle, hot water, deep shit, or just up the creek without a paddle? You in a tight spot, hot spot, or a tough spot? You comin' undone, unglued, or unzipped? You between a rock and a hard place, got your tail in a gate, or your tit in a wringer?

"We in for some tough sleddin' ahead. We caught in a squeeze play, or is this caper nothing more than a little hot grease for the old Road Dog?

"Let's open Pandora's Box and see what we got in there: a can of worms, a kettle of fish, a hot potato, a can of peas, or just another cold turd.

"It's multiple choice time: pick one or all of the above, sister. You messed up, screwed up, hung up, hard up, jacked up, jammed up, or worse of all: Did you, by chance, buy a ticket to the Big Empty? Which is it?" My *Glad Eye* was twitching like a whore in church, waitin' for the lightning to strike, when I finished with that little bit of rag chewin'.

"Mr. Gumshoe, is there something wrong with your eye?" she wanted to know. Me—with the bad back, piles, emphysema, and trick knee—felt for my eye, hoping against all hope that I hadn't suddenly developed yet another earthly affliction. She was right! My left eye, the one without the patch over it, was twitching like a Spider monkey hopped-up on Mountain Dew. But, after feelin' around a bit, I smiled through my gaped teeth (too many Jaw Breakers at an early age) when I fancied my vision still intact.

Sensing that I had some serious clinical issues that I was still dealing with, Huda Kookalova got up to leave. Again, anticipating the loss of an easy mark, I managed—this time—to rise up out of my chair. It was here that I noticed my fly was open. *Hell's Bells! Must have dressed a little too quickly this morning*, I thought. *Don't want to scare her off so early in **our** date.* In my mind, I had subconsciously begun to label this interview: Our First Date. Almost in tears, I called after her: "Wait! **PLEASE!**" The combination of urgency and desperation in my voice—and probably the impending expectation of seeing a grown man so emotionally humbled, groveling, frustrated, and crying—most likely brought her back. And, I do get emotional at times; you should have seen me at the end of "<u>Free</u> <u>Willy</u>." Trying to pick up the loose ends and salvage this clambake, I babbled on: "So, what's haps?"

"Haps?"

"Happening. What's happening? You know, like—" She held up her gloved hand for me to stop. "Let's not go there again, please. I get it; I get it," said the Puffer. Only one of her hands had a glove on it. She was wearing a formal, long-sleeved, opera glove up to her left elbow; the fingers on her other flipper were all individually swaddled in blue Band-Aids. The lacerations didn't look too bad; I'd been cut up worse just havin' sex.

Shaking, she reached into her cigarette case and pulled out another Virginia Slim. I fumbled through my desk for that elusive lighter, but Ms. Peroxide waved me off; instead, she pulled a gold lighter out of her handbag. I immediately sensed a big fee. "A gift," cooed the Puffer as she lit her own cigarette; this time Popeye, the Sailor Man skipped the smoke ring show. "I want you to conduct a thorough background check on my boyfriend," she explained. "Well, actually he's my fiancé. I'm engaged to be married and well, you know,"—here she looked pointedly at me; me, sitting there on my piles—"I don't wanna marry a loser."

"Funny; that's what my ex-fiancé said about me. That and how I wouldn't commit to a *serious* relationship. I said I would. Actually, when I said I would, I taught she had said I wouldn't commit to a *series* of relationships. (I was a little hard of hearing at times due to a punctured eardrum I acquired while playing golf when I was a teen.) Next, she wanted to know when. Well, she had me cold there on that one. I just stumbled and stammered about so much that she left me. Her last words, out the door, were: "When? I'll tell you when. When you're in a nursing home, that's when you'll finally decide to settle down and have some kids."

Okay, back to the subject at hand, I thought to myself; I was beginning to drift off there a tad.

I repeated her request: "A background check, huh?" Befuddled, I added: "You mean, like follow him around and things?" That meant I'd have to leave the office.

"If that's what it takes, that's what I mean."

"Let me ask you something, Puffer. Do you suspect him of anything?"

"Like what?"

"I don't know. Like, maybe he drinks too much. Runs around with other women. You know, the typical things *all* guys do." See, I was being to wonder what violence might lie ahead for me. In today's age, women have not only reached equal rights, they have far surpassed them. They have become a violent breed. Believe me I know all about violent women. I was once shacked-up with a Mexican spitfire named Lupe Gomez, but that's another story best saved for another time.

You read about their foofaraws and rampages every day in the newspapers: how this woman cut off her husband's big toe with an axe while he was barbecuing chicken at the family picnic. She calmed, in court, that it was "all a silly mishap" and that she was merely chopping up some more wood for the fire; never mind, he had a mistress and three children by another woman. "That had nothing to do with this; this is all one big mistake!" she protested on her way to the Big House.

Or, you read about the woman that claimed her boyfriend accidentally shot himself, six times, while he was checking the deer rifle (making sure it had a full load) that he was going hunting with the next day. He got a full load all right. I can't help but wonder what in the hell he must have done to deserve that.

Women, in the old days, would just sit and pout in a corner while viciously mumbling under their breath, all the while gnashing and grinding their teeth together, when their husbands had an affair; now, they arm themselves and not just seek total revenge, but only an abundance of mayhem and disfigurement, along the way, will satisfy their thirst for blood. Whatever happened to: "Vengeance is mine," said the Lord. Personally, I don't believe a person should be fooling around with knives and firearms in the bedroom. Period!

Women have become equal all right; equal opportunity murders. It's come to the point where a fellow has to sleep with one eye open at night, least he wake up with his testicles in a mayonnaise jar next to the nightstand. Women have added a new meaning to the phrase "safe sex." It used to mean protection; well, it still does but, in a new way. It's no longer about whether the guy is wearing a condom or not, but rather if he's wearing a bulletproof vest.

"Who cares if he drinks or whores around? I want you to initiate a complete background check on my Sugar Daddy and see if he has any money. And I mean: REAL MONEY!"

The light bulb inside my head flickered on; it flashed, *GOLD-DIGGER!*, in neon. She looked like the type that could steal the gold outta your teeth while you were chewin' gum. I, however, saw a chance to get rich. "That'll cost ya."

"How much?"

"Some big bucks, as they say. Mucho dinero. Big-time do re mi. I'll need a bankroll, some foldin' green, a little happy money, a few smackers, something for my poke. Some scrip, wampum, dead presidents, shekels, rubles, a big boodle of moolah—whatever the market will bear. Some—"

She held up her gloved hand and waved me off, again. "I get the picture. It's just that I'm not a very wealthy woman . . . yet."

Here it comes, I thought.

"I mean, I hope to be someday, but—as of yet—I'm still a struggling, young woman trying to make her way in this cruel world."

I saw the handwriting on the wall: No squeezing this tomato. "How 'bout five hundred to get us started?"

"Five hundred . . . DOLLARS?"

"Of course, dollars" I responded. "What'd you think I had in mind . . . Confederate money?"

It was here that the blonde-haired circus clown threw up her nose and went sideways: She fainted, dead away. This was a real inconvenience for me as I had all this trouble getting up and out of my chair. Somehow, I managed to get my hands on a bottle of water and lightly sprinkled some onto her face. As she came out of her faint, I thought: *This ain't gonna work and bein' how I hadn't had much to eat in the last few days, I'd better lower the ante.*

"How 'bout a six-pack of Bud and a TV dinner?"

As she got up off the floor, she eyeballed me with a rather dubious look, as if the cheese had slipped off my cracker a long time ago. "I was hoping you'd do it pro boner."

I looked down at my fly, which I distinctly remember closing. "Pro what?" was all I could think of to say.

"Pro boner. You know . . . for free. That's what lawyers do."

"They do? To tell you the truth, I never heard of lawyers doing anything for free, and I think you mean pro bono, which I can't afford to do, at the moment."

Looking one more time at the eye on my door, she exited through it. I yelled after her: "Don't you want me for your Private Dick?!"

"Hiring you would be like going deer hunting with an accordion," she yelled back.

She had me yet again. And now, she was gone forever. This entire episode seemed to have, somehow, sizzled up in my face.

There went any hope of me having hot monkey sex. Ah, it probably wouldn't have worked out, anyway; Huda Kookalova was nothing but another money grubbin' kook . . . I sure could've used that six-pack though, I thought. And talk about hungry! I'd been on a budget, lately. I was cutting back on a few of the frills in life . . . like water.

As I reached down, to hunt through my trash basket (I just knew I threw a little bit of left-over doughnut and some Garbanzo beans in there last week), I slid off the cushion on my rocking chair and landed on the floor with a THUD. I gathered myself up, checked my vital signs (I had to be bleeding . . . somewhere), when a sudden brainchild burst forth: *Man, I gotta take a whiz, BAD!* I had a friable bladder to go along with all my other infirmities.

Well, my body may not be in the best of shape, but—at least—I've still got my mental health. I knew all about emotional maladjustments. I once read an article by a clinical psychologist in an issue of the

Journal of Medical Ethics where this shrink proposed that happiness should be classified as a psychiatric disorder, arguing that happy people suffer from impaired judgment that prevents them from acquiring a realistic understanding of their physical and social environment.

But, all things considered, I've got a lot to be thankful for in life. I should get down on my knees, if only I could (an arthritic kneecap prevented that), and thank my lucky stars I don't belong to *that* group of people . . . happy, mentally ill people. I cracked a smile from ear to ear: Gee-Me Gumshoe, Private Dick—that's me!

"Nothing is foolproof with a sufficiently talented fool."
Bumper sticker

*****

"Fools get away with the impossible."
Robert Mitchum
from
His Kind of Woman

*****

Plato Kohlslaugh– Polak Daredevil

"Hey, Doc! Take a gander at this guy on the gurney they're wheeling in now," giggled Ms. Birdie Waters; Betty (Elizabeth was her given name), but everyone at Allegheny General just called her Birdie. Birdie was Black, a droll spirit, and a blithe survivor of the cosmos, but her forte was an uncanny ability, coupled with the acumen, to see the world for what it was; not as a stage—as Shakespeare would have you believe—and we are not mere actors making exits and entrances, playing many parts. From her perspective, as a nurse in the emergency room for the last thirty-five years, this was no game. She knew the universe wasn't full of noble sentiments and ping-pong balls. This could be one cruel world from which you exit in a hurry, if you weren't diligently paying attention to the minutest of details; and, sometimes, the last part you ever get to play is that of a sorrowful victim on a lonely operating table in some mysterious hospital, surrounded by strangers in white surgical masks and green scrubs, wondering: *Christ in high heels! Whatever made me think that ugly-lookin' dude with one arm, dressed in camouflage pants, a tank top and wearing a black ski mask, while maniacally whirling around a double-barreled shotgun in the 7-Eleven (that I just happened to walk into for a cup of coffee and a jelly roll on my way to the office) and simultaneously screaming,* **"I'M GONNA KILL ALL YOU MOTHER FUCKERS!"** *at the top of his lungs, was just some poor misunderstood underprivileged minority—one of God's little children who was just temporarily down on his luck—and would never shoot me in the stomach like this, leaving such a big-ass hole in it?* And, as you fade into the sunset, your last thought is: *"I wonder what Hell is gonna look like? Gonna be there in about ten seconds."*

Doctor Mohammad Mahmood—an austere Pakistani who only recently immigrated to Pittsburgh, after passing his Pennsylvania medical boards—got up from behind the desk at the nurses' station, where he'd been reading the chart on a seventy-six year old father; father—as in priest from three counties away—who would never have ventured into his local hospital, not in the condition he was in. It seemed the reverend was a Viagra addict who tooled in with his *Johnson* wedged in the hose of a Hoover ("The cleaner that puts you in charge of how, when, and where you want to clean") vacuum cleaner (the Self-Propelled Wind Tunnel Ultra Upright Bagless model), along with a smokeless candle that was partially melted into his old vestibule. In a singsong Middle East accent, the Pakistani intern—who was wearing a black patch over his left eye, due to light sensitivity from the lingering effects of pink eye—replied: "Yes, Nurse. Where is this gentleman?"

"Over yonder," snickered Birdie as she pointed to a man in his late thirties with premature white hair. He was dressed in bedraggled, grayish-green tights, knicker lederhosen (leather trousers)—held up by suspenders—and a jester's cap, complete with jangling bells. Oh, yeah. The jester was being held upright, by two male orderlies, because of the arrow lodged in his head. "You don't see sumthin' like that every day." A pause. "He sorta looks like a young Steve Martin, don't he?" remarked Birdie.

"How do you know this Steve Martin, already? He just gets here."

"I don't. What I said was, 'He sorta looks like a young Steve Martin.'"

"Who is this young Steve Martin? Is he Billy Martin's brother?"

"Billy Martin? You mean that guy in the seventies who was the manager of the Yankees?"

"Who these Yankees? Like 'Damn Yankees?' Like Yankees in 'Gone With the Wind?' Those Yankees?"

"No, the baseball Yankees."

The M.D. scratched his head and muttered, "Bazeball? Bazeball? What is this bazeball? I mean the Billy Martin who sing all those Eyetalian love songs on my records."

"You mean Dean Martin?"

"Who is this Dean Martin?"

The R.N. shrugged and wondered how this immigrant ever got a medical degree. "Never mind. It's not important. I got a feelin' we could be here all day.

"We'd better go over and look into William Tell's head there; see if he's got any wetware inside, or just applesauce."

As the doctor and nurse approached their new patient, down the aisle scurried a blond in her twenties, dressed in a Swiss maid's outfit like Heidi; she looked like she just came from a full day of milking cows and churning cream into butter. "Plato, Plato. You feeling any better, babe?"

The befuddled man, holding the arrow in his head, looked up from the fog he was in. "Not much. You park the car alright?"

"Don't worry about that silly, old car; it's okay. I mean, how can you hurt a twenty-year-old Yugo? Brand-new, it cost less than $4,000.00," said Heidi.

Snatches of conversation could be overheard from two male orderlies, who were scurrying around and straightening up the emergency room: changing bed sheets, sweeping around—over and under medical equipment—tossing out ripped-up pieces of what were once garments (now soiled with blood, excrement, and various gastric juices) into hazardous waste disposal containers.

ORDERLY # 1: "I never met her before. A friend introduced us at one of those oxygen bars that serve herbal teas and rice cakes. You know, those places that charge you a dollar a minute to suck down O2 through some plastic tube called a cannula. Can you believe it? They sell you flavored air: peppermint, bayberry, cranberry, wintergreen—whatever you want. She looked like she might be some fun, so I asked her out."

ORDERLY # 2: "Uh-huh."

The R.N. nudged her boss, "We got us a real combo here with Robin Hood and Maid Marian."

"Ssshh," replied the general practitioner, then turned to his new patient. "I am Doctor Mohammad Mahmood. How can you help me?"

The Tyrolean couple looked at each other, dumbfounded.

"He means: How can he help you?" proffered Ms. Waters, by way of explanation.

The Swiss maid was first to regain her composure and speak. "What are you, his interpreter?" Without waiting for a reply, she turned toward the intern. "Are you the duck that runs this place?"

"Precisely," said the physician, then he smiled.

A short pause.

"Well Doc," continued Heidi, "in case you haven't noticed, my boyfriend just happens to have an arrow in his head!"

"Precisely," responded Mahmood, again . . . then he smiled, again. A big, wide smile that showed glittering, pearly whites that twinkled like stars in the sky on a clear night. He just stood there. Smiling.

The young Steve Martin attempted to smile back, through what was left of a smile: his front four choppers were missing.

The M.D. gasped, then whistled. "Holy Cow!" he blurted out. "You don't get teeth like those from standing still."

After an extremely long pause, Maid Marian continued. "You have no idea how hard it was to get here, crammed in that old Yugo with my main squeeze and total babe here—he's a hottie—hanging half out the window with the wind blowing in and—"

"Who squeeze your babe? Where your hot baby on fire?"

"He's," pointing to her hottie, "my baby."

"Oh, that kind of baby. I see. I see. Why was your *baby* hanging half out the window?"

"The arrow wouldn't fit in the car with the window closed and we didn't want to dislodge it for fear of damaging something inside his head."

"He needn't have worried on that account," interjected Birdie.

ORDERLY # 1: "Boy! That just goes to show you how wrong you can be about somebody; they don't turn out to be what they appear to look like they're gonna be . . . sometimes. I mean, this woman just couldn't take a joke. I wasn't really gonna rape her. What did she think I was? Some kinda barnyard animal?"

ORDERLY # 2: "Uh-huh."

The blond nervously was twisting her hair into knots. "Yes . . . well, we made it this far. My name is Gretchen and this is—"

"Plato. Plato Kohlslaugh (pronounced Coleslaw), Polak Daredevil," interrupted a brassy Robin Hood as he whipped out a calling card from his tights and handled it to the physician.

Mohammed stepped back and squinted at the card.

Geez, in addition to being an idiot, we got us a one-eyed surgeon who looks like a pirate to boot, thought Maid Marian.

"Kohlslaugh. Like in the shredded cabbage?" asked the pirate.

"The same," blathered the young Steve Martin.

The nurse leaned over and whispered in the doctor's ear, "Polak Daredevil? Isn't that an oxymoron?"

"I heard that!" exclaimed their patient.

"Ssshh," murmured Long John Silver to his parrot.

"That's okay. I've heard all the jokes. Oxymoron, huh? Did you hear the one about the Polak kamikaze pilot who flew forty-eight successful missions?"

ORDERLY # 1: "I mean, I just stuck it up through the bottom of the popcorn box is all—when she wasn't lookin'—as . . . sort of a gag. It was dark in the theatre and the movie was a dud. That ain't no rape. Everybody knows that!"

ORDERLY # 2: "Uh-huh."

"So you're Polish, are you?" continued the Pakistani as he physically examined the injury to his patient's head.

"Full blooded, and I'm proud of my heritage. In fact, if you'll take a closer look at my card, I even bill myself as a Polak. That's how proud of the fact I am."

The general practitioner scrunched another squinch at the card. "It says on here: 'The best *this side* of the Monongahela.' Which side?"

"Which side what?"

"Which side of the Monongahela River are you the best on?"

"That's just an expression: 'The best this side of the Monongahela.' I got gigs all over the West Virginia Hillbilly Circuit."

Nurse Waters quickly posed a question, which was just as quickly followed by an opinion. "What's that mean? All them . . . *gigs and circuits* with hillbillies. I heard about them. That's some kinda sexual thing with them peoples down there, all havin' intercourse with farm animals, ain't it?"

Kohlslaugh looked at her rather suspiciously. "What was your name again? Dirty Waters?"

"Birdie Waters!" she corrected him.

Ignoring her, the Pole continued palavering with the intern about his peripatetic lifestyle. "You know, places like: Beech Bottom, West Virginia—population 606; and Paw Paw, 524; or Lost Creek, 467; and don't forget Harper's Ferry—population 307. Harper's Ferry is kinda famous. That's where they caught up with that John Brown abolitionist fella back in '59 and hung him from a tree."

"They were still hanging people from trees in this country in 1959?" inquired the physician.

"No. In 1859. And maybe it was a scaffold."

ORDERLY # 1: "She didn't have ta go start all that screamin' and hollerin'. I mean, right in the middle of the flick. People were tryin' ta have a good time, includin' me, is how I looked at it. And she goes and ruins it."

ORDERLY # 2: "Uh-huh."

"And what are you *the best* at?" wondered the MD.

"The best daredevil, of course. I mean, I do it all."

"By *all*, what do you mean?"

"Prestidigitation and Death-Defying Feats of Magical Disbelief. That's what I like to call 'em."

"I can believe that disbelief part 'cause I'm still havin' trouble believin' that dart in your head there," butted in Birdie, as she twanged the feathered tip protruding from his cranium. "But, what is that presti—, presto—whatever part?"

"Prestidigitation. It's defined as the performance of tricks by quick, skillful use of the hand."

"You must still be practicin' them, 'cause with that big dart in your noggin you don't look like you're too quick . . . or too skillful."

Pushing forward, William Tell explained. "Those people— back there in the woods of West Virginia—are in such dire need of entertainment, any kind of entertainment, that they don't much care what I do. Nevertheless, to succinctly answer your question, I perform

Prestidigitation and Death-Defying Feats of Mystical Disbelief in gas stations, bowling alleys, behind outhouses—

"*In* outhouses?" asked Ms. Waters with an angelic smile on her face.

"—places like that," continued the bohemian patient without missing a beat. "They draw the line at too much violence. Sometimes, with all the blood and cussin' from me over my self-inflicted wounds, a lot of the little kiddies run from the tent in a frenzy, shriekin' like all hell fire. Them little ones don't hold up well when you accidentally sever one of your major arteries and that red people juice comes a pourin' outta your veins, all over the place. I can't begin to tell you, Doc, how many times I've been told to come back when I've perfected my act a little better. I try and warn 'em. At the beginning of each performance, I tell 'em how I am a *professional*—"

"A WHAT?!" interjected Birdie.

"—and don't be tryin' this at home. But, do you think they listen? Naw. You know, Doc, as a side-note, a lot of them small towns don't have no hospitals in 'em at all. I nearly been done in several times by the lack of proper medical facilities."

ORDERLY # 1: "I told her: 'You're actin' like a fool.' That's what I told her, over all her screamin' and hollerin'. 'You're actin' like a fool, I says.'"

ORDERLY # 2: "Uh-huh."

Cutting some of the audacious thrill-seeker's hair away, the intern continued. "Like, what are some of these death-defying things you do? Like, give me an example of what you were trying to do here when you got this missile stuck up into the side of your head like this, for instance."

"That was partially my fault," cut in his assistant.

"How's that, Miss?"

"I sneezed at the last minute when I let it fly."

"Oh! So, you shot him?"

Kohlslaugh turned to his archer who started sniveling. "Now, now. Don't blame yourself. If I wasn't blindfolded, I could have gotten out of the way."

"BLINDFOLDED?!"

"It wouldn't have been no death-defying feat if I could see, now would it, Doc? You forgot who you're dealing with—"

34

"I didn't," murmured Ms. Waters.

"—here. I'm livin' in the Big Time."

"Well now, slap my ass and call me Sally. Did you hear that, Doc?" The RN poked her boss in his ribs. "He's livin' in the **BIG TIME**! And he's got a **BIG TIME** dart in his **BIG TIME** head to prove it."

"What exactly were you trying to do here?" wondered the physician.

"I was trying to catch an arrow in mid-flight, which was traveling at 135 mph, with my right hand . . . while blindfolded."

"Piece of cake," muttered Birdie.

"What is the trick?" inquired the MD.

"Obviously, there ain't one, Doc. Look at him!" exclaimed the nurse.

"Ah, but there is. I rely solely on my sense of hearing," protested Kohlslaugh.

"You must be deaf then," suggested the RN.

ORDERLY # 1: "She didn't have ta go callin' them cops the way she did. You know how embarrassin' that was when they turned them lights all the way up in that theatre and went down the aisles lookin' fer me?"

ORDERLY # 2: "Uh-huh."

"Gretchen stands seventy-five feet away from me," explained the Guru of Abracadabra. "I remain relaxed, focusing on nothin' but sound. I hear the string go twang, and when I perceive the feathers go whiz through the air near me, then—"

"You musta not heard that last whiz too good." Ms. Waters smiled.

"—I know where the projectile is, and I merely reach out my hand and grab it."

"That's simple enough. You're in the wrong line of work, Doc. Why don't you give this Bohunk here a run for his money? Call yourself Doctor Mohammad Mahmood—Pakistani Daredevil. Call yourself 'The Best on the *other* side of the Monongahela', and do all them Presti-whatever and Death-Defying Feats of Magical Disbelief on the Doctors' and Nurses' Circuit. You could do surgery with a blindfold on."

"What are some of the other feats that you do, Mister Polak?" asked the intern. "You seem to have some serious scars on your body that are very hard to disbelieve."

"Scars! You wanna see some scars, Doc?" spouted the *professional*. "Wait'll we get around to takin' my clothes off. I'll—"

"Can hardly wait," interjected Birdie.

"—show you some real scars, then! Right, Gretchen?" She nodded. "Let's see. Some of my feats." A pause. "Well, let's see. What are some of my simpler tricks?" A light bulb went on in his head. "I can suck spaghetti into my mouth and blow it out my nose."

"So could all my kids . . . But, I'll tell you where you could 'blow it out' of that would really grab my attention fer sure," blustered the RN.

"Ssshh," said her boss.

Feeling challenged, the feckless adventurer pushed on: "I can burp at over one hundred decibels." He looked at Ms. Waters for approval. She lowered her eyebrows. "Keep goin'. I'll let you know when you hit somethin' my kids ain't never done."

"I can squirt milk outta one of my eyes while lifting a sixteen-pound bowling ball by my testicles."

"That must make for great public entertainment."

"I once skewered one of my biceps like a shish kebab over a hot barbeque."

Birdie piped up, **"On purpose?!"**

"Of course, on purpose. Ya gotta take some chances in life, if ya wanna run with the big dogs."

"None of my kids *ever* done that!"

Feeling proud of himself, at finally having achieved some measure of success in the nurse's eyes, the beleaguered hotspur plunged forward with his braggadocio. "I can balance a running lawn mower on my face. Juggle chainsaws.

"Now, mind you, I ain't sayin' I was always successful on my first try at these stunts. But, I did do them."

Gretchen pulled on his leotards. "Well, at least he attempted them. At least, once," murmured his assistant.

"I know! I almost escaped plastic wrap mummification. Thank God, Gretchen was there that time." She sympathetically patted his shoulder as he grinned back at her through his gapped teeth.

"Once I escaped from a washing machine—that was in full operation—while restrained in handcuffs and leg irons. How 'bout that?!

"And you heard of doing a wheelie on a motorcycle. Well, I did—what we, professionals in the business, call—a *'stoppie'*, at over 100 miles per hour. Of course, that wall did help me . . . somewhat.

"And I once dove off a platform from thirty-nine feet up into six inches of water. Now, that one, even I'll never try again!" He was directing his right index finger to where his front teeth used to be when he made that last remark.

ORDERLY # 1: "They never would have found me hidin' under them seats if it wasn't fer that little bugger of a kid who kept pointin' at me with his Popsicle."

ORDERLY # 1: "Uh-huh."

"Well, Mister Polak, there is an ancient proverb in my country that says: 'If true happiness can only be achieved through a state of nothingness, you are going down the right path,'" quoted the Pakistani.

"What does that mean, Doc?"

"It means: It's time to pull up our socks and get outta here, is what it means," volunteered the RN.

"Huh?"

"It's almost time to get off-duty, which means the Doc here can go home and listen to all his records by that *Eye-talian* singer, Billy Martin."

"Lean back now, Mister Polak," said the MD. "Hang on to the side of that litter there, real tight now, while we wheel you into surgery." And with that, Doctor Mohammed Mahmood and his trusty sidekick grabbed the sides of the gurney and away they all went down the main aisle of the emergency room as Nurse Elizabeth Waters yelled: "We're livin' in the **BIG TIME** now!"

ORDERLY # 1: "You ever spend a night in jail? Well, I'll tell ya. It ain't pleasant. Just me and my popcorn box amongst all those weirdoes."

ORDERLY # 2: "Uh-huh."

(Excerpt from the poem: *RICHARD COREY*)

"Whenever Richard Cory went down town,
We people on the pavement looked at him . . .
And he was rich - yes, richer than a king -
And admirably schooled in every grace:
In fine, we thought that he was everything
To make us wish that we were in his place . . .
And Richard Cory, one calm summer night,
Went home and put a bullet through his head."
by
Edwin Arlington Robinson
December 22, 1869—April 6, 1935
(American who won three Pulitzer Prizes for his work)

*****

"The claw of the sea-puss gets us all in the end."

F. Hopkinson Smith

*****

Till Death Do Us Part

"Who are you?"

"I'm Mr. West, Frank. Christian West. Don't you remember me?"

"Who's Frank?"

"Why you are, Frank."

"I'm Ham."

With a troubled look on his face, Mr. West tilted his head into a question mark. "Okay Ham, if you say so; but your real name is Frank. Frank Dietz. Doctor Franklin Dietz, to be precise."

Doctor Franklin Dietz looked at his smartly trimmed fingernails, the fingernails of a prosperous man, as he pondered this last bit of information. "I'm not Frank Deitz. My name is Ham. Hamish Bridger."

The middle-aged man with the impeccable manicure, who called himself Bridger, looked around the room; it was sparsely furnished: a table with chairs, with a nearly empty glass on it; a bed with a night table and lamp; a bookshelf with some medical books and bric-a-brac. The room had a sanitized look about it, like a hospital, or . . . a clinic.

That's it, a clinic, he thought. He was sitting at a table, in a clinic, across from an unknown man who called himself Christian West whose only distinguishing features were a birthmark on his left ear and the bow tie that he was wearing. And the only thing between them was a just-about-empty glass on the table with some insignificant ashy remains of a chalky essence in the bottom of it. Ham swallowed. He tasted a powdery film around the edges of his mouth. "Just, who are you, and exactly where am I?"

"You're kidding me, right Frank?" Mr. West squinted across the table with a jaundiced eye. "You know, Frank, this is really not the time to be joking around. Rather it's a most somber time considering—"

"I keep telling you, I'm not this Frank person you keep referring to. I'm Ham Bridger."

Suddenly, a light bulb went on inside the head of the gentleman with the birthmark on his left ear. "Ah, yes! I was told you might show up, Frank. I mean, Mr. Bridger."

"Mr. West, could you humor me for a minute. Just explain to me who you think I am and why you think that?"

The gentleman in the bow tie stared at the middle-aged man, sitting across the table from him, shrugged his shoulders and said: "Why not?" as if granting one last wish to a dying man. "I know you're Frank Dietz and that you're a doctor—actually an obstetrician—because when you arrived here, about two weeks ago, we did an extensive background check on you, and well . . . you are who you say you are."

"Background check on me? What for?"

"You don't think we allow people to do what you're doing without first checking to see if what they told us is true or not, do you?"

Ham Bridger was at a loss; nevertheless, he pushed ahead. "Is this some sort of clinic?"

"Physically, we're in one of a series of flats. We refer to it as a . . . place of peace."

"Where exactly is this *place of peace* that I'm in?"

"Switzerland. Zurich, since you wish to be exact."

"Switzerland?"

"More than two-thirds of our patients are foreigners."

Hamish stifled a yawn with the back of his hand. "What do you do here, Mr. West?"

"I'm a volunteer, actually."

"No, I mean: What is your job here?"

"I'm a registered nurse, Fra—. I mean, Mr. Bridger."

"What do they call this a 'place of peace'?"

"Pax Pacis is the name of our organization."

Ham mulls this over in his mind. "Peace?"

"Yes, peace . . . In this case, peace for Frank Dietz."

"We keep getting back to this Frank character, don't we? You want to tell me a little more about him?"

"Okay, but just a little. Actually, that's about all we'll have time for . . . is . . . *a little*."

"Sorry, I don't follow."

"You will shortly, Mr. Bridger. You will shortly."

Hamish rubs his eyes with the backs of his hands as Mr. West continues. "Doctor Frank Dietz comes from a wealthy family. He's a graduate of Duke Medical School and has, or rather had, a nice practice in Durham, North Carolina. Just goes to show that money doesn't always buy you happiness."

"How's that?"

"Well, you see . . . Frank has a problem."

"And what, pray tell, would that be?"

"You."

"Me? How can I be a problem for Mr. Dietz? You just got done telling me I was Dr. Dietz."

"You've always been a problem for him." Seeing the confusion in the well-to-do man's eyes, the gentleman with the birthmark continued. "You see, Mr. Bridger . . . Doctor Dietz has Dissociative Identity Disorder." Hamish began to interrupt, but Mr. West waved him off. "It's a habitual disease; he's had it all his life. It seems he's constantly at war with himself and well, he's finally had enough."

"Hasn't Doctor Dietz ever heard of that expression: 'Physician, heal thyself?'"

"Believe me, Mr. Bridger, he's tried. His decision is final."

"Decision? What decision?"

"Up until 1994, the American Psychiatric Association referred to Dissociative Identity Disorder as Multiple Personality Disorder."

"You mean, where two or more personalities live in one body."

"Actually, people with this disorder suffer from not having *more* than one personality, but rather from having *less* than one personality. Their failure lies in the fact that they are unable to integrate various aspects of identity into *one* unified personality.

"You see, Mr. Bridger, when I said that Doctor Dietz was constantly at war with himself, I meant that he and you are the same person and he's been at war with you for the last forty years now."

"What? That's absurd! I've never even heard of Mr. Dietz?"

"I wouldn't expect you to be aware of him, but he certainly knows about you."

"What about this Dissociative Identity Disorder? And what has it go to do with me?"

"Dissociative Identity Disorder is born out of chronic, repeated trauma which leads to separate personality states in childhood that continues right up into adulthood. Anxiety and stress are the causes and the results are the spontaneous switching of personality states. The disease allowed Frank to dissociate himself from his immediate circumstances by becoming you, as a means of protecting himself from overwhelming mental pain. The reason you don't remember Doctor Dietz is because you are his *other* personality state, the one he wishes to get rid of."

"Anxiety? What stress?"

"*You* are the anxiety and the stress, Mr. Bridger."

"You said this was chronic. To me, chronic means unremitting, having an ailment for a long time; it doesn't mean terminal." Hamish stifled a big yawn and rubbed his eyes again.

Mr. West nodded towards the glass on the table, with the insignificant ashy remains of a chalky essence in the bottom of it. Ham swallowed again and tasted a dusty coating around the inside of his mouth and down his throat. "Frank has decided to make it terminal . . . I think you'd better lie down, Mr. Bridger, it's about time."

Mr. West got up from his chair, helped the American from the table to the bed, then looked directly into his eyes as he spoke. "Pax Pacis is an assisted suicide clinic. That glass on the table contained a fatal dose of barbiturates that Doctor Dietz drank, voluntarily, about five minutes ago. I'm sorry."

Ham Bridger struggled to right himself in the bed, but was barely able to support himself with one arm. "You're sorry? I don't want to hear you're sorry! You have no right to do this to me. I didn't agree to take that glass of poison of my own volition. This isn't suicide, it's murder!"

The volunteer from Switzerland sympathetically shook his head. "Frank tried to warn me about you; that'd you'd be like this and to prepare for you. That's why he signed this notarized document." Mr. West extracted a folded manuscript from his pocket and held it aloft. "This document states—in terms which cannot be misconstrued, and which allow Doctor Dietz to carry out his wishes, even in the face of opposition—that it is his declared intent as a patient of this clinic that his request for assisted suicide be honored."

Ham Bridger fell back onto his pillow, his eyes started to close. Still, he violently spat out the words, "You're Death . . . and you've come too soon."

"Isn't that always the way in life, Mr. Bridger?"

"You can't do this to me. I know my rights. I'm from America!"

Mr. West took a deep sigh. "Ah yes, America. I don't understand America. That's where women have a constitutional right to do what they want to their bodies as they see fit. Frank told me all about it. Roe v. Wade, he said, was the Supreme Court decision, back in '73. Legalized abortion on demand for *any* reason. Second opinions are never required, ninety-nine percent of abortions are for non-medical reasons, surgical training is not necessary, no informed consent is legally necessary, and burial is in a garbage can."

"This isn't fair. I didn't do anything to deserve this. Why should I be tied to a guy, who I don't even know, and he gets to decide my fate?"

"Why should those poor babies, who never did anything to deserve their fates, be tied to women who they don't even know? I guess there are a lot of things in this world that aren't exactly . . . fair."

"And you go by the first name of Christian. You're anything but a Christian."

"A Christian, Mr. Bridger? We're talking burial in a garbage can here. That doesn't sound too Christian, or very dignified to me. Not for a progressive civilization like America with all of its . . . *rights*!

"Let's see: How many children? Oh, I'm sorry, they like to call them *'pregnancy tissue'* in America. Let's see: How many pregnancy tissues have been terminated since that infamous Roe v. Wade case? I guess pregnancy tissues don't have any *rights* in America."

The male nurse appeared to be mentally calculating figures in his head. "About 1.8 million per year, but then again, all states don't report their statistics. But, if I had to guess, I'd say probably in the neighborhood of fifty million plus. That would mean about every third baby conceived in America is *murdered* by an abortion."

"Murdered, you say? No, not murdered. That's how the law reads. That's God's will."

"Oh, so you believe in God now, do you Mr. West?"

"Let me just say this, Frank, or Ham, or whoever you think you are. God didn't create your Supreme Court, or America's law, which said Roe v. Wade was legal; men did. It's not God's law that puts these unborn to death, nor is it God's will. It's man's law; it's man's will. Fallible, misguided, feeble, and at times, a very sick evil man. God is to whom this sick evil man runs to in times of trouble, or when he wants to . . . *pray* for something.

"As for me, I personally struggle with the concept of God. I often wonder about God . . . often wonder. For, if you believe in God, you must believe that God doesn't protect the weak, the young, the infirmed, or the dying. So, who are we blindly praying to? Who does He then protect? Anyone? If no one, then why do we pray to Him and refer to Him as a . . . *God*?"

Struggling to keep his eyes open, the rich man—with the neatly buffed nails—managed to mumble, "This wouldn't be legal, to do this to me in America. There is no justice here."

Mr. West thought to himself, *Maybe in Heaven, Mr. Bridger; maybe there'll be some justice there*; then, his thoughts metamorphosed back to the parable of the rich man trying to get into Heaven and how that was as difficult as a camel trying to pass through the eye of a needle.

Mr. West looked down upon his patient, "Yes, America. According to Frank, it's all nice and legal there when the doctor tears a fetus from its mother's womb; a fetus that has progressed to term and is healthy, breathing, and viable. Then, they toss it—all alone and in a panic—into one of those dark trashcans with a lid on it and wait . . . as it slowly suffocates to death; wait . . . as its muffled whimpers beg for help, and then, Voila! The fetus finally dies . . . about forty-five minutes later. That's called: Pro-Choice, I believe. Pro-Choice for whom is the question.

"Where is the justice there, Mr. Bridger? Is that the America you're talking about, with all of its Christian values?"

"Where's the morality then?"

"Now that's what I really don't understand about America: its system of morality. Why is it okay for an adult, in your society, to do away with a healthy and helpless child—excuse me, *pregnancy tissue*—in such a grotesque and cavalier manner? On the other hand, it is considered inhumane, and even cruel and unusual punishment, to execute—with a painless injection—that same adult if he were convicted of killing a newborn, cutting it up with a buzz saw, and then eating its body parts. To put him to death, in the name of justice, is wrong in your country. How is that, Mr. Bridger?"

The indignant, righteous-talking American could no longer hear what the male nurse was saying to him; his eyes were glazed over, dilated, and fixed like a pair of doll's eyes.

And so died Doctor Franklin Dietz—the obstetrician—on a bed in a flat in Switzerland, taking Mr. Hamish Bridger with him.

Mr. Christian West leaned over the deceased one last time. "Mr. Bridger, Doctor Dietz wanted me to tell you: 'Till death do us part.'" Then, almost as an afterthought, the gentleman in the bow tie bent his body down lower—next to the physician's head, the physician who had just healed himself. In a conspiratorial whisper, he breathed into the corpse's ear, "And oh yes, one last thing, Mr. Bridger. He said to tell you that he thought of himself as the obstetrician and he looked upon you as the abortionist."

"Friends help you move. Real friends help you move bodies."
Unknown

*****

"All of man's troubles come from his
inability to sit quietly in a room by himself."
Boardwalk Empire
(HBO Series)

*****

How Wild Bill Lost His Tooth

If you're thinking Wild Bill is some six-year-old kid that lost his tooth or that this story has something to do with Wild Bill Hickok, you'd be wrong; it's not and it hasn't. The real Wild Bill—the real one I'm talking about—is sixty-seven years old (Yup, he lived that long) and has calmed down quite a bit. He's not nearly as wild as he once was, especially after he lost his tooth. It was his right front tooth, in case you were wondering which tooth it was. People get like that, you know: they just can't follow along with the narrative. Gotta get way out ahead, wondering. Gotta know all the answers, like which tooth Wild Bill lost, when they're only into the first paragraph of this potboiler.

First, let me tell you where this megillah took place. Was in a small town called New Smyrna Beach. For the majority of you and the Joe Six-packs that live there who, for the most part, have absolutely no idea where in the hell they are (either physically or mentally), it's in Florida.

New Smyrna Beach is one of those sleepy, seaside whistle-stops on a barrier island about fifteen miles south of Daytona Beach. It's relatively undiscovered; although, each year it gets more and more discovered. It, once upon a time, billed itself as the Safest Beach in the World; now, it's the Shark Bite Capital of the World.

It's not a bad place to live, if you discount the people that live there; taxes are low, homes are relatively inexpensive as are the other commodities of life i.e. food, electricity, and entertainment; if entertainment, to you, consists of watching other people stomp around on top of each other's feet (that's called line dancing) while some inbred country group named *Disposable Penis*, out at Billy Bob's Barbie-Q, sings *My Baby's Just Flat*.

Wild Bill would often say, "They ought to construct one of those huge signs over the entrance to this city that reads: 'Welcome to New Smyrna Beach, Where Ignorance Is Bliss.'" Then he'd add, as an afterthought: Along with that sign, they ought to administer some sort of I.Q. test once someone seeks residency on this patch of sand. Here, an eighth-grader graduating from middle school would be considered gifted if he read on a sixth grade level because normally that eighth-grader would be reading on a fourth grade level.

As far as politics are concerned, New Smyrna Beach is rhubarb on the seashore; it's run by a city manager whose main claim to fame is that he owns the local fruit stand, the kind that sells rubber alligators and nectarines. Don't know if he can figure out a budget, but he sure knows how to package a mean crate of kumquats. And, one of the City Commissioners insisted that a disgruntled group of aliens put the snatch on him and while he was in their spaceship, they operated on his brain; or maybe they ate his brain. Who knows? Anyway, they talked about his sanity for several months, but finally re-elected him anyway. This town is not going to let little things like running a fruit stand, or abduction by aliens hold back good men from public office. For those of you with inquiring minds, there isn't any local chapter of Mensa here and P. T. Barnum could have retired for life with all the suckers hibernating here.

New Smyrna Beach is a great place to live, if you go there with money; if you were born there, good luck. The wages are meager from the cops to the candlestick makers. "Bad news for the people trying to make a living; good news for the people who retire there and are exploiting the 'cheap help,'" as Bill was fond of saying. "I used to have a measure of sympathy for the people making the low wages; that was until I lived here for about a year, then, I understood why the wages were so sub-standard. That's all the help deserved to be paid; in fact, they were probably being overpaid . . . substantially."

Fortunately for William "Wild Bill" Wilding, he wasn't born in New Smyrna Beach, and he wasn't trying to make a living there. He was, however, trying to survive which was proving most difficult with each passing year because of the "cheap help" situation.

William Wilding was born in New York and migrated to Miami over forty years ago. For twenty-five of those forty years, he managed to sock away some shekels "working for the man ev'ry night and day," as the song goes. Then, he moved on up the line to New Smyrna Beach where he's been retired for the last twenty years.

Wild Bill moved to New Smyrna Beach to escape the hustle and bustle of Miami; he pictured himself on a tropical beach, away from the big city push-and-shove and the parking lot traffic. He got away from the traffic all right, but what replaced the big city push-and-shove was the small town chiseling. Nearly everybody in New Smyrna Beach was a scam artist, or thought they were. But, Wild Bill knew better; after all, he was from New York. The city that never sleeps. Where the art of the hustle was born in 1624 when Peter Minuit stole Manhattan from the Lenapes Indians, who had owned the land since 10,000 B.C. Minuit turned the island into New Amsterdam for sixty Dutch guilders (twenty-four American dollars to those non-Dutch speaking people out there) worth of duffel cloth, wampum (seashell beads), and jew's-harps—which is a sound, musical instrument played with the mouth. When young William learned of this transaction in a grade school history class, his first thought was: "Who were the Lenapes Indians and what would they want with a bunch of jew's-harps?" I guess ole Peter figured the Indians needed some musical accompaniment while they danced the *minuet* (a little pun there) around the campfire.

When Bill first put down his roots in New Smyrna Beach, he moved in next to a rental. Over the Fourth of July holiday, the renters—amid all the black-market fireworks and hell raising— illegally parked their twenty-five plus vehicles all over the street including Bill's driveway. He called the cops; one showed up all right (about an hour and forty-five minutes later), but the cop said he didn't know how to write a parking ticket. Talk about a Barney Fife police force. The sheriff was ever so proud of the fact that he was an Andy Griffith fan, even going so far as to purchase a 1962 Ford Galaxy for the department (for about six thousand dollars, not including all the thousands of dollars needed for the repairs necessary to get it to run), just like the one used in Mayberry P. D. "Money, better spent," said some taxpayers. As far as Bill was concerned, he thought buying the Ford for a squad car was a stroke of genius as most of the female officers on the force had a butt the size of Aunt Bee's and needed a vehicle that big just to get behind the wheel. So much for the cops in New Smyrna Beach.

Building contractors know all about police presence, or rather the lack thereof. Bill, on numerous occasions, eyeballed many a construction workers illegally park their trucks in a moving lane of traffic—going the wrong way, no less—and leave them . . . ALL DAY. On one occasion, when a patrol car did in fact come by, it drove around the construction truck—just like a tourist would—and continued on its merry way.

Bill never expected to be treated so unfairly by these country folk. That's what they all liked to say, "We're *jesta country folk* here, y'all." He could always tell when he was about to get raked over the coals, and charged triple by the cheap help, when the jasper on the job would preface the economic mutilation, that was about to take place, with: "I'm jesta country boy who jesta loves the smell of the barn." But, these here folks in New Smyrna Beach were about as country as Donald Trump eating biscuits with gravy in the Ozarks. "Country folk in New Smyrna Beach? No way! But I'm up to my arse in goobers though," was how Bill was fond of putting it.

Bill's first debacle was the house. He bought a nice, little beach cottage, but it needed a little work. An exterior paint job was the first item on his list of must-do's, but for the price he paid ("priced reasonably" according to Bubba, the *jesta county folk* real estate agent, who sold Bill the house), he figured he'd get a couple of coats after he moved in. Big mistake. First on his list of must-do's should have been the hiring a good shrink who was not adverse to writing prescriptions for massive doses of Valium.

Bill accepted the first painter's bid on the house (Another big mistake!): ten thousand dollars (This was in the mid-nineties). When the slop the workmen put on faded, then started to peel off, within the first year, he figured he'd be covered by the twenty-five year warranty. The paint was covered all right, but not the labor. The store told him they sub-contracted out the labor. Bill would have to continue to pay them, but they couldn't fix anything; he'd have to get the sub-contractors to re-paint the house . . . again . . . once he tracked them down, of course.

"Of course," said Bill.

Looking back, Bill thought it was odd when two Cubans (Salvador Dali and Pablo Picasso, neither of whom spoke more than a handful of sentences in broken English, but they smiled and grabbed their crotches a lot) showed up to put a couple of coats on the place. Two Cubans in New Smyrna Beach was about as likely as Martin Luther King secretly being the Imperial Wizard of the K.K.K.

Bill finally did catch up with the two Latinos, and they did come back out to his humble abode. However, all they did was slather over the bad spots. So now, Bill had a two-tone house: spots consisting of a worn out, faded texture next to freshly applied spots. It looked like a bad Jackson Pollock lithograph. Oh, it was all the same color all right, "jesta sum was more a freshner than other part of house," was how one of the Spanish workers put it. Bill figured he could have had the house slopped-over four times for what that job cost him.

Bill was hopping mad, to say the least, and he told the *jesta country folk* down at the paint store just how he felt in language that even the Village Idiot could understand. The stickup artists at the outlet finally settled for the six thousand that Bill had already ponied-up (which was about two and a half times the price of painting a conventional house) and washed out the remaining four grand. Nice of them, especially since Bill had to turn around and get another company to re-do the entire house for a third time. He figured it was easier than chasing down those two crotch-grabbin', Cuban artistsans. Well, nobody got hurt, at least not physically. John Law didn't have to be called, as if they would have done any good. And, this was not how Wild Bill lost his tooth.

Next came the interior painter. After the mess Bill got himself in with the facade of the house, he decided to paint one room at a time, starting with the downstairs bathroom. How big is a bathroom, right? It's only one room (five by nine) with a sink, a tub, a toilet, a big mirror on the wall and a closet; not a lot of wall space to paint. Bill figured he'd be smart this time and get estimates from BOO COO painters; he called up twenty, but only two actually showed up.

Bill decided on the interior decorator, Mr. Wartham, because he didn't have the smell of liquor on his breath; however, Mr. Wartham did have this lazy eye with some sort of milky discharge coming out of it. The eye looked out over Bill's right shoulder towards Saturn in the night sky. Mr. Wartham also had this exaggerated, dippity-doo, spit curl hanging down from a receding hairline and this big-ass wart—about the size of a corn dog—on the tip of his nose. Bill was so mesmerized by the wart that by the time Mr. Wartham was wrapping up his estimate, Bill had absent-mindedly started calling him Mr. Wart, much to everyone's embarrassment. "It was that left eye, really," Bill would later explain to his wife. "What intrigued me was that it didn't blink . . . not once."

Bill wanted the bathroom painted in one of those designers patterns from Ralph Lauren; one of those linen-type weaves where they put down a base coat of paint (Parchment), then brush over it with a glaze (Safari Vest). All this weaving about with a base coat and glaze should have been the tip-off. No painter in New Smyrna Beach—drunk or sober, dead or alive—was going to be able to pull that off, especially since they couldn't even apply a simple coat to the outside of the house. After five days of newspapers taped down all over the floor, ceiling, and walls, the painter finally got the base coat and glaze on. What boggled Bill's mind was: *What was the big deal that it took five days to paint this bathroom?* Everything in the room seemed to be covered up with cloths and tape. It was only a five by nine room, not the Sistine Chapel.

Well, the linen effect Bill had hoped for didn't exactly look like linen; it looked more like a series of bumps. That wouldn't have been too bad if they were small bumps . . . maybe evenly spaced throughout the room. But, they weren't. No. No. Not gonna happen. These were BIG bumps (turn quickly and you could put an eye out); and they were all clumped together, in massive clusters all around the room, sort of like the topography on the moon. Well, chalk another one up.

Bill had to ultimately resort to hiring a painter with liquor on his breath. He came in, got a gallon of paint (a Muenster yellow to drown out the two-tone browns of Ralph Lauren), and re-did the entire discombooberation. To this day, Bill hates to go in the room and only does so for emergencies, like when he went to Mexico and came back with a monumental case of dysentery; the rest of the time, he'd rather go outside to drain the dew off the lily. All this for a five by nine bathroom that ended up costing eight-hundred dollars to paint. Bill figured if he ever befriended a blind person, he'd invite the guy over, feed him some beer, wait till he had to take a whiz, then tell him there's an old treasure map in Braille on the wall of the bathroom, which gives the location of a Spanish galleon that went down in the early 1600's. And, if it's not too much trouble, since Bill can't read Braille, if he could just feel around a bit—as long as he's in there anyway—and figure out the hidden message on the wall, then Bill would be willing to split the booty with him. Bill figured he'd just sit back and watch the fun; no liquor required.

Hey!, need a good tiler? Don't use Mr. Goowie & Company, as Bill unfortunately found out. Bill contracted them to tear up the existing carpeting and replace it with tile. "It'll take the better part of a week." Bill put half the money down. Dare I say about here: another big mistake?

They tore up the carpeting all right—the first day on the job—and threw it into Bill's front yard. And there it sat, in the rain, the heat, and the dark of night for three and a half weeks until Bill finally hauled it off himself.

Some days the tilers would come early in the morning; some days they'd come late in the afternoon; some days they wouldn't come at all. "Depends how the fishin' is," said the older of the tilers and the owner of the company; a fellow who went by the name of Trojan Goowie. He had this annoying habit of stopping in the middle of a sentence, licking his fingers as if they had gravy on them, smacking his lips, and then continuing with his conversation.

Bill couldn't understand the New Smyrna Beach work mentality. He was used to working five days a week. EVERY WEEK. The concept of a workweek in New Smyrna Beach was to scratch by until you had enough money for this week's bills, then go fishin', or surfin', or just go drinkin' beer while pickin' your good, old, country boy ass.

One day Goowie and his buddies came at eight in the morning, stayed twenty minutes, went off to another job . . . and never came back for three days. I guess the fishin' must have been real good those days.

Bill complained to the salesman that this was turning out to be one hellava lousy job and he was inclined not to pay. Another big mistake. The clerk turned around and charged the final half of the job (which wasn't even completed yet) to Bill's credit card without his authorization, or knowledge. I guess that's *jesta* how them *country folk* done things in Florida: screw you, before you can quit them, on a bum job that they were doing to "y'all."

Two more weeks of startin' and stoppin' and the job was finally completed. On the last day of the job, Goowie—while packing up his power tools—turned to Wild Bill.

"Well, we finally got her done. Iffin' the—

Goowie stopped and licked his fingers.

SMACK.

"—bluefish was a runnin' today, I was a fixin' ta take one more day. Good thing they ain't, huh?"

"Yeah, good thing," was all Bill could manage through the steam fuming out his ears.

It was a good thing it wasn't hunting season either, thought Bill.

Last year, a couple of hunters went into the woods—just west of town—and shot this poor hick's Cocker Spaniel, thinking it was a rabbit. When the judge asked them about it, the one said, "Well, he was a might big and sorta slow for a rabbit, but then again, I jesta figured it was our lucky day. We jesta happened upon a fat, dawdling rabbit is all."

The judge turned to the other hunter and asked him if he didn't notice anything odd about the Cocker. He said: "Well, slap my ass and call me Sally. Now that you mention it, Judge, I did think it a bit unusual fer a rabbit to be a wearin' a scarf."

Well, no harm/no foul during the tiling job and this was not how Wild Bill lost his tooth.

Bill's problems didn't stop there. About a week after he arrived and set up his banking account, he went to the local grocery market. It was one of those big chains that operate throughout Florida where the checkout girls are impatient sixteen-year-olds. They can't wait for the cash register to accept your ATM card and feel it's necessary to swipe your bank debit card through the machine twice . . . jesta be sure. Bill thought he was being charged for three hundred dollars worth of food. And he was. TWICE! He immediately went looking for the manager, a fellow that went by the name of Buddy. Not Mr. James Boozoloonie, as was his given name. Not Jimmy. But Buddy. Buddy Boozoloonie. At least it wasn't another Bubba. They actually named their kids here Bubba; they're proud of that name. Bill met one local named Bubba and his kid was Bubba Junior.

Buddy was easy to find: he was six-foot-four and was standing in the middle of the Bakery aisle, scratchin' his nuts. Buddy was not, however, much help; he wasn't able to figure out how this happened. In fact, Buddy had some trouble figuring out how to even swipe the bankcard, and Buddy was the manager. *Hell*, thought Bill, *at least, the sixteen year-old teenybopper could do that. She did it wrong, but at least she could do it.*

Unable to straighten out the mess with Buddy Boozoloonie, Bill trucked over to his bank, figuring he'd rectify the situation there. Mrs. Kimo Jones was the whiz-bang executive manager in charge. Her advice: "Wait a couple days and see if it fixes itself."

Bill, trying extremely hard to control his rising anger, asked: "How will the bank computer know to 'fix' something if you don't tell the computer how or what to 'fix'?" To which Kimo answered, "No need to get smart about it; I'm only tryin' to help here."

Well, five days later, and numerous phone calls to the main office in Merritt Island (some sixty miles away) and the account had finally . . . *fixed itself*.

The attitude of Buddy Boozoloonie, the manager of the grocery store, seemed to have trickled down to his employees. What's that expression? The tone is set at the top. A week had passed after the debit card incident and Bill went back to the same grocery store (the only one in town) looking for some peanut butter; only this time he brought cash. No sense taking any chances with a debit card. He couldn't find any chucky Peter Pan (his favorite), so he asked one of the sixteen-year-old stock boys with zits where the peanut butter aisle was. Too busy to find out, the pimpled kid merely replied, "They discontinued it."

WHOA! Fuckin' A! Discontinued peanut butter? What kinda town is this? Bill wondered.

It wasn't just the grocery store. Bill went to the local jeweler; the wife needed the settings rebuilt on her engagement ring where they'd been worn down from forty years of hand wringing. Mookie Hardpepper ran the establishment. The country folk around town jesta called him "the Mook."

Well, the Mook figured it would cost "around a hundred twenty-five dollars, American," was how he put it, as if Bill was going to pay in pesos. Bill was especially nervous when he said that "around" part.

Nobody ever wrote anything down in this town like a food order or an estimate for a job, lest they be indicted. What Bill should have been worried about was not the "around" part, but the fact that the Mook never told him when the setting would be ready. You see, what Bill hadn't discovered yet in New Smyrna Beach was that the country folk didn't operate with an American calendar, but rather with the change of seasons. Four subsequent visits and ten days later, Bill found that out when he asked for his ring back and the quite indignant Mook responded: "I can't work miracles here," as if Bill was expecting him to turn water into wine, something evidently far more complex that merely re-setting the wife's engagement ring. Bill demanded his ring back, went to Daytona Beach, and got it re-set in one day, for fifty dollars less.

At least the Mook didn't try to sell him something he didn't need; the merchants in New Smyrna Beach were always trying to do that. He wouldn't have considered it the least bit odd for the Mook—a jeweler by trade—to try to sell him a couple of pairs of women's bikini panties from the bottom drawer of his shop, right next to the mood rings.

Next stop: the plumber. Yup, you guessed it. Bill sprung a leak. As he was washing his socks one day, Bill noticed the ceiling in the laundry room was drooling water.

A light bulb went off in Bill's head. Right over the laundry room, on the second floor, was the shower for the Master Bath.

Out of twenty-five calls Bill made to various plumbers in the Yellow Pages, four actually showed up. *I guess that's probably better odds than the painters, and the plumbers weren't drunks*, was how Bill figured it.

"Of course, we're gonna have ta pull up the old shower pan, put in a new one," said P.U. Leak, the plumber.

"Of course," said Bill.

"But jesta a little shower pan."

"No doubt," Bill mumbled.

"No need to go a tearin' up your whole damn house," said P.U.; then, he snorted a laugh that was right out of one of those Halloween horror movies. Mr. Leak had a bluster to him all right, but it was all horse feathers and gunsmoke.

"And, of course, that means ya gotta put in all new tile where the old ones used ta be."

Of course, thought Bill; instead, he just said, "Can you do it?"

"Don't do tile work. Gotta get someone else for that. Be careful who you gets fer tilers though. Some of 'em do shoddy work."

"I know," was all Bill could manage.

Well, twelve weeks, umpteen calls (mostly to find some new tilers) and several thousands of dollars later, there stood the new shower.

Fast-forward ten months. Bill was in the laundry room . . . drip, drip, and drip onto the old noggin. It turned out—after Bill paid ANOTHER plumber to put in ANOTHER new shower—that P.U.—the first plumber who put the "little" shower pan in—also put a BIG nail hole in the liner in the "little" shower pan which, in turn, caused this new little leak.

You say: *Why didn't Bill go back to P.U. Leak and have him repair it; afterall, it must have been under warranty, right?* You're right. It was under warranty and Bill did go back to Mr. Leak. He called him and told him that the shower was percolating into the laundry room . . . AGAIN!

"Must be the shower door leakin'."

"Couldn't be," said Bill. "I stuffed towels all around the door and ran the water. Doesn't leak."

"Must be the shower handle is a leakin'. Sometimes they springs a leak and water will drip down the inside of the wall."

"It ain't dripping down the inside of no wall. The leak's comin' from three feet off the wall and over my head."

"Must be the tile then. The tilers probably forgot to caulk it. I warned ya about them tilers."

"How could they forget something so major like caulking the tile?" I asked him.

"You'd be surprised."

"No I wouldn't."

"Well, you know the old saying: 'You get what you pay for,'" replied the plumber.

"Words to live by. In which case, I should be living in the Taj Mahal!" Wild Bill took a deep breath. "Anyway, it ain't the tilers. I already called them and they've been to the house. They say it's you. Say you put a nail through the shower pan."

"See. I done warned you 'bout them tillers. Always blamin' someone else for their shoddy work."

Feeling the beginnings of a Grand Mal seizure taking hold, Bill violently grabbed his temples. "How do you know it's the tilers and not you? How can you do all this diagnosis over the phone without even coming over to see what the problem is? You could have—"

"Don't need to," interrupted Leak.

"Let me finish!," Wild Bill yelled back. "First, you blame the shower door, then the faucets, then the tilers. It's everyone's fault but yours. **I have a warranty!**"

A long pause.

"Ya finished?"

"Yeah!"

"It's the tillers. Got a warranty with them?" Then P.U. hung up.

It didn't stop there; Bill could go on, and on, and on.

Bill took his clothes into the dry cleaners; they lost them. Oh, they were going to reimburse him all right, at two cents on the dollar. "What's fairer than that?" said the manager.

It wasn't just the cheap help; it was the, so-called, *professionals* too.

Bill had a friend that cracked a rib while sneezing. Are you listening up, folks? He cracked a rib . . . **SNEEZING!** I don't know about you but, right about here, a red banner would have gone up the old flagpole for me. He was forty-nine years old and literally three weeks away from death. He had colon cancer; it had spread via his lymph nodes into his liver, spleen, kidneys, gall bladder, and all throughout his bones. His doctor suggested pain management therapy. Now there was a doctor at the top of his game.

It was the people. It was always the people in New Smyrna Beach that drove Bill to the brink of psychosis. And they lived everywhere. You couldn't get away from them, no matter where you went.

Some lived on the river; they just moored their boats in the middle of the river and set up a home. They never paid any taxes for schools, roads, whatever. They lived the good life on the river; dumped all their garbage and sewage into the river for the rest of us to drink. If, and this is a BIG IF considering the bureaucracy of New Smyrna Beach, anyone from city government came by to check on them, they just up and moved down the river and set up house all over again. One boat owner had his twenty-five foot cabin cruiser sink under him, so he just abandoned it. There it laid, half submerged . . . on its side . . . in the middle of a shipping lane . . . for months on end.

For such a small town, driving can also be a real problem. A contractor, on one of those condominium construction sites, put his dumpster in the road—in one of the turning lanes—and left it there, to be filled up later with debris. The police never said a word.

When the snowbirds from up North—with their blue hair and twenty-year-old Cadillacs—come down for the winter, they drive in the middle of the road at fifteen miles per hour to all the early bird specials. This slows everyone down except, of course, the local Bubba on his way to a fish fry in his black pick-up, which is all tricked-out with Yosemite Sam mud flaps with "**BACK OFF**" emblazoned on them; he just barrels into the opposite lane of traffic, going right around that little old lady with the blue hair.

And then, there was Amy Breezy—the local soccer mom—who made the front-page of the newspaper, after causing six thousand dollars worth of damage to the front end of the family car. She was smoking a cigarette, talking on the cell phone, and applying her make-up while—allegedly—driving her Chevy Trailblazer home from a game. The said car contained her youngest daughter, Mindy, and two of her schoolmates; all were eating pizza in the rear with the family dog, a hyperactive poodle named Nutley, who was trying to hump little Mindy's leg.

Normally, the natives don't even bother to slide to a halt at a stop sign—that's a given. And the driving instructors teach the residents how to make illegal U-turns, "soes as they won't git hurt." Despite the locals knowing about the meaning of red lights, something evidently went terribly wrong on this particular day as Amy Breezy failed to see this particular red light and collided with a van from Mr. Chips, the snack food deliveryman. Her response to the investigating officer—when he told her that he didn't think she was a very safe driver—was: "But, I had my seat belt on." To top this already highly charged confrontation off, Mrs. Breezy became extremely indignant at the officer for—what she later reported to Internal Affairs as—his "insensitivity to my predicament." Allegedly, this boorish motorcycle cop, while straddling his Harley writing her a ticket, couldn't resist whistling Willie Nelson's song, *"I Can't Wait To Get On the Road Again."*

Want a great deal? Go to any of the antique dealers in town; they're the people who sell other people's worthless junk, once they mark it up five times the customary value. Antique dealers; that has a respectable ring to it. Thieves would be more apropos. *Hey!, if the dumb tourists wanta buy this crap,* is how the merchants saw it; it was jesta another opportunity to enrich themselves; no big deal.

Speaking of the merchants here, most run their businesses like a hobby: come in late, go home early; work only four days a week; close for lunch, or just plain leave the business unattended with a sign that reads: "Gone to Post Office" with no time given as to when they may return . . . if ever.

Speaking of the Post Office. Bill went there one day because he needed some five-cent stamps. He was mailing several letters that fell between the normal postage rates. They were out. The post office! Out of stamps! They were out of ten-cent stamps too.

"How could that happen?" he asked. "You're supposed to be a Post Office. That's what you do. Sell freakin' stamps."

"We don't like to keep a big inventory on hand," said the female clerk. Duh! Bill couldn't believe it. When he asked to see the manager, he was told that there were two, but they were both unavailable. Bill asked if they were in.

"Oh yeah, they're in alright," said the same female clerk, the one with the perpetual smirk on her face and a band-aid over the side of her mouth that was partially covering some sort of doohickey of cosmic proportions that had morphed into an oozing fungus. "It's just that they're busy in the morning, doing their work, and don't like to be disturbed. So, you'll have to come back in the afternoon."

Next.

What dumbfounded Wild Bill was how the newspaper would print an annual section entitled: BEST AROUND PLACES.

The merchants would literally *pay* to have their particular advertisements placed in the local paper saying that they were the best of this, or the best of that. For example: Best All-Around Middle East Food. Now I ask you: How many All-Around Middle East Food stores do you think there are in New Smyrna Beach? You got it. ONE! And, it's the Best. Could be it's the Best . . . and the Worst.

Another place lists itself as: Best Szechuan Food. I'd give odds that nine out of ten people in New Smyrna Beach have no idea what Szechuan Food is, much less, where this place is.

They've got some rather ridiculous categories too: Best Lo Mein, Best Mandarin Food, Best Menu Selection, Best Vietnamese Food, and Best Shepherd's Pie. And, it's just not limited to food.

They have Best Exercise Psychologist, whatever that is. Here again, I wonder if there are even two of these clowns in New Smyrna Beach.

How about Best Equipment for Disabilities and Best Dome Ceiling Sales? Yup, you got it. That's a real place and a real ad.

What hypocritical people, Bill thought. They give you the worst product—along with the worst service in town—and have the audacity to put out a brochure (that each Mom and Pop turnkey operation in town *pays* to be in) describing how they're the BEST. Then, the townies get upset when a Super Wal-Mart wants to move in and service the people 24/7 for a third of the price. They claim it will destroy their environment. What they really mean is: It will destroy their lazy work ethic.

Then, there are the SPECIAL EVENTS in Volusia County. Oh, the Special Events.

There is Speed Week that culminates with the running of the Daytona 500. There's Spring Break; the Turkey Run Car Show and Swap Meet; Biketoberfest in October, and Bike Week every February. And last, but not least, there's Black College Reunion where thousands of Black drug dealers—who call themselves "college students" and are anywhere from eighteen to eighty years of age—come to town, drive their cars endlessly up and down A1A (with their radios on ear-splitting, ear-poppin' super high), drink beer and urinate on everyone's front lawn.

Bike Week. Now there's an event. A better way to describe it would be a Moby Dick-sized gathering of trailer trash with artificial limbs. I never saw so many people in one place decked out in head halos and back braces; so many without arms, without legs, without . . . teeth. The sad thing is that the people in the neighborhood—while having to contend with all the rowdiness, noise, and traffic congestion—end up having their taxes raised because of this event. The homeowners ultimately end-up paying for all of this tomfoolery. It cost over a million a year, in additional clean-up fees, to tidy-up the mishmash that this group alone makes, so the hotels, restaurants, and bars can become as rich as Croesus.

And the women in New Smyrna Beach? Why, they're tougher than a Texas boll weevil. They all seem to have tattoos, somewhere on their bodies: curving around their calves, circling their thighs, up their ankles, down their legs, stuck on their backs, rolling over their shoulder blades, popping out of their navels, spreading throughout their fingers and between their toes, on the back of their necks, crawling over their breasts, and climbing out of their butts. When the women aren't getting themselves tattooed, they usually can be seen around town welding steel into non-traditional "art" (and I use that word loosely). Weird.

The ultimate in bizarre behavior came one day when Bill went to the men's room in the local Cineplex. This buckaroo, wearing short pants and cowboy boots (nice combo), literally was hoisting himself up in the air over, or rather into, the urinal next to Wild Bill. Instead of answering nature's call in the normal manner by opening one's fly, he was stretching his pant leg and trying to urinate out through the side. He ended up splashing urine down the side of his leg, over his boot, and onto the bathroom floor. Wild Bill shook his head and thought to himself: *These country folk sure are strange when it comes to hygiene. In fact,* he thought, *this whole damn town must have been some whack, generic experiment that went awry and ended up breeding mutants; they all walk around as if they have Mad Cow Disease. The entire town seems to be one toke over the line. If you wanted to give the world an enema, New Smyrna Beach is where you'd stick the nozzle.*

It happened at a red light, coming back from the movie theater. Bill, in his SUV, pulled up in the outside lane. There was one of those itsy-bitsy, white, Miata sports cars in the inside lane waiting for the light to change.

SNAP!

To this day Bill swears, "I don't know what came over me."

The Gestalt Theory makes the claim that the whole is greater than the sum of its parts. I guess that's what happened to Bill. It must have been a combination of painters, tilers; or maybe just the general, all around, poor excuse for what tries to pass as country folk in New Smyrna. The cumulative effect in quantitative aggravation was greater than the sum of all the cheap help collectively, if you catch what I'm trying to say here.

"It was at this traffic control device, I believe, that Bill gently—but forcibly—slipped off the tracks and careened over the edge. Maybe he wasn't getting enough fiber for his colon, or maybe he was getting too much sugar in his diet. Who knows?

"You had better cut back on some of those pop-tarts for breakfast, so you won't vent like that again," said the doctor in the psychiatric ward where Bill was eventually booked under the Baker Act.

All the driver, in the car next to Bill, seemed to have done was just smile and wave to Bill. Apparently, for reasons only known to God, Bill rolled down his window. Slowly, and ever so gingerly (so as not to splatter any on the side of his car), Bill poured his orange-pineapple flavored, Double-Big-Gulp Slurpee—that he just purchased at the 7-Eleven—out his window and onto the passenger side door of the white Miata. Big mistake.

What happened next was the biggest bubba monster, this side of Loch Ness, got out of this teensy-weensy Miata. When he asked Bill what was his problem, Bill's response was: "I *jesta* know a *country folk* like you is gonna try and sell me some wampum and a jew's-harp that I don't need."

All Bill remembers seeing, before he went toes-up into this wet, oily spot in the roadway . . . face first, was that this big daddy—who was dressed in these Oriental flip-flops and had overgrown hammerhead toes (this was definitely not the type of dude you'd meet at the local spa getting a volcanic mud wrap)—breathing extremely hard while grabbing his crotch and simultaneously scratchin' his balls, all with one hand. Bad, bad sign.

Any second guessing on the part of Bill? You bet. After the incident, Bill told the emergency doctor that sutured up his front lip, which now covered a white enamel stub that used to be his right front tooth: "When that huckleberry stepped out of that mini-car, the thought did cross my mind that maybe I'd gone too far. When he hit me, it felt just like I'd grabbed onto the third rail of a subway track. I'll tell you something: "You don't learn to fight like that in yur basement."

And, **THAT'S** how Wild Bill lost his tooth.

So, what's the moral of this story, you ask? I'll tell you.

In today's world, where incompetence rules, you'd better be able to do it all. You've got to be your own **BEST ALL-AROUND, EVERYTHING, GET IT DONE PERSON**; a man for all seasons, as they say.

You need to be your own cop, contractor, painter, tiler, interior decorator, grocery store clerk, banker, jeweler, plumber, dry cleaner, and merchant (for any and all products that you may need from toilet paper to a Hot Fudge Sundae).

You'd better be able to deliver your own mail and most important of all, you'd better be able to bend over—when the circumstances become necessary—and with the aid of a flashlight and mirror, give yourself a colonoscopy; you had better do the latter when you first arrive in New Smyrna Beach because if you don't the "country folk" there sure will.

I think I'll add dentist to that list of things you had better be able to do. Then again, maybe I'll save that for the sequel to this story and call it: "HOW WILD BILL GOT HIS TOOTH CAPPED."

"I used to be a dreamer, but marriage changed all that."

D'Artagnan Bloodhawke

*****

"The one charm of marriage is that it makes a
life of deception necessary for both parties."

Oscar Wilde

*****

"Marriage is the equivalent of trying to live
with a bug perpetually up your nose."

D'Artagnan Bloodhawke

*****

"Women; the supreme masters of the bait and switch."

D'Artagnan Bloodhawke

*****

A Woman Run Amok

I should have known my Sweetie was a birdbrain when she said,
"I follow football, religiously." That was right before she asked me,
"What's a first down, again?" Hey, what did I know? I was twenty-two,

fresh out of college. If you've been married longer than two weeks, you get the picture, I'm sure.

I was married in 1969. Big church wedding, sanctified by the devil. I might just as well have gotten married by a Ute medicine man—in the backyard, standing on a rock—for all the good a church wedding did me.

From the outset, we never seemed to be paddling in the same direction. We were like chalk and cheese; just didn't go together. She wanted us to be registered at stores like Tiffany's and Saks Fifth Avenue; whereas, I was in favor of registering at Crate & Barrel. Little did I know that'd it'd all come to such a sticky end.

Got divorced in 1980. That's about it. Eleven years. Eleven long, very long, years under the elephant's tail. There was a lot of drama along the way. It was like living on top of a volcano; it had a sense of high adventure to it every day. And no one was exactly hand feeding me Mai Tai's with watermelon on some South Pacific island with tropical breezes blowing by.

When the divorce came, then things really got a little wormy. The wife and her divorce attorney decided that she should live in *my* house and that I should take up residency on the street . . . in a different time zone. Between the two of them, they did everything to me except harvest my organs. And boy!, do women change in a hurry. To see those evil convulsions her face was making, it was like looking at something that sprang from the seed of Chucky. To say I was at an all time low would be a gross understatement; I was most definitely at the bottom of the birdcage. My divorce was like a knife fight in a telephone booth: up-close and personal and I needed that about as much as an ass-load of hamburgers. I just stood there in court, thinking to myself: *This is how horror movies start.* I learned a lot about life and marriage that day in court. I learned that life is not a "box of chocolates," as Forrest Gump would have you believe; but rather, in life you never know what you'll uncover once you lift the lid. Divorce can be utterly ridiculous, like two bald men fighting over a comb.

Women! Huh! You'd soon as trust them as put a pistol to your nuts. I leaned one thing though: Marriage to a woman is a full time job. But, what's a guy to do? Dissolve?

We got back together in '81. Big mistake. Like I needed that same, special, certain someone in my life to tie knots in my tail, all over again. We were separated in '83, back together again in '86 and the final dust-off (fingers crossed here) came in 2007. Nothing like a clean, sharp break. We never did actually remarry any of those times; I'm not certifiably stupid. Talk about a life diddled away!

As you can tell, it wasn't all moonlight, roses, and gypsy violins; it was pretty raw. Like living in a box with a snake. Hey, I'm not saying the ex hit the Mother Lode when she married me, but I'm what you get when you're looking to walk down that *Yellow Brick Road* to Oz and into a lifetime filled with ease.

She was beautiful to look at, but hell to live with. She should have been a picture on the wall; marriage would have worked out a whole lot better for me. It doesn't matter now anyway; the only thing I remember about her, after all of these years, is that she had long feet and was constipate most of the time.

Marriage! It would have been a whole lot easier in life to have had a heart transplant, or for me to have given away a kidney—or maybe both kidneys—than gone through a marriage. Now, don't get me wrong; I never allowed myself to get so psychological distraught that I'd ever consider procuring the services of a High Priestess of Santeria to conjure-up a mystical spell to have my ~~turbobitch~~ Lambie Pie's stool turn to concrete, or anything like that. In the end, I just guess some guys just aren't cut out for Holy Matrimony. Holy Matrimony; now, there's an oxymoron for you.

Bitter? What me, bitter? Get outta here. Pshaw! Why be bitter over thirty-eight years of your life down the rathole. If you get bit by a snake, what are you gonna do? Blame the snake? Hell no; it was your own freakin' fault for getting so damn close to that snake.

Has it been frustrating for me? You can bet the farm at Caesar's Palace it has. Will I ever remarry? At this point in time, and at my age, why tempt the gods now? With that all said, let me tell you how I *really* feel.

Statistically, fifty percent of all first marriages in this country end in divorce; eighty percent of all second marriages and ninety percent of all third marriages. For the life of me, I can't possibly imagine what type of DNA a person must possess to endure three marriages; you'd have to be one tough son of a bitch with testicles made out of titanium and a single digit I.Q.

I'm not going to snivel or whine over the little stuff in life that we all go through in a marriage, that would be petty of me. Like the time I had to explain to ~~(my lawfully wedded nightmare)~~ my lovely bride how to cook scrambled eggs on our honeymoon. The young missus wanted to know what you put in the bowl with them. Water? And, do you just crack the eggs into a container (I can only presume she thought you ate them out of the same receptacle you cooked them in), or just put the yokes on a plate? Apparently, her original idea was not to even cook them; but, just . . . sort of . . . scramble them all up . . . in something. They ended up tasting like a boiled ferret. We progressed way beyond that in our ~~(debacle)~~ relationship, but not—even at our final demise—to the point of investing in a cookbook. But, like I said: I'm not gonna get all petty here; after all, I'm not a petty person.

Fast-forward thirty—eight years. By then, she could pretty much heat up a frozen pizza, sort of. She still had some difficulty deciding which rack to put the pizza on, the first or the second. I caught her one day moving her finger back and forth, from the first to the second rack, while singing to herself:

"Eeeny, meeny, miny, moe,
Catch a tiger by the toe.
If he hollers, let him go,
Eeny, meeny, miny, moe.
Your mother told me to pick the very best one, and that is Y-O-U!"

I kept putting a post-it note, next to the bake button on the oven, reminding her it was the second rack, to no avail.

Snuggle Puss burnt one of her gastronomical delights to cinders one particular day. When I heard the smoke alarm go off (that's usually how she timed-out most of our meals), I told her I was cocksure that whatever she was cooking was done. She told me: "It still has three minutes to go yet, according to the automatic timer." It came out looking like something from an industrial accident, or maybe something a kid would pick up off a subway floor. Well, at least it wasn't radioactive.

Her cuisine, to say the least, was just marginally better than hunger. Moreover, the ingredients she came up with, for most of her dynamite cremations, were picked at random using the "one potato, two potato, three potato, four" method of decision-making, learned at the Beavis and Butthead School of Intestinal Delights. Listen, I don't mean to be petty, but I don't think meat loaf should glow in the dark. What's that old adage? Brush your teeth after every meal. I used to count mine! I'm sure glad I'm not petty.

I really didn't mind the expense, nor the waste the ex created; it was the aggravation, 24/7. My ~~Brain Scrambler~~ April Rose would toddle into a room, to get her purse, then put on the fan and light, and immediately saunter out, leaving the fan spinning round and the light ablaze for the next ten hours. She'd do this with every alcove she wandered into and usually, by noon, all the fans and lights in the joint were working overtime. By nightfall, we'd be lit up like an all-night liquor store and cooler than a cucumber. One time, Baby Cakes even managed to leave the light, for the icemaker, on in the refrigerator door. Imagine that, if you will. How she accomplished that is nothing less than an engineering marvel. At our house, the electric meter was whirling away like an out-of-control freight train headed, full-steam ahead, down Pike's Peak.

Or, my significant other would come home and open all the windows and doors: "to get some air into this stuffy old place"; she wouldn't even bother to check if the air conditioner was already on or not. And, what was Turtledove's response when I ask her why she'd been cooling the great outdoors for the last three hours: "It's no big deal," she'd say in that whiny voice, which was not unlike the braying of a jackass.

When I first got married, I noticed one of my socks was wearing a tad thin in the heel, so I asked her if she could fix it. I don't know what I was thinking at the time. I've never used drugs, so it couldn't have been that I was under the influence. You know what it was. I was spoiled. I had a great mom who could do it all (cook, iron, clean house, darn socks, etc.) and I just assumed that *all* women were taught these domestic tricks that I took for granted, like darning. Another big mistake.

Back to the socks. About a week later, when I was putting them on, right after a shower. I kept pulling, and pulling, and pulling— sweatin' up a storm. I was in a hurry and figured: *Maybe they'd just shrunk a bit from all the scrubbings.* That's what I figured, until I put my sneakers on, stood up, and tried to walk around. I had this massive lump on the bottom of my right foot like some cancerous growth gone wild. It was like trying to walk with a rock in your shoe. What Dear

Heart had done was take the worn-out part on the heel of my sock, lump it all together in one gigantic mass, and just sew it all off at the end. That's why I didn't have any room to get my ankle through the neck of the sock; it was all sewed together. I needed that like a plague of locusts and boils. Best not to dwell too much on the past; after all, it was only a silly wardrobe malfunction. "It's no big deal," right? And besides, I'm not a petty person.

The wifey got mad at me early on in our marriage, when I wouldn't let her have her own checking account. I got to feelin' bad. Maybe it was me, I thought; so, I gave in. I thought everything was going slide-by-easy until (the Chief of Staff) Honeybunch called me one night, from a gas station, in tears. The manager called the police: they took her credit card away, right at the pump, for non-payment. Angel Face wanted me to talk to the cop, so she wouldn't have to spend the night in the hoosegow. I couldn't understand what had happened until we sat down at the kitchen table and went over her checkbook, which consisted of page, after page, after page without a balance. Debits weren't even entered. Dream Puss "had meant to" record them, but "got busy." My (block and tackle) Sweet Patootie logged them all down, she assured me—somewhere.

We did find most of them: on microscopic pieces of paper that were stuffed in her handbag along with paperclips and pennies, shoe polish and lipstick, and enough pens and pencils (what they were for I have no idea; she never wrote anything down, like . . . a note) to provision the Pentagon. Honey Buns didn't have any idea what the balance was in the checking account; thus, she was apprehensive about paying *any* of the bills for fear the next check would bounce, so she just let the accounts (and there were several of them) lapse into default. I tried not to be too hard on her. I got to thinking: Maybe she's not getting enough fiber in her diet, or worse yet, maybe she was missing a gene; you know, like the one you get for . . . *intelligence.*

That's another thing: How unfair the laws are in this country concerning the handicapped. Do you know the Driver's License Bureau won't give you one of those disabled parking stickers for being mentally challenged? I went down to the Department of Motor Vehicles and tried to get one for (the old lady) the Living Doll. I gave them example after example of why she should qualify. They sympathized with me but, no go. That would have been nice; would have gotten me a closer parking space at Wal-Mart, the movie theater, or Dairy Queen. Let's move on, folks, before I slash my wrists.

To say ~~(the old ball and chain)~~ my sweetheart wasn't exactly a mechanically wizard, nor was she on the cutting edge of modern technology would be an understatement to the nth degree; she's still trying to square a circle. Once, I procured this cheap toaster. I bought it because it only had one button on it, which ranged from one to seven, to lightened or darkened the bread. One morning, I caught her turning the toaster upside down, with crumbs falling every which way, in an attempt to get the burnt toast out. She looked like a monkey playing football. I demonstrated to her how one has only to lift the lever on the side to the up position and Voila!—the toast would automatically pop-up. What's that maxim? You just can't fix stupid. My ~~(freak mama)~~ helpmate called me a "know-it-all" and the toaster "confusing." It was like being married to Lucy Ricardo on Crack.

I'd learned early in our marriage to go for the "uncomplicated" when it came to mechanical devices. I once bought a washing machine with a gazillion dials and switches on it. Returning home from work one day, I watched ~~(the old broad)~~ My Little Geranium struggle to operate the appliance. She looked as if she'd taken a fit, talking for the most part in strange tongues, while trying to untie the Gordian knot. However, I distinctly remember hearing her say, every so often, "Abracadabra; bippity, bobbity, boo. I got the mojo." I half expected to find a forklift in the pantry and ~~(the she-wolf named Satin)~~ the Sugar Lump trying to lift the washer upside-down to retrieve my underwear, which ultimately came out a sort of dingy gray color. I ended up taking my T-shirts to the laundry, so I wouldn't be mistaken for one of the homeless when I went shopping.

They say women are the weaker sex. It takes six men—tried and true—to carry a man to his grave, it only takes *one* woman to put him there. Somehow, that doesn't sound like weak to me.

I, literally, dreaded the purchase of a new car. She drove the salesmen nuts with her constant calling (some even refused my repeat business), getting them out of meetings to explain where the horn was. I'd spend hours going over the owner's manual with the little woman. I pretty much had to set aside one Saturday out of every month (for at least the first few months, anyway) for remedial training. We'd go over safety issues like: Where to insert the ignition key, the adjustment of *all* mirrors (even the ones she claimed she "didn't need"), the air conditioner (Yup, my companion through life liked to drive around with the sunroof open and the A/C on), and lastly, seat alignment.

When we got our last new Honda—for the longest time—she would slump down (so only her eyes would peek over the dash), straighten herself out like a yardstick, and extend her foot along the floorboard in order to reach the accelerator pedal; she was several inches short. My ~~old millstone around my neck~~ missing rib didn't know how to fine-tune the car seat and "the instruction booklet wasn't too clear on that." Why didn't she just ~~nag me~~ ask me about it, I wondered?

"I didn't want to bother you," ~~the anchor~~ my little peach said with her barbed tongue. At times, it was hard to keep track of who was in the boat and who was in the water.

Not too long ago, I got up in the middle of the night—on the wrong side of the bed (much to my regret)—to go to the bathroom and nearly broke both ankles (along with my back, neck, and tailbone) tripping over one of her pumps. My roommate had twenty-seven pairs of high-heels (none of which—by the way—are "comfortable," according to her) stuffed under or near her side of the bed. ***Twenty-seven freakin' pairs!*** And, that doesn't include what she has in her closets. Notice how I used the plural, *closets*. Once, she had so many clothes jammed onto *one* of the racks in *one* of her closets that the sheer weight literally tore the plaster off the walls when it collapsed. My ~~cellmate~~ soul mate used under the beds—along with every other niche, cranny, and cubbyhole—for storage. The flophouse I lived in was a Feng Shui nightmare. "A place for everything and everything in its place" is right up there next to her gourmet cooking.

The woman was never happy. My ~~old gasbag~~ little biscuit could sizzle on for hours about how this is not right and that needs fixing (She had a list somewhere) and then punctuate the end of her sentence with . . . "but, I'm not complainin', mind you," as she gave me the old stink eye.

Our conjugal life together? It was probably the closest I'd ever come to a near-death experience. Did you ever see that sci-fi flick, "Night of the Living Dead?" Let's just say our—me and the kitten's—bedroom forays weren't exactly jam-packed with cheap, meaningless, hot monkey sex. I don't want to imply that it was dull but, I wasn't exactly getting laid like it was Helen of Troy with her ass on fire. As a matter of fact, on several occasions, I could remember that even dust in the bedroom would distract me. In fact, we both—mutually agreed—to a sort of metaphysical approach to sex to wit: *Less is more and none is perfect.* Enough said.

Since being married, I've always tried to live by this one simple truism: "Women; you can't live with them." Period! That's it. I think Jesus said that.

I used to wonder where all those eighty-year-old widows came from; you know, the ones you'd see on TV, or read about in the newspapers, who were swindled out of their life savings by some unscrupulous roofer who ripped them off for eighty-thousand dollars and gave them a leaky roof in return. I look at the ex and now I understand exactly where they all came from.

I have this enduring and endearing (forgive me, God, for I know not what I say) vision, burnt into my brain, of the (sourpuss) Sugar Puss in her eighties, with all her belongings (piled high in one of those Wal-Mart shopping carts; the one with the broken, squeaky wheel), eating cat food out of a dumpster; her sagging, torn panty hose puddled down around her orthopedic shoes that were made necessary by the oodles of bunions, coupled with a bazillion big-wiz corns, Moby Dick sized ingrown toenails, bookoo shin splints, a mess of major league heel spurs, as well as a few well-placed metatarsal stress fractures and something called subungual exostosis; all from years of wearing *uncomfortable* footwear from under our bed. With her tootsies in the condition that they were, I certainly do hope that *Yellow Brick Road* isn't farther than the next 7-11 because she couldn't get from here to the end of her thumb. She's hunched over, laboriously and hurriedly shuffling along—as if climbing Mount Everest while trying to stay upright—so she won't be late getting to her sleeping spot under the bridge. To put a period on all of this, I have absolutely no idea what path the ex has traveled down since are our last meeting; but if—by some fortuitous stroke of luck—she did make it to that *Yellow Brick Road*, I do hope, when she gets to Oz, that the Wizard has another brain he can give out.

I don't mean to be petty, but then again, I guess life pretty much is all about petty when you boil it down, isn't it? And, I truly don't mean to rant on, nor aggrandize the state of affairs I went through; I'm just trying to tell you how the cabbage got chewed around my house. We became like tennis players who taunted each other over the net. My *"better half"* seemed to have selective hearing when it came to—

"Yoo-hoo. Oh, yoo-hoo." I heard the snapping of fingers. "You were staring off into space, again."

"Yes, nurse," I said, as I bent over in my wheelchair, trying to retrieve the plastic spoon for my oatmeal that I'd dropped on the hospital floor.

"And how are we feeling today, after our little old nervous breakdown last month?" replied Mrs. Toenut, in that singsong tone of voice, as she wheeled her medical cart into my room.

"I'm not exactly laughing all over myself . . . but, I'm not *complainin'* either; that would be *petty* of me."

"That's not what the doctor says. He says you've been doing quite a bit of complaining lately; making *'much ado about nothing,'* as he likes to say."

"You mean Doctor Finger, that headshrinker?"

"The one and only. Now, guess what?"

"It's time for my enema."

"No, silly boy."

"I'm gonna be a future bed pan user?"

"No. It's time for our little old medicine."

"Ah, geez!" I said, slightly perturbed.

"Now, now. You know how upset yon can get without it."

"But, it's so hard for me to swallow all those pills at once."

"Ssshhh, now. You're complaining again. You know it's not all that difficult."

I pointed to my head and just mumbled: "Helmet. It's the helmet; it so hard to swallow all those capsules with this helmet on."

"But, you know, you have to remain helmeted; especially after that last incident where you tried to bash your brains through that steel grate on the wall that covers those windows over there."

"Ah, geez!" I snapped back, as I reached for her fistful the pills. "When am I gettin' outta this asylum, anyway?"

"Now, you know we don't refer to Happy Times Nursing Home as an asylum, the nuthouse, a dump, or any of those other quaint expressions that you're so fond of using. We like to think of it as your . . . home away from home.

"As far as your release date goes, that'd be up to the doctor. He does say, however, that you're making remarkable progress. It ain't often we have a patient out of their straight jacket and sitting up this quickly, especially so soon after electric shock therapy.

"I remember the brouhaha you caused on the night you were admitted. You kept yelling—over and over again—at the top of your lungs, in a Cuban accent, no less: **'Lucy, I'm home.'** You've come a long way since then."

"It feels like . . . like . . . like a lifetime ago," I managed to respond between swallowing down multi-mouthfuls of sedatives and narcotics.

"Oh, it hasn't been that long. But, enough of those bad thoughts of yours; I've got some good news for you. Your ex-wife is coming to visit you today," said Nurse Toenut as she vigorously grasped both my jaws, squeezed them to the point where I felt my back molars would explode through my cheeks; and then, popped the final tranquilizer—the size of a horse pill—into my mouth herself. While she did that, all that kept pounding, and pounding, and **FUC---G POUNDING** through my brain—like a runaway jackhammer—was: "I hope, Sweet Jesus, she's not gonna follow me to the grave."

"Sir? Oh, sir? You're drooling all over yourself again, sir. And, what did I tell you about that twitching? We don't want to have another little old seizure . . . again, do we?"

"LUCY, I'M HOME."

"Every boy should have two things when he's growing up:
a dog and a mother who'll let him have one."

Unknown

*****

"In your lifetime, try and be the person your dog thinks you are."

Unknown

*****

"In coelo quies."

[*There is peace in Heaven.*]

Epitaph on William Bligh's tomb
Captain of the HMS Bounty
St. Mary's Churchyard
Lambeth, London
1754-1817

*****

Paris On A Sunday

Christmas, 2013

Cemetery comes from a Greek word meaning "a sleeping place."
They got that right.

Here I sit. Alone. On a cold, granite bench in a cemetery in Florida on Christmas Day. It's where I've been sitting for the past fifteen Christmases. And Thanksgivings. And Mother's Days. And, on July 22ⁿᵈ, that was my mother's birthday. And, on January 25ᵗʰ, that was the anniversary of her death.

> *"They are not long, the days of wine and roses;*
> *Out of a misty dream*
> *Our path emerges for a while, then closes*
> *Within a dream."*

That's the epitaph etched on her tombstone (it's from a poem by Ernest Dowson, 1867-1900), along with her date of birth and death; mine's there too (my date of birth, not my death . . . not yet), as I have the adjoining plot.

Christmas, 1997

I sat holding my mother's hand as she lay in bed, drifting in and out of sleep, one month away—to the day—from dying of ovarian cancer (which her mother died from when Mom was only four). Bing Crosby was crooning *I'm Dreaming of a White Christmas* on the radio. I thought she was going to make it; I really did. I guess I wanted to believe that. Just like I wanted to believe in Santa Claus as a kid, the Tooth Fairy, God, and that you will live forever; it's everybody else that dies, not you. And, not your mom. She must have believed otherwise though: After a few months, she discontinued her chemotherapy (she said it made her too sick, but I wonder now). Near the end, when we were out for a walk—I was pushing her along in a wheelchair—she turned and said: "I know everything is going to be all right; but, if by some chance, things don't work out, maybe I should be cremated and just be done with it. What do you think?" I knew she was facing the inevitable, even if I couldn't.

"A cemetery isn't just for those who pass away," I told her. "It's for the living too. It's a place to go for those left behind, who want to sit and be with their loved ones . . . to talk to them. If you're cremated, it's almost as if you weren't even here. Where would I go to talk to you? Besides, I don't have anyone: no kids, no wife. I was hoping to be buried next to you." With teardrops trickling down her cheeks, Mom smiled with those "happy eyes" (they always seemed to twinkle with sunshine), then hugged me. "That sounds like a wonderful idea. Let's do that," she said.

1950

My first memories were of Mom, when I was growing up in Poughkeepsie, New York. I remember one day how she dressed me in a clean pullover and sent me out to play, told me to be home by noon for lunch. I asked: "How will I know when it's noon?" I couldn't tell time yet. Mom said to look up and when the sun was overhead, come home. I must have gotten it right; she never berated me for being tardy. Always had peanut butter and jelly sandwiches ready; they were my favorites. Still are. Some things never change. Then, I ran outside and stood under the second-story porch of the house next-door (for reasons still unknown to me, to this day). The neighbor proceeded to open the window, then dump out a basin of water, right on my head; the general public did things like that in those days: dump fluids out the windows, instead of down the kitchen drain.

Right after the war, you could let your kids play in the neighborhood without fear; let them go, unattended, to the corner store: the one that was darker than a cave inside. It had wooden planks for floors; was run by an old, short, hunched-over, wrinkled-up, Polish lady (she looked as if she were one-hundred years old to a four-year-old) with gray hair, who was *always* attired in a black dress—that plummeted to her ankles—and who used to reach for the cereal boxes on the top shelves with "the grabber," a wooden pole that had a claw-type hook on the end.

I grew up in a town that had a "5 & 10 Cent Store"—that was actually the name of the store—and you could literally buy things for 5 and 10 cents! Amazing isn't it, compared to today.

I grew up in an era where "grass" was mowed; guys didn't wear earrings; "Aids" were helpers in the Principal's office; where anything that had "Made in Japan" on it was junk; where "Coke" was a cold drink and "pot" was something your mother cooked in. Today, any female, who has reached the age of twenty-two and has never owned a fur coat, has had a terrible upbringing.

1951

I have committed to memory my first day in kindergarten, walking to W. W. Smith School on Church Street. We didn't own a car; we hoofed it everywhere: to church, to school, to the bank, to stores, to the movies—everywhere. I stood outside; wouldn't go in when the bell rang. I stomped my feet and nearly came to tears. When Mom left, I followed her down the street. She had a hell of a time getting me inside to finger-paint. I was so used to spending the day with her; it was the first time we parted—even if it was for only half a day—and I dreaded the experience.

Christmas, 1954

Silently . . . behind the scenes . . . Mom always tried to secretly intervene—in an effort to try and balance out the harshness of life—as she did for me on Christmas Day, 1954.

When I was a kid, my favorite TV show was "The Adventures of Wild Bill Hickok" starring Guy Madison as Marshal James Butler "Wild Bill" Hickok and three-hundred pound Andy Devine as his sidekick ("Wait for me, Wild Bill!"), Deputy Marshal Jingles P. Jones. Wild Bill had two guns, which he wore backwards in unique holsters. I wanted that gun and holster set so badly, but I figured we couldn't afford it; we didn't possess Fortunatus's purse. Not only did I get them, I also got a buckskin jacket with leather fringe that dangled from both sleeves, just like Wild Bill wore. I just know, my mother had everything to do with making that Christmas a most remarkable one; the memory of it is seared into my brain and just reflecting upon it makes up for all the future Christmases that never came.

February, 1956

The terrain had long since frozen over in the Hudson River Valley. It was *real* winter; the type where your nostrils frosted together and the steam from your breath would solidify in the air; if you took a hammer to the vapors, they would shatter like glass, all over the ground. Even the Cream of Wheat that mom made you eat before school (diluted with plenty of milk to make sure there were no lumps) wouldn't warm you up.

I heard: "Here's your dog, lady," as I was getting ready for grade school one morning. I quickly peeked between the banisters on the second floor. A tall stooped-over man with enormous ears—who was older than dirt—stood below me in a winter coat, the stripes on it having washed out a long time ago. His gnarly fingers were cupped around a tiny ball of light brown fur. "My dog jest had a litter, 'bout three week ago."

My mother stood at the front door . . . speechless. It was obvious, from the expression on her face, that she had absolutely no idea what this elderly man was talking about; he saw her expression and continued.

"Name's Denton. I work with your husband down at the machine shop; he said to save him a pup . . . as a birthday present for the boy." My tenth birthday was on the seventeenth of the month and I wanted a dog ever since <u>Rin Tin Tin</u> aired on television. The man's grizzled hands opened. He held a tomtit of a mongrel that he proceeded to hand over to my mother. "For the boy," he said.

Rin Tin Tin was the best buddy of Private Rusty, the orphan boy on the TV series, whose parents were massacred by Indians. Rusty lived on the cavalry post at Fort Apache, Arizona with Lieutenant Rip Masters, Sergeant Biff O'Hara, and Corporal Boone. Rinty followed Rusty everywhere and together they saved the townspeople's lives of nearby Mesa Grande. I wanted to live in that TV show.

As I knelt at the top of the stairs, peeking through the banisters at this pathetic piece of fluffed-up fuzz with big brown eyes, I could hear the words: "Yo ho Rinty!" (the canine attack command that Rusty would yell to Rinty in times of danger) bouncing around in my head as I imagined myself romping around the block with Rinty, saving the lives of my neighbors.

But this dog!, flopping around on the floor where my mother had put it, was barely able to properly walk. It was a scrawny-looking runt—not a big, strong, dependable, heroic German Shepherd.

From the upstairs window, I watched the old dog—who had just dropped off the young dog—leave. Denton climbed into a clunker of a car that looked more primeval than he was; it was from the thirties and had running boards on the sides with only a rust colored primer on it, which was way beyond faded.

I went downstairs to meet my birthday present. Mom still hadn't spoken a solitary word; she just stood there, frozen in the foyer, staring at this fuzz ball that was wobbling about. Then, the fuzz ball took a tinkle on the throw rug. Mom spoke then! Most of which I shall not repeat for the sake of my mother's memory; after all, she was a saint, you know.

I wanted to skip school and stay home with my new pup, but Mom would have none of that. In those days, you had to have double pneumonia coupled with polio; or, at the bare minimum, the inability to hobble—even with the aid of metal leg braces—through an electrical storm, for her to let you stay home. Okay, okay; I was exaggerating a little there. I'm sure if I blew a blood vessel in my brain, Mom would have let me stay home. I spent the next eight hours in school, daydreaming of what to name my newfound friend.

Mom and Dad went 'round that night over "the animal," as Mom called *it*; *it* being a female, by the way. This upset Dad, as he specifically told Denton he only wanted a male.

"I've a good mind to take 'it' back; Denton knew better," he said. Mom smiled. I was more concerned than upset; Rinty was a male. What could a female do (I had watched my younger sister for years and she couldn't do much) to save the lives of my neighbors? My father relented. Mom frowned. Dad then managed to come up with a name, Sandy, which had about as much originality as owning a black dog and calling it Blackie.

To say Dad had a predilection towards being a tightnutter would be an understatement of apocalyptic, biblical proportions; he wouldn't have paid twenty-five cents to watch Christ ride a bicycle, much less have paid a similar amount to own Rin Tin Tin.

We weren't soup kitchen poor. What little we had, we kept because the old man believed in an ascetic standard of existence: no *extravagant* wasting of hard-earned money on *luxuries,* such as dining out in restaurants (not even for birthdays, anniversaries, or graduations); no new dresses, nor diamonds as big as horse turds for Mom; no frivolous vacations, or *any* form of entertainment. And, all of us, in the family, were suspected of being *extravagant spendthrifts.* If we got caught running the hot water in the shower—just a smidgen longer than he felt was necessary to get clean—he'd go down into the cellar, giggling, and turn off the hot water off; we'd have to finish the shower in cold water and learn not to waste the hot water next time. He showed us! It wasn't as if we wanted to see Elvis wrestle Satan, purchase a big, honkin' sports car, or anything of that magnitude; we just wanted some hot water to get clean.

The bottom line: He knew "the value of a buck" and tried to teach it to me at an early age; and, he surely wasn't going to spring for a purebred German Shepherd when he could easily get a co-worker to give him a mongrel, for free, as a birthday gift for his son.

*****

Nothing was ever done first-rate for my father; there were never the least little nods or shrugs of approbation. When I built my first model airplane (which I had to buy with my own money because it was considered an "*extravagant* waste of money" for a ten-year-old), he told me it was "a terribly, botched job": I'd splattered too much glue around the cockpit. He stressed his disappointment at what a failure I was to be in life.

A mother's love knew just how to realign my center of gravity. "That tiny bit of paste is fine. It's your first one, don't worry; it's a good job."

Spring of 1958

One Saturday, I went to mom for a dime to go to the movies. She didn't have one. Back then, women didn't work for a living; they didn't have their own income. They had to depend on the good will of their husbands and Dad left her penniless. She told me to ask my father. I did. He turned me down too, but not because he didn't have a dime. His explanation: He was brought-up in the depression with eight brothers and sisters and wasn't "given" anything as a kid; he had to make his own way. He had to collect firewood from the Hudson River to burn in the stove for heat—not as a luxury, but to survive. His family grew vegetables in the back yard; not as a hobby, but to survive. His father was committed to an insane asylum (he died there, forty-one years later), just after the ninth child was born. His mother (my grandmother) put several of the younger siblings in a foundling home while she held down a full-time job in the day and scrubbed floors at night; she worked those jobs until she could get her children out. He worked as a paperboy (until he was eighteen) and gave the money to his mother; many of his brothers and sisters had to leave school (one only got to the sixth grade; only two ever completed high school) to work, so the family could eat.

"Life is a war; if you're a weak soldier, you die." I would have "to learn the hard way," just like he had, about "all the disappointments in life," about "the value of a dollar." If I wanted to go to the movies, I would have to "go out and get a job; don't expect others to pay your way." He summed up by saying that it was about time I learned it's up to me to make my own way in this world, by myself, and not to depend on anyone else, because no one else in this world is gonna care what happens to you. A hard lesson for a twelve year old. I guess he figured since he didn't have a happy childhood, I shouldn't either; that way I'd learn.

My first job was as an errand boy after school. I would grocery shopping after school at the local A & P for Mrs. Dennis, a lonely widow in her eighties without anyone to talk to except me, as I later found out. Mrs. Dennis never paid me for my services until after I went down memory lane with her concerning tales of her youth, of her being trapped up a tree with her kitten in the Johnstown flood. She paid me fifteen cents for my labor, enough for a Saturday matinee and a box of Juju Bees. I shopped at the supermarket and cut grass in the neighborhood until I got a paper route.

My father claimed to be a devout Roman Catholic; but, I'm not all that sure that the Church was that keen, or that enthusiastic about claiming him . . . as anything, much less devout, and much less as one of their own. I always thought he was a bit of an ogre. He made sure I followed "the Lord": confession every Saturday (Whatever could a twelve-year-old boy get into that he needed to go to confession every week?), mass every Sunday, novenas every Monday, and the family knelt on the floor—every night—and said the rosary.

The majordomo was one of those emotionally (Ah, the rantings! Ah, the fire and brimstone!) and physically abusive men. Despite being six-feet tall and weighing 225 pounds, he was a "*little*" man. Evening meals consisted of my father quoting the Bible or Scriptures (he used both words interchangeably), usually about what I had done wrong that day and why I was headed straight for Hell. He would work himself into a frenzy: eyeballs rolled back, wild demons bubbling-up inside his head like a madman. Ranting and raving, veins a poppin' in his forehead, while waving his hands about—over his head—towards the Almighty, he would scream at the top of his lungs: **"The truth shall make you free!"** He would bang his fists so hard on the kitchen table—as if it were on a church pulpit preaching a sermon to a congregation of heathens—that the silverware would bounce into the air and plates would rattle about the tabletop. It would frighten Sandy who sat underneath the table, waiting for the scraps of food that I did not particularly care for. You knew you were in for a bumpy dinner whenever he prefaced the meal with, "The Bible says . . ." And, somewhere during the course of the meal, he'd make it crystal clear to me that the Bible said the only thing he was obligated to provide for me was food, clothing and a roof over my head.

The Preacher, as I nicknamed Dad, believed in a literal translation of the Bible. He would talk of sin: "According to the Scriptures, 'If your eye offends you, pluck it out.'" Then, for emphasis—at a decibel level that only a supersonic jet could approximate—he would spew forth from his blowhole: **"PLUCK IT OUT!"** According to him, if you sin with your eyes, pluck them out; the same for your hands, arms, legs, ears . . . or whatever bodily organ was deemed offensive. I consider myself fortunate in life that I left home with all the digits on my extremities intact . . . and with both eyes functioning

My father reminded me of Raymond Massey in the movie "The Santa Fe Trail," which I saw one Saturday at the Stratford Theatre. Errol Flynn and Ronald Reagan were the leads and Massey played the abolitionist, John Brown: an intense, religious zealot who believed God directed him to wipe out slavery by murdering all those who opposed him. That was the Preacher: trying to be Christ-like, all the while inflicting pain—with his fanatical ways—wherever he went.

Summer of 1958

Sandy was a kind and timid pooch by nature. She got that way after a couple of frightening episodes in the early stages of her development. On one occasion, in her first summer, a group of us were playing softball in the street; Sandy wanted to join in on the fun and bounded into the middle of the roadway. She had no inkling of what an automobile was, much less the damage it could do to a dog's body. A little old lady in a Ford ran over her. Sandy went down; fortunately, none of the wheels struck her. The cars in the fifties were much higher off the ground than todays; she bounced and skidded under the middle of the sedan, got up, and ran for her life. How she escaped any injuries is still a mystery to me, but she did.

We used to open the door and let Sandy out to do her business in the back yard. In the first winter she was with us, being a pup, she sniffed and dawdled her way up the sidewalk until she must have turned around in a panic, knew she had wandered too far and was lost. We looked for her; the neighbors looked for her; everyone looked for her, for days on end. No Sandy. I ate my Cream of Wheat in a state of despair. She may not have been Rin Tin Tin, but she was my first dog. About ten days after her disappearance, Dad was on his way downtown (We walked everywhere: to school, to church, downtown, as we didn't have a vehicle). When he was about two blocks from home, he happened to call out Sandy's name. What for? He had no idea. She climbed out from under a porch and there she stood, shaking. How she lived ten days under a porch is yet another miracle. Home she came, and home is where she stayed from then on; her traveling days were over. She never wandered off her immediate property or into the street again.

When I first got Sandy, I let her sleep on my bed, just as Rinty used to sleep with Rusty. She was small and I hardly knew she was there. However, she grew. And grew. And, grew some more. By the time she was a year old, Sandy was close to seventy pounds. She had gone from a nondescript cur to approximating something like a greyhound with her curved chest. I moved her to the landing, but she left a spot on the wallpaper from her shiny coat, so I had to move her to the cellar which had no heat, nor light in the winter. How tragic, looking back. From a warm bed to a dark, cold cellar. What must that dog have thought? But, Sandy accepted it all in good stead.

It was about this time that my father proclaimed that Sandy had to get fixed and that I "had to pay for the operation" since I "took on those responsibilities in life by wanting this dog."

"Wanting this dog?!" I wanted Rin Tin Tin.

The procedure cost twenty-five dollars, which in 1958 was a lot of money, especially for a twelve-year-old boy. I saved my birthday money, also the money I got from mowing lawns and running errands. The day finally arrived.

Dad gave me the name of a veterinarian whose office, down by the Hudson River, was about a five-mile trek. I walked Sandy on a rope to this foreboding, grit-covered building with wood planking on the floor, which stood on the side of the hill on lower Main Street. The vet walked with a twisted cane that had knots on it, and he looked in worse shape than Denton's car. It was with some trepidation that I gave "the Doc" my twenty-five, hard-earned dollars. He told me to come back in four days. I came back in two to visit Sandy. She looked in low spirits as she got up in her cage to greet me. I said hello and patted her through the cage. I came back in another two days and we left. I felt bad for her, having to walk five miles after being spayed, but she seemed happy just to be going home. I tried to carry her, but she was too heavy and we made too many stops for water.

Winter of 1958

It was about this time that the beatings began.

"The Bible says: 'Spare the rod and spoil the child'"; that's how my father liked to put it. He felt I had not "properly owned up to my responsibilities in life" and, now that I was older, a stricter form of discipline was required. I guess he figured his tirades at the dinner table weren't getting through to me. The discipline turned to corporal punishment; it started simple enough: an occasional, swift backhand that progressed into several slap shots to the head, the belt followed, and then the beatings; they continued, regularly, until I was about sixteen years of age.

Once, the slave driver was remodeling the kitchen floor with linoleum. I was the *go-fer*. I was in charge of going-fer the cleaning rag, or the linoleum knife; whatever it was, I'd go-fer it. I was going-fer something, one day during this major project, when I accidentally stepped on one of the linoleum squares that had just been glued down; it slipped sideways, making a mess.

Dad went dark in a hurry; it was like uncorking a bottled monster with monkey pox. I found myself on the receiving end of a first class pounding. Simon Legree threw a double-duck fit, then slammed me against the wall with such force that the house shook; he was a man with a lot of crush. I felt as if I were going over Niagara Falls in a barrel. Then, out came the belt. He pummeled my bedraggled body for what seemed like an eternity, but was probably closer to five minutes. There were a whole lot of body parts flocking about in the red zone that day. I was tossed around that kitchen like kernels of popcorn in a hot kettle; I sorely wished I had a time-out in my back pocket.

This was the other side of living; this was living on a knife-edge! It was all pretty raw, navigating those swirling waters, but Mom tried her best to intercede. I heard her shrieking: "Holy Aunt Hanna! (She actually used that expression.) Not his face! Don't hit him in his face!"

"BE QUIET, WOMAN, AND LET ME HANDLE THIS!" bellowed the Imperial Potentate.

He had a proclivity for violence and callous strictures; getting him to agree to *anything* was like pulling teeth with your fingers. Short of force-feeding you Sprite and llama urine, then taking away bathroom privileges; or hogtying you to a pickle barrel; or practicing the ancient torture of "Breaking on the Wheel," everything was considered fair game.

I was a bit cast down that day, to say the least, but I managed to gather my umbrage and walk out of that tenebrous room, not bowing and not crawling away, throwing mud. I had some good color in my cheeks (What more could a boy of twelve ask for?), didn't need a cut man or a plastic hip, and there wasn't any blood in my urine or bones in my stool which is always a good sign.

June of 1960

The beating I remembered the most was when I graduated from the eighth grade. A classmate—Johnny Mancuso—threw a party at his house one Saturday night. My father said, "Be home by eleven o'clock." Now, when my father said: "Be home by eleven o'clock," he did not mean eleven-fifteen, eleven-ten, or even eleven-oh-one; what he meant was eleven o'clock, ON THE DOT! Just so we're clear on that. I knew that Deuteronomy is the fifth book of the Old Testament and is Moses' explanation of God's Law. I could quote chapter and verse, so I knew that the Fourth Commandment said: "Honor Thy Father and Thy Mother." That meant to Dad: in all things, in all ways, at ALL times; there were no exceptions, no excuses; the Scriptures did not allow for any.

I had to walk to the party, a few miles, which meant I would be walking home too. When it was about 10:15 at night, I was saying my good-byes when Johnny said: "Hey, my mom and aunt are taking a bunch of kids home. We go right by your place. We could drive you home too." Being apprehensive, I asked Mrs. Mancuso—who was sitting at the kitchen table with her sister—when she'd be leaving, as I didn't want to be late.

"I'll be leaving in a couple of minutes; just as soon as I finish this cup of coffee."

I guess Mrs. Mancuso figured if she told her kid to be home by eleven, and if he got a ride with the parents of the party-giver, and if he was a little late, well . . . that was a good excuse. Evidently, Mrs. Mancuso was a heathen, who had never read the Scriptures, nor studied the Ten Commandments.

Mrs. Mancuso had a second cup of coffee that night and I got home at eleven-fifteen.

My father was waiting for me. He saw me exit the vehicle outside, but never asked: What time is it? Why were you late? Who drove you home? Once inside the front door, he hit me on the side of my head; the blow was so overwhelming that it knocked my feet from under me. Holding me by the ankles, he dragged me up the stairs—deliberately banging my head against each step—until we reached the second floor landing; then, he threw me onto my bed and hammered me with his fists. Then, out came the belt, which he proceeded to thrash me with, mercilessly.

"Yo ho Rinty!" Sandy to the rescue. The tiny ball of light brown fur had become a big ball of light brown fur that leapfrogged onto the bed, getting between Dad and me. She growled, showed her teeth (though everyone in the room knew she wasn't going to bite anyone), and ricocheted around the sheets; no matter which way Dad turned Sandy was there: snapping, jousting about, and fending off the blows. He threw her onto the floor; faster than a speeding bullet, she was back. Finally, he gave up and walked away rubbing his fists. As he reached my bedroom door, he turned, "I said: 'Be home by eleven o'clock.' The fourth commandment says, 'Honor Thy Father and Thy Mother.' That'll teach you to disrespect your parents."

Far worse than the weekly batterings was the daily fear of them. Being abused as a child changes you; it robs you of developing into the person you might have been.

Sometimes I'd forget to let the dog out and she'd relieve herself in the cellar that Dad used as a workshop. My father would beat me and I, in turn, would beat the dog. She would look at me with those big brown eyes as if to say, *What have I done to so enrage you?* She forgave me however, the minute the buffeting stopped; I know because she licked my hand with her pink tongue; she was too much of a good dog to have done otherwise. Through my own shameful disregard, I took out my frustrations on a poor, dumb animal that only had the utmost love for me. Had I turned into John Brown from *The Santa Fe Trail?* Or, to quote the Bible: ". . . I was my father's son . . ." From then on, I tried to be the opposite of what my father preached and more like an uncle I had, who became my early mentor, my role model in life.

The czar of our household was a man, badly made, but the kind you didn't dare flip off: a carbon copy of Mom's father, both of whom could make you grind your back teeth to a knub. Mom and I shared a tacit identity: When she was eighteen, to escape her domicile in Washingtonville, New York and an emotionally abusive and neglectful father (he so ignored her dental hygiene that by the time she approached eighteen, she needed a full set of false teeth—uppers and lowers—to replace *all* of her decayed ones), she married an emotionally abusive husband, thirty miles away. Little did she know she was walking always from a dimly lit flame and into a raging fire. Both men were about as deep as a puddle; neither was noted for his ability to charm the birds out of the trees, and you never wanted to stick your hand in either's cage. Talk about a couple of truculent, Alpha males with high testosterone levels; they made Robert Mitchum look like a sissy boy. Both were out of their autocratic senses—avoiding some real clinical issues—and needed to be on medication of some sort. God should have raised the bar a tad more when it came to creating these two beings, possibly a little bit more in *HIS* image and likeness.

*****

87

Happy Eyes—never the warden—gifted me with her loyalty and devotion; taught me a value system: that accounts not balanced in this world must be carried over into the next. The things she taught me weren't about high-tech, problematic issues like how to untie the Gordian knot; but rather, about *the little stuff in life*. Like walking along the outside of the sidewalk when escorting a date home; don't sharpen your tongue with a whetstone, then sit on the sidelines and spear your friends; it's an honest man that talks slowly; to open and hold doors for females; she even taught me the box step before I attended my first sock hop.

I must have learned how to waltz pretty well (I did have a good teacher) because the girls would line up to *ask me* to dance. I once turned one down: I was all danced-out. Mom heard about it, and over breakfast one morning, gave me this cogent and sage piece of advice: "Don't be so quick to turn a girl down." When I asked "Why not?; they turn me down," she replied: "That school shindig might have been important to her; she could have been lookin' forward to that for months, maybe even bought a new dress for the occasion (they didn't have any sports, or outside activities, for young ladies back then). Consider how embarrassed it makes you feel when a girl turns you down. You know how hard it is for you to go up and ask them to dance, and you're a young man."

Sensing something coming my way, I hesitatingly responded with: "Ye . . . ah."

"Well, how hard do you think it must have been for that girl to ask you—a boy—to dance? Imagine how she must have felt when you said, 'No thanks.' You don't want her feelings hurt like that, now do you?"

I didn't have anything to compare those sentiments to, so I thought about how I felt when the boss man would upbraid me, and then I had an idea of how hurt those feelings must have been. I never turned a girl down again, even though I haven't danced now in over twenty years; not being asked much lately.

*****

Throughout the years, Mom was *always* there for me: When I got the croup—which was every year when I was in my single digits—she nursed me back to health. Through all the tears from the cruel and pejorative taunts and teasing of classmates, she bolstered my confidence. She was the one who sewed the torn knees in my school pants, darned my socks, who was with me at the hospital for those stitches in my head (eyebrow, back, chin; you get the picture). She cooked, cleaned, sewed, and worked a part-time job. She was the dietician who made me eat my prunes, so I'd be "regular." I never knew what "regular" meant until I started eating prunes. Then, from handouts from under the table, Sandy also found out what "regular" meant.

Mom was the most optimistic person I have ever met in my life; she could put the most advantageous spin on the most unfortunate of circumstances. If she had been the Captain of the Titanic—when it hit that iceberg in 1912, in the middle of the Atlantic Ocean, and stopped dead in the water—she would have, cheerfully and confidently, addressed the panic-stricken passengers, over the P.A. system—in the most assured, unflappable, angelic of voices—by calming announcing to all: "Don't worry about a thing; we just stop to pick up a little ice for the party tonight." She was always telling me not to dwell on the negative, but to "look for the sunny side of life. Who knows? It just might be right around the next corner."

She was also the nurse who would hurdle herself between my father and the thrashings, trying to maintain peace (and save my life); a banker (for loans that never needed repaying); a confessor and best friend—who listened to my aspirations and dreams, then tucked me into bed at night. As she put out the lights, she would always say, in her dulcet voice: "Sweet dreams."

As I grew older and moved through life, I tried to keep a centered equilibrium coupled with a sense of humor. I always believed that your future happiness may well depend on your ability to leave the past behind.

I went to college, got married, then moved to Florida.

My grandmother took Sandy to her job as a live-in cook at a retreat house for the Sisters of Charity in rural Stanfordville, New York. Sandy loved it there: total country with loving nuns to fuss over her, all day long.

My mother called me one day in the early seventies. "Sandy died," she said. Mom always tried to ignore the unpleasantness of life and put some positive spin on a bad situation.

"She had a good life and lived to be seventeen. Grandma and the nuns buried her in the garden, out back by the chapel."

How apropos for Sandy, I thought. A perfect, peaceful place for a perfect, peaceful dog. It wasn't until thirty years later that my father told me the real story: Sandy was old, nearly blind, and had trouble walking. He took her to a vet on Manchester Road and had her put to sleep. She ended life in a garbage dumpster. What a tragic end, I thought. She deserved better than that. She deserved that grave in the garden that only existed in Mom's imagination.

It was then, fifty years after that tiny ball of light brown fur first arrived, that I realized what I truly had as a lad. I wanted Rin Tin Tin and was disappointed when it turned out to be this silly brown mutt, but what I got was better that Rinty. A Heinz 57 that was timid and shy, but when the chips were down, she rode to my rescue ("Yo ho Rinty!") and hurdled herself between my father and the thrashings, trying to maintain peace and protect a boy from the beatings he got in his youth. A dog that slept with, and comforted him. A dog when shunned, locked away in a dark cold cellar and beaten, stood up for that abused boy with a never-ending love. I look back today; don't even have a photo of Sandy, only the memories. I had a dog that had more loyalty for me than I ever had for her and for that, I am ashamed. I've since adopted this philosophy on life: the best way for a man to live up to his full potential, as a human being, is to try to become the person his dog thinks he is.

The older I've gotten, the sadder the world seems; but, every so often, you get to look back at a bright spot and smile. I look back to a wintry morning in 1956 and into those big brown eyes, with the little dog soul deep within them, and smile. I miss that puppy breath on my face and the dog spit on my pillowcase. Now that I am closer to the end than to the beginning, I am full of repentance over a sandy-colored friend and savior. I believe what that great American humorist, Will Rogers, once said about dogs: "If there are no dogs in Heaven, then when I die I want to go where they went."

When you're young, time goes so slowly. The days in grade school seemed to drag on, forever, before you were finally able to go home and play with your first puppy, a brown dog named Sandy. Then, in high school, all you wanted to do was play football, kiss a girl (you had forgotten about the dog by then), and drive a car. Sixteen seemed as if it was never gonna come, so you could get your license. Then, you couldn't wait until college: to join a fraternity, drink, and have sex with women. No more girls; it's women that you were after then! Fun, fun, fun, interspersed with a limited amount of work. Very limited.

Then, all too abruptly, you're out of college. You get your first job, get married, buy your first house (and all the bills that go with it), and that's when things begin to gather momentum; you can't seem to slow the universe down. It becomes work, work, and work, interspersed with some fun, like when I turned forty in Paris at the Moulin Rouge. It was Utopia: the Louvre; the artists in Montmartre; the Place de la Concorde; sauntering under the L'arc de Triomphe and over the cobblestone walkways in the Latin Quarter; up the Eiffel Tower; across the Seine, via the Pont Neuf, to the Ile de la Cite. To me, meandering through the four-hundred year-old Jardin du Luxembourg on the Left Bank, then down the Champs Elysees on a Sunday afternoon, was as close to Heaven on Earth as it got.

*****

In later years, I went on to become a cop in Miami; worked the Vice Squad (the real, shoot-'em-up Miami Vice) for thirteen of my twenty-two years on the force; saw a lot of creation's wretchedness and despair, a lot more than I care to conjure up.

And learned a lot.

I learned that the world is a double-hard place to live in; you've got to have a tough pair of rubber nuts to get through it. For me, it's been a big disappointment, a lot sadder than it's been happier. As you make your way along this earth, the sadness follows you: the death of my first dog, your relatives, your friends . . . but, through it all were those set of happy eyes. Then, you come to that point in your existence when you realize that you're not going to live forever; that you're a lot closer to the end than to the beginning. Life is like a roll of toilet paper: the closer you get to the end, the faster it spins. And then—suddenly—it's over, when it should just be beginning. Mind you, I'm not complaining; I'm just telling you how the cabbage got chewed, is all.

Christmas, 1997

On her deathbed, my mother held my hand, and choking back her emotions, told me how she regretted she couldn't' have done more to save me from that flogging over the linoleum, forty years earlier.

(I knew that women in the forties and fifties had little choice, if any, than to stick it out with the man they married in life; the Catholic Church forbad divorce and also birth control; women didn't have the job skills that men did, nor the opportunity to obtain them; and employers just plain discriminated against women when it came to hiring them over a man; so, what could a woman do with a couple of kids, no job, nowhere to stay, nor a means to put food on the table? Marriage to the wrong man, back in those days, was the equivalent of a death sentence.)

I told her that she was the best mom ever; that she gave me all the encouragement I ever needed to succeed. And, if it weren't for her, I'd probably have run away in my teens. I only endured the beatings so as not to break her heart. I told her to rest easy; she had done more than her best.

Secretly, I always felt she never had much of a life as a child, nor throughout her marriage. I felt she gave me a better childhood than she ever had, and I truly appreciated the sacrifices she went through to give it to me. And, I tried—especially when times got the hardest—to always "look for the sunny side of life. Who knows? It just might be right around the next corner."

Christmas, 2012

I probably could have done without a father in life (you only get one; sometimes, it's just the wrong one; you don't get to pick) for it is from him that I learned about anger and intolerance in this world; abusive people are like that: They project onto you whatever they don't like about themselves. I realize now that a lot of his anger, which was directed towards me, was because he had tried to climb inside my head and make it his own, but I would never let him. It was this castigating man that was the true failure in life: he failed at all that *he wanted to be*, at all that was *important to him*: as a husband, as a father, and as a Christian.

And, Dad now? Well, the Preacher Man is ninety-three now, an old man with liver spots, limping along on the edge of his grave. His hands shake like a paint-mixing machine at Sears; can't take a pee in the toilet without hitting the floor; has that grandpa smell about him; scabs on his knees and elbows, as if he'd been dragged behind a car on a chain; but, if I'm not mistaken, he still has his First Communion money. And, as far as the old tyrant ever getting the truth straight about the Bible or life, for that matter, he reminds me of that character Tom Cruise played (Lt. Daniel Kaffe) in the 1992 movie, *"A Few Good Men."* Cruise, while cross-examining Jack Nicolson (Colonel Nathan R. Jessep) in court, asks him for the truth. Nicolson responds: "You can't handle the truth!" Funny how life works out, isn't it.

*****

I know I could have done without a father in life, but I know I could not have done without Sandy; it's from that dog that I learned to accept things as they are in life and to keep on loving to the end; all from a brown dog that lived in the cellar.

I also know I could not have done without Mom, for it is from her that I learned about loving to the core and patience; to me, she still is all things, both bright and beautiful, in this world. I read somewhere that you never really die if someone remembers you. I hope that is true; then, Sandy and Mom's spirits will live on.

If I remember my Bible, which I ought to after all of the evening suppers spent with the Preacher drumming it into me, Jesus said: "Blessed are the peacemakers, for they shall be called the children of God." Wouldn't that be wonderful place: a world full of Sandy's and mom's like mine.

There's a pedestrian apothegm: "Time heals all wounds." Not true. Some things you just never seem to get over; they're all you ever had, and all you're ever gonna have.

Here it ends, with me sitting in a cemetery on Christmas Day with these deep feelings, eating a peanut butter and jelly sandwich (some things never change), trying to find the sunny side of life while thinking about all *the little stuff in life*. It all seems many a million dreams ago now. Funny, isn't it, how it only took a moment . . . a moment to go from Wild Bill Hickok to the grave. Then, I realized, for a little while—when Mom was here—why it always felt like Paris on a Sunday.

Sweet dreams, Happy Eyes.

"I hope that life isn't just a big joke because I don't get it."
Deep Thoughts by Jack Handey

*****

Sampson And Lila

(a one-act play)

Cast of Characters

Winston "Winney" Bumpus

In his late fifties; strictly blue-collar, all the way;

works for Dandy Doodle Pies; married thirty-four years to wife, Lila.

Lila Bumpus

In her early fifties;
Irish/Catholic (born in Ireland);
harried housewife;
spouse of Winston.

Stanley Stonebreaker

In his mid-sixties;
Superintendent (for the last thirty-five years) of the apartment building where the Bumpuses live.

<u>Setting</u>

The entire action of the play takes place in the modest kitchen of a Bronx, New York apartment where Winston and Lila Bumpus live.

<u>Time</u>

The present.

Act One

The time is now, early evening.

The scene is a small kitchen with a stove, refrigerator, mirror on the wall, a kitchen table with four chairs in an apartment complex in the Bronx, New York.

As THE CURTAIN RISES, we see LILA BUMPUS; she is the typical harried homemaker who is scurrying around a cluttered kitchen, cooking dinner.

The door opens and her husband, WINSTON "WINNIE" BUMPUS, enters; despite his aristocratic first name, he is completely blue collar in every respect. He is wearing a cap and a uniform jacket with a logo on it that says: "DANDY DOODLE PIE COMPANY." He is carrying three pies.

LILA
(*in an Irish brogue*)
Aye, the pie man is home . . . finally. And look! Just watt wee be a needin' in this house . . . more fuckin' pies. They must put a sign, on every third pie that toddles down the line at the Dandy Doodle Pie Company:
(*Stretches her hand above her head, as if picturing a sign*)
"Deliver to the home of Winston and Lila Bumpus."
(*a beat*)
I got pies coming out of me ass, I do . . . Oh well, find yourself a place to put them down . . . somewheres. I suppose you'd be a wantin' your supper now . . . to go with them pies.

WINSTON
(*in a thick Bronx accent*)

Well, I—

LILA

I know. I know.

WINSTON
(*Looking for a place, amidst the disarray in the kitchen, to place the pies*)

Ya know? Ya know what?

LILA

I know watt yur'd be a thinkin', I do.

WINSTON

How would ya know what I'm thinkin'? I jest walked in the door. I don't even know what I'm thinkin'.

LILA

Because.

WINSTON

Because? Because what?

LILA

Aye, because I can tell by that look on yur face there, Mr. Bumpus.

WINSTON
(*Studying his mug in the wall mirror*)

What look?

LILA
(*Busing herself putting plates and silverware on the kitchen table*)

That look on there . . . There on yur face. I know. I know.

WINSTON

Ya know what?

LILA

I know watt you'd gonna be a sayin' next.

WINSTON

Now, how do ya know what I'm—

LILA

Yur tired, yude had a rough day at work, and yur hungry.

WINSTON

How do ya know?

LILA

Because yur always tired, yur always be a havin' a rough day at work, and yur always hungry. That's how come I know.

WINSTON

Well, as a matter of fact—

LILA

Like I'm not?

WINSTON

Not what?

LILA

Tired, had me a rough day, and hungry.

WINSTON

(*WINSTON puts the three pies, next to three other pies, atop the refrigerator.*)
I didn't say—

LILA

I know. I know.

WINSTON

Didn't we jest go through all that? Now you're supposed ta say: "Like I ain't."

LILA

Meaning?

WINSTON

Meaning . . . like you're tired, had a rough day, and are hungry too.

LILA

That'd be it. Go ahead. Make fun of me, like you always be a doin'. Washin', cleanin', and slavin' away here . . . all day . . . over this hot stove. This is not a picnic going on around here, you know. Keepin' up with those two kids of yurs—

WINSTON

They're your two kids too, ya know.

LILA

I sometimes wonder, watt with the genes those two be a havin'.

WINSTON

If anybody should be wonderin' about their genes, it ought ta be me . . . I mean, if anybody should know if those kids are their's, you'd think it'd be you; after all, ya was supposedly there when they were conceived.

LILA

Aye . . . well, maybe I got bored, as usual with you, and fell asleep and don't remember.

WINSTON

Don't remember? Ya delivered 'em. I saw ya! I was with ya, in the hospital . . . both times, when ya delivered those kids. How can they not be your kids too?
(*WINSTON takes off his cap and jacket and tosses them onto a chair.*)
Jesus!

LILA

Don't be goin' askin' Him fer no help. He ain't gonna help no sinner the likes of you.

WINSTON

What?

LILA

You heard me.

WINSTON

Now, how'd ya come to that conclusion? Christ.

LILA

Now, there ya be a goin' again, with the prayin' to the Lord.

WINSTON

I ain't prayin' to no Lord.

LILA

Then, ya are a blasphemin', which is a worse thing yet.

WINSTON

Listen. How did ya manage to turn this whole thing around and make it be about me?

LILA

What whole thing you be a talkin' 'bout?

WINSTON

(*WINSTON gets up, opens the refrigerator and pops open a beer.*)
There ya go again.

LILA

That'd be it. Go be a gettin' drunk, why don't you . . . again. That'll solve everything for you, won't it? Go searchin' for your identity in the bottom of a beer bottle.

WINSTON

God Almighty, woman. Yu'd drive the Lord, and His powers to be, down the path to alcoholism. And He'd probably thank Heaven ta go. Just soes He could put a smile on His face again.

LILA

That'd be your answer to everything.

WINSTON

What is?

LILA

Alcohol and the denial it brings.

WINSTON

Who's in denial?

LILA

You are.

WINSTON

No, I'm not.

LILA

SEE!

WINSTON

(*WINSTON sits back down at the kitchen table; both of their voices grow louder.*)
Hey! I'm not in no denial. I'm very much in the present . . . unfortunately. I'm here all right. If I was in denial, I wouldn't wanta be here . . . trapped . . . like a rat—

LILA

AH HA! At last, we be havin' the right word for you.

WINSTON

What word's that?

LILA

A rat.

WINSTON

My, oh my, on my. How ya sure can twist things around.

LILA

It's not me be a twistin' things around. It's you, yurself, that used that very word, just now, to describe yurself, you did. And a better word one could not find in the entire dictionary for you.

(*LILA heads to the stove and continues cooking. She points her finger at WINSTON.*)

And, don't be takin' the name of the Lord in vain again, just because you hung yourself on your own petard.

WINSTON

Hung myself on my own what?

LILA

Petard. Petard. Go finds yourself a dictionary and look it up. Get educated.

WINSTON

Since when you been readin' the dictionary? Ya daffy witch of an Irish woman.

LILA

Oh, so now I'm a daffy witch, am I?

WINSTON

A man just can't win with ya. Listen. Havin' a couple of beers, after a hard day's work, is my only pleasure in life, anymore.

LILA

(*LILA begins to slam pots and pans about the stove, turns the heat up and down, and is generally fuming.*)

Oh, so I don't be givin' ya any pleasure in life no more, do I?

WINSTON

That's not what I meant.

LILA

Oh, it's not, is it? That's what it sure sounded like from where I'd be standin'. Poor man. Poor, poor man. You're a regular martyr 'round here, yude be.

(*a beat*)

So, where would yude rather be then?

WINSTON

What do ya mean?

LILA

You just said, when you was describin' how you was a rat . . . a trapped rat, at that . . . and I'll be a quotin' ya here and now: "If I was in denial, I wouldn't wanta be here." Thems your exact words, they be.

WINSTON

Well, I don't know. I haven't had much time ta think about it.

LILA

Oh, you haven't, have you? Well, how 'bout I take off with the kids . . . and the supper, and give you plenty of time to be a thinkin' 'bout it.

WINSTON

Let's not go gettin' all rash here.

(*a small smile; trying to get back in LILA's good graces*)

Besides, you jest got done sayin' how them kids ain't yours anyways. Why would ya want ta haul about with a bunch of kids that ain't yours?

LILA

(*Still fiddling with the pots and pans on the stove and moving about, madly, between the stove and the kitchen table*)

Hmm.

WINSTON

(*trying to inject some humor into the conversation*)

Ya know, watchin' ya cook is sorta like watchin' a dog work a doorknob.

LILA

If ya be so unhappy with your lot in life, why don't cha be enterin' one of those Buddhist monasteries, way up on a Tibetan mountain top somewhere, where they all bees wearin' them hair shirts? You'd look right smart in one of them hair shirts . . . Or better yet, maybe the monks'll let you wear a sackcloth and ashes. You could shave your head and point it towards heaven while contemplatin' your navel . . . since I don't be givin' ya any pleasure in life no more.

WINSTON

You'd like that, wouldn't ya? Me walkin' 'round with a shaved head. You'd just love ta turn me into a Sampson ta you're Lila, wouldn't ya?

LILA

It's **Dee-lila**, you idiot.

WINSTON

Now, who's makin' fun of who?

LILA

I'm not makin' fun of you; I'm just tryin' to help educate you.

WINSTON

Oh, is that it. Well, answer me this. Why is it when I merely mention ya havin' a rough day, ya throw up your nose and go sideways? Ya say I'm makin' fun a ya. But, it's all right for ya ta call me an "idiot"; that ain't makin' fun of me. No, that's . . . "tryin' ta help educate me," accordin' ta you.

LILA

You wantin' to know why?

(*LILA stops her cooking and glares at WINSTON; she is waiting for a reply. WINSTON just continues to sit in his chair with a blank stare. Finally . . .*)

WINSTON

Well, okay. I'm just waitin' ta hear this one . . . Why?

LILA

Well, okay. I'll be a tellin' you why, since you asked.
(*a beat*)
I call things the way they are. Jesus said: "The truth shall make you free." I'm not in no denial like you. Yule see the light, once you get up in that Buddhist monastery, on that Tibetan mountain top, with yur shaved head pointin' to heaven. Yule be able to read all about it in the Good Book there.

WINSTON

Hey!, if tellin' the truth was all it took ta set me free of this fresh Hell here,
(*Looks at LILA, then around the kitchen; folds his hands, towards heaven, as if pleading to God*)
I'd be prayin', in a church, night and day, with a crucifix in one hand while sprinklin' myself with holy water with the other hand.

LILA

And, watt would you be a knowin' 'bout prayin'?

WINSTON

A lot, that's what. I get down on my hands and knees every night and pray ta God.

LILA

For watt? Your next six-pack?

WINSTON

No, for an early death, so as I can end all this misery.

LILA

Let me tell you something, Winston: the cheese slipped off your cracker a long time ago. No need to go be a prayin' 'bout it.
(*WINSTON starts to peruse the newspaper.*)
When'd you start prayin', anyways?

WINSTON

On our honeymoon. It's thirty-four years later and I'm still hopin' God will pick up the phone.

LILA

God works in mysterious ways, he does.

WINSTON

I gotta question fer ya. A sorta philosophical question, since ya knows it all . . . If a man makes a mistake in the forest, and there's no woman around ta see it, is it still a mistake?
(*Both of their voices are really starting to carry now.*)

LILA

He was a probably up to something he shouldn't have been up to and therefore, he shouldn't have even been in the forest, in the first place, to even make a mistake.
(*sarcastically*)
A philosophical question, indeed. And from the Dandy Doodle Pie Man, of all people. You out to go on that TV show, *Jeopardy*. You'd stump 'em all, what with your sly wit and superior knowledge.

WINSTON

Well, there's one thing my superior knowledge tells me and that's that we need ta be on a budget 'round here. You live an extravagant life style, you do.

LILA

Is that right? Well, you haven't exactly been keepin' me in jewels around here, you know. Pies, yes; jewels, no!

WINSTON

Well, all's I'm sayin' is that we need ta cut back on a few things 'round here.

LILA

Like what? Water! That's just about all that's left to cut back on around here. We've cut back on everything else . . . except maybe PIES!

WINSTON

Ya could have done better with your lot in life? Then, why'd ya marry me in the first place?

LILA

Actually, I married you for your money. Well, it's thirty-two years later and what I want to know is: When do I get to see some of it?
(*thinking to herself; then, coyly*)
I had me my chances, though.

WINSTON

Yeah. Like who? That Brian Mendelwitz you wuz datin'? I could just see ya now as a rabbi's wife. With a shawl around yur head. Or, how 'bout that biker dude ya went out with? Talk about goin' from one extreme ta the other. You thought he was cute because he had a beauty mole under his ear . . . till ya found out it was a tick!

LILA

Hey, Mr. "Can't Keep the Women Away" Stud. I could mention a few of the beaut's you went out with.

WINSTON

Like who?

LILA

Like that divorcee you took a shinin' to. That Shirley . . . that floozy, or whatever her name was. The one that wore a dog collar.

WINSTON

She wasn't so bad.

LILA

Are you kidding me? She had a face like the back of a hairbrush.

WINSTON

I'll have ya know she wasn't no floozie, as you would have one believe. She was a Chinese heiress.

LILA

Oh, that's right; I forgot. A Chinese heiress. Right. And her last name was "Hop On," not Floozie. That's right; I got it all straight now.
(sarcastically)
Chinese heiress, my sweet ass. And I'm a bein' the long lost daughter of Maureen O'Hara.
(contemptuous laugh)
Chinese heiress. To use a pun: that's *pie* in the sky thinking. What do you a do: Wake up each mornin' and turn off that part of your brain that thinks? She was a gold digger if ever I saw me one. She could steal the gold out of your teeth while you was a chewing gum, she could.
(a pause)
Far be it for me to be a sayin' unkind words about a person, or to be castin' stones or aspirations, or aspersions, or whatever they be a callin' them. And, far be it for me to be a sayin' that she was a tad overweight, but I heard her first husband had to hire a rodeo clown to distract her when he brought home the groceries to put in the refrigerator.

WINSTON

Now, *that* was unkind! No need for fat jokes here.

LILA

Unkind? Hey, she's' the one—not me—who slept with a slab of bacon under her pillow every night.

WINSTON

Yeah, well. Look who I ended up with instead: a woman with Irritable Bowel Syndrome coupled with Mad Cow Disease!

LILA

Yeah, well. That street runs back and forth, two ways, ya know. Look what I ended up with: Brainless the Second, the accomplished dreamer . . . Son of Brainless the First.

WINSTON

Okay! Okay! **ENOUGH!** Your voice is beginnin' to grate on me; it sounds like quarters droppin' in a slot machine.
(WINSTON heads for the refrigerator and gets another beer.)
I think it's time fer another beer; I ain't had enough.

LILA

You don't know what enough is till you had more than enough.
    (*There's a **LOUD** knock on the door. WINSTON and LILA look at each other.*)
Who is it?

STONEBREAKER (O.S.)

Mr. Stonebreaker.
    (*LILA walks over to the door.*)

LILA

Who?

STONEBREAKER (O.S.)

Mr. Stonebreaker, the super. Open up.
    (*LILA squints through the peephole in the door, then lets him in.*)

LILA
(*Shouting to WINSTON*)

It's the . . . SUPER-IN-TEN-DENT, Mr. Ballbuster.

STONEBREAKER
(*correcting her*)

Stonebreaker.

LILA

Whatever. What is it you'd be a wantin', Mr. Ballbuster?

STONEBREAKER
(*quite irritated*)

I got a complaint about all the noise up here.

LILA
(*to WINSTON, derisively*)

He's . . . "gotta complaint . . . about all the . . . **NOISE** . . . up here."

109

WINSTON
(to LILA, calmly)
UP HERE? Naw. There must be some kinda mistake.

LILA
(LILA to STONEBREAKER: hollering, although he's standing right next to her.)
"Up here? Naw. There must be some kinda mistake."

STONEBREAKER
Yeah, up here. Who else could be makin' all of this noise?

LILA
(to WINSTON, mimicking STONEBREAKER)
Mr. Ballbuster wants to know: "Who else could be makin' all of the noise?"

WINSTON
(to LILA, placidly)
Could be **THE KRANTEZES** in 10-B; they just got one of those Rhesus monkeys in their apartment?

LILA
(to STONEBREAKER)
"Could be the—

STONEBREAKER
I can hear. I can hear! You don't have to shout; I ain't deaf, ya know.

LILA
(to WINSTON)
He can hear you. He can hear you! You don't have to shout; he ain't deaf, ya know.
(WINSTON walks over to STONEBREAKER.)

WINSTON
(to LILA, serenely)
I'll handle this.

(*LILA heads back to cooking at the stove. WINSTON turns to STONEBREAKER.*)

WINSTON

Can I help ya?

STONEBREAKER

The noise. All this yellin' and screamin'. You've gotta hold down the noise. I've been gettin' complains from your neighbors.
(*A long pause. Just the clanging of pots and pans from LILA. STONEBREAKER continues, awkwardly.*)
Look, if there's one thing I've learned—mostly from being the Super of this building for the last thirty-five years—it's not to dig around too much in other people's lives; you're liable to break your shovel but . . .
(*a pause; STONEBREAKER wonders whether to continue or not*)

WINSTON
(*sarcastically*)

Yes, please do go on. I'd like to hear what life's *really* all about; after all, I'm only a mere deliveryman for a pie company. What would I know about life?

STONEBREAKER
(*motions WINSTON in closer; in sotto voice*)

Look, buddy. I can understand you—

WINSTON
(*cutting in, sharply*)

You ain't gonna charge me for this advice, are ya . . . **buddy**?

STONEBREAKER

Of course not.

WINSTON
(*mockingly*)

Thank God. What a relief. Lots of time, advice like this don't come free . . . nor cheap. I'm just so thankful we's **buddies**, or else I might have ta take out a loan ta pay fer it; times is tough enough around here without that. We're goin' on a budget, ya know.

LILA
(*butting in*)
Yeah, we be a cuttin' back a wee bit on all the extravagances we got goin' on around here. Even cuttin' back on water. You know, I just thought of something: Eatin' all this pie, without any water, is goin' to taste a tad bit dry from now on.

STONEBREAKER
As I was saying . . . I can understand you got your hands full around here.
(*nodding towards LILA*)
As a matter of fact, if I was in your shoes, I'd have put one in my bonnet by now,
(*points his hand, in the shape of a gun, with his thumb cocked, to his head and simulates pulling the trigger*)
or brodied off a bridge a long time ago,
(*bends his knees and pretends he's taking a Swan dive off a train trestle*)
if you get my meaning, buddy.
(*winks at WINSTON*)

WINSTON
Oh, I get your meaning, all right. What's that expression ya used a moment ago? Oh, yeah. I think you just . . . "broke your shovel . . . **BUDDY!**"
(*WINSTON gives STONEBREAKER an exaggerated wink; opens the door; picks STONEBREAKER up, by the seat of his pants; tosses him out into the hallway; then, yells after him*)
NOBODY BAD-MOUTHS MY WIFE THAT WAY!
(*WINSTON slams the door shut. LILA, who has been watching all of this from the stove, runs over and hugs WINSTON for standing up for her.*)

LILA
Oh, Winney! I think that calls for a drink.

(*LILA highballs it over to the refrigerator, pops open a beer and gives it to WINSTON who sits back down at the kitchen table.*)
I think I'll even be joinin' you.
(*LILA gets herself a beer and sits next to WINSTON.*)

WINSTON
(*indignantly*)
The nerve of that guy. Badmouthin' my wife like that. Who does he think he is? Me!?

LILA
(*giggling like a schoolgirl*)
Indeed! He must not know who he is a dealin' with here.

WINSTON
And, who might that be . . . Pumpkin Puss?

LILA
Why, my Sampson, of course.

WINSTON
Any you're my Lila.

LILA
That's **Dee—lila**, you idiot.

WINSTON
(*mimicking LILA*)
"I know, I know."
(They click beer cans in a toast, have a little swig of the brewski, give each other a little smooch, then laugh like a couple of kids that just pulled one over on the teacher.)

Curtain Falls

The End

"All comedy is based in tragedy."
(I think someone famous said this;
if not, then I'll take credit for it.)

D'Artagnan Bloodhawke

*****

*"Life is what happens to you while
you're busy making plans."*
John Lennon

*****

Deaf, Dumb And Blind

(A Play in Three Acts)

Cast of Characters

<u>Danielle "Dani" Goodwright</u>	Attractive single woman in her early forties; works as a pharmaceutical clerk.
<u>Lillian "Lilly" Goodwright</u>	Seventy-eight year old mother of Dani; widowed for the last thirty years; has early onset of senility.

Bustan "Buster" Wolfowitz	In his eighties, nearly stone deaf; wears a hearing aid in each ear and drinks cheap wine; has been Lilly's boyfriend for the last twenty-five years.
Mildred "Millie" Macduff	Seventy-six year old sister of Lilly and Dani's aunt; has heavy New York accent; is as close to total blindness as one can get; gets around with the full-time aid of a walker.
Bruce Wigley	Fifty-eight year old boyfriend of Dani; is afraid of emotional commitment; career oriented; employed at First Commercial Mercantile & Dairy Farmers Bank for past thirty-six years; currently is the Head Teller and hopes to make Assistant Manager soon.
Dr. Augustus "Gus" Praetorian	Dani's obstetrician; handsome, in mid-forties.
Father Patrick "Patty" O'Shea	Local, semiretired, Irish priest; in his late seventies; lives in the rectory at St. Bartholomew's Church of the Apostles; born in Ireland and speaks with an Irish brogue.
Police Officer #1	Male (one line, minor part).
Police Officer #2	Male (one line, minor part).

The Scene

The entire action of the play takes place in a fifth floor, walk-up, rent controlled apartment in Greenwich Village, New York City where Dani, Lilly, Buster, and Millie all live.

<u>Time</u>

the beginning of the Twenty-First Century, early evening.

<u>Synopsis of Acts</u>

ACT I: The time is the beginning of the Twenty-First Century, early evening.

ACT II: A Saturday afternoon, six and a half months later.

ACT III: A Sunday afternoon, one year later.

Act 1

Deaf, Dumb And Blind
ACT I

The time is the beginning of the Twenty-First Century, early evening.

The scene is a fifth floor, walk-up, rent controlled apartment in Greenwich Village, just a short walk past Washington Square Park. Rundown would be too harsh a word for this humble abode, and elegant too nice; turn of the century-which century would be debatable—OLD world would be more appropriate.

It is the home of an attractive, working class woman in her early forties named DANIELLE "DANI" GOODWRIGHT who lives there with her seventy-eight year old mother, LILLIAN "LILLY" GOODWRIGHT, who has been widowed for thirty years and suffers from the early onset of senility. Sharing their domicile is LILLIAN'S gentleman friend for the past twenty-five years, BUSTAN "BUSTER" WOLFOWITZ, who is rapidly approaching total deafness; yet, he still manages to hear what he wants to hear. Not wanting to leave anyone out, a MILDRED MACDUFF also inhabits this dwelling; what she brings to the party is the fact that she's the seventy-six year old, blind, spinster sister of LILLIAN. Despite all of the infirmities the three of them individually possess, together they equal one fully functional human being.

The apartment is on two floors. The lower floor consists of a living room/ dining room area with a large table and four chairs; a large sofa or couch; an oversized lounger; a love seat; a TV set; a curio cabinet holding knickknacks, bottles of liquor, a portable phone, etc. Next to living room/dining room area is a kitchen, a bathroom and a door leading to DANIELLE'S bedroom. A stairway leads to an upper loft with a long hallway, off which is a door to the bedroom of LILLIAN and BUSTER, and another door to the bedroom of MILDRED. Between these two doors is a hall window with an outside fire escape. Farther down the hall is a second bathroom.

As THE CURTAIN RISES, *we see* MILDRED "MILLIE" MACDUFF *wearing Coke bottle eyeglasses and struggling—always with the aid of a walker—to get down the flight of stairs in one piece. It's obvious by the way* MILDRED *is battling with the staircase, often at times dangerously close to falling, that her eyewear is mostly decorative, as it most certainly does not have any practical application.*

MILLIE
(in a panic)

Lilly? . . . Lilly?

*(We see BUSTER WOLFOWITZ. In his early eighties, he is a robust and highborn looking gentleman despite his having a large hearing aid protruding from each ear; he has two levels of responding to all conversations: LOUD and **LOUDER**. He walks out of the kitchen with a glass of red wine and sits down at the dining room table with his back towards MILDRED. BUSTER may have an aristocratic bearing, but his tastes run cheap, as he's drinking Mad Dog 20/20 Red Grape Wine.)*

MILLIE
(continuing)

Lilly? . . . Lilly! . . . **LILLY!**

(BUSTER looks around, unsure if he hears something or not.)

BUSTER

Billy?

MILLIE
(raising her voice to a distress level)

LILLY!

(BUSTER turns and sees MILDRED.)

BUSTER

Billy? Who's Billy?

(MILDRED finally makes it to the bottom of the stairs.)

MILLIE

Lilly! . . . Lilly, not Billy.

BUSTER

That's right.

MILLIE

LILLY . . . My sister and your . . . your . . . whatever the two of you are.

(MILDRED shuffles over to the table and stands next to BUSTER.)

120

BUSTER

Lillian and me, we're like . . . married.

MILLIE

LIKE married? What is *LIKE* married like? You either are or you aren't married. You're not . . . *LIKE* married.

BUSTER

You want to hear something?

MILLIE

From you? Not really.

BUSTER
(*mimicking* MILDRED'S *voice*)

Not really.

MILLIE

Not if the entire asteroid belt around Mars was headed for Greenwich Village, would I want to hear from you.

BUSTER

Well, I'm going to tell you anyway. Those glasses you're wearing don't help you to see, Mrs. Magoo; they just keep the dust out of your eyes. You ever notice that?

MILLIE

Yeah well, let me tell you something: Every time you can't hear someone, you always say: 'That's right,' when you haven't the foggiest idea what people are talking about. You ever notice that?

BUSTER

That's right.

MILLIE

See!

BUSTER

What are you implying?, that I'm deaf?

MILLIE

No, not at all, **Mr. Miracle Ears**.

BUSTER

I can hear just fine; it's you people who can't enunciate properly. You mumble.

MILLIE
(*impatiently*)

Well, have you seen her or not?

BUSTER

Who?

MILLIE

Lilly! You old goat.

BUSTER

No, I haven't; it's not my turn to watch her . . . And I'm not an old goat.

MILLIE

Anyone who thinks it has to be ***his turn*** to watch out for a senile, old lady can't be anything but an old goat.
     (MILDRED *begins to channel her frustrations out on* BUSTER.)
If she was under you makin' the sheets sing, you'd know where she was. You wouldn't be the least bit concerned about it ***not being your turn*** to watch her; you'd be watchin' her pretty damn good then.
     (*looks at* BUSTER *with loathing*)
Horny, old fool.

BUSTER

I heard that!

MILLIE
(to herself)

I doubt that very seriously.

(*Silence as each eyes the other like two gunfighters from the old West squaring off.*)

You know, she's been missin' now for about the last hour or two?

BUSTER

Who?

MILLIE

LILLY!

BUSTER

When did you last see her?

MILLIE

I can't see her.

BUSTER

Well then, how do you know she's missing?

(MILDRED looks at BUSTER in disbelief; utter stillness within the room then. In through the front door comes DANIELLE, wearing an attractive work dress, with LILLIAN, who is clad in a housecoat that is turned inside-out.)

MILLIE

Who is it?

BUSTER
(to himself)

Blind, old bat.

MILLIE

What'd you call me?

BUSTER

What are you, DEAF?, in addition to being blind.

DANI

Buster. Aunt Millie. Stop it. Can't I even go to work without the two of you getting at each other's throats?

LILLY
(out of breath)

Phew! Each year we live here, those five flights of stairs seem to get longer and longer; they're beginning to feel more like fifty flights of stairs.
(fanning herself with her hand)
Boy, is it hot in here!
(LILLIAN *sees* MILDRED *and, in a dither, runs over to her.*)

LILLY
(continuing)

Millie, where have you been? I've been looking all over for you.

MILLIE

Right here, Lilly; standin' right next to your . . . Mr. Wonderful.

LILLY

You're not thinking of stealing him away now, are you Millie?

MILLIE

Hardly. No, this catch here,
(nodding towards BUSTER)
he's *all* yours, Lilly.
(LILLIAN *smiles at* BUSTER *and takes a seat next to him at the dining room table.* MILDRED *sits down next to* LILLIAN.)

LILLY
(looking at BUSTER, admiringly)

Bustan Wolfowitz.

BUSTER
(puffs out his chest)

As I live and breathe.

> ### LILLY
> (*said with a schoolgirl's passion*)

Oh, Wolfie.

> ### MILLIE

Geez-O! I think I'm gonna be sick.
 (LILLIAN *is still periodically fanning herself with her hand.*)

> ### LILLY
> *(to* BUSTER*)*

Phew!, is it hot in here, or are we going through the change?

> ### BUSTER

I know I changed; right after my first divorce.

> ### LILLY

No seriously, Wolfie, is it hot in here?
 (coyly adds)
Or, is that just because I'm sitting next to you?

> ### BUSTER
> (trying to be hip)

I'm smokin', baby.
 (singing while snapping his fingers and swaying from side to side)
'Come on baby, light my fire' . . .
 (LILLIAN *and* BUSTER *giggle to themselves like a couple of school kids.*)

> ### MILLIE
> *(to* BUSTER*)*

You're just catnip to the ladies, all right.
 (pause)
You know, I've always wanted to ask you: What does your first name, Bustan, stand for?

> ### LILLY
> *(answering for* BUSTER*)*

It's the Jewish name for garden.

(lovingly)
To me, he's a beautiful garden of earthly delights.

MILLIE

Uh-huh. Some garden; it must be full of Poison Sumac.
(pause)
Bustan. No wonder he calls himself, 'Buster.'
(DANIELLE *walks over and stands behind the trio seated at the table.*)

LILLY

So, why does everybody look so worried?

MILLIE

Because you were lost, Lilly.

LILLY

No, I wasn't; I knew exactly where I was.

BUSTER

Where'd you go, Lillian?

LILLY

Oh, just out for a little walk, Wolfie.

DANI

I just happened to find Mom wandering through Washington Square
Park on my way home from work.

LILLY

I wasn't wandering, Danielle.

DANI

Oh no. What would you call going from parking meter to parking
meter, Mom?

LILLY

I wasn't going from parking meter to parking meter. You make it
sound like I'm some kinda half-baked loonie.
(*All heads in the room turn towards* LILLIAN.)

DANI
(to herself)
Not half-baked; *completely* baked.

LILLY
I was only going to the expired ones.

DANI
Why, Mom?

LILLY
(matter-of-factly, as if everybody should know the answer to that silly question)
I was putting money in, as a sort of nice concerned citizen gesture, so those poor people wouldn't get ticketed.

DANI
Those poor people around here are a lot richer than you or me, Mom. But, that's beside the point; you were trying to stuff peanuts into the meters, not money.

LILLY
No, no, no, Danielle. The peanuts were for the pigeons in the park.

MILLIE
(interrupting; trying to avoid an upsetting argument)
Close enough, Dani. Money, peanuts. What's the difference? Just as long as Lilly's back.

BUSTER
(seconding the motion)
Aye-aye! Just as long as Lillian's back.
(to LILLIAN)
Come on, Lillian, let's go upstairs to bed.

MILLIE
Horny, old fool.

BUSTER

I heard that!

MILLIE
(to herself)

I doubt that very seriously.
(BUSTER *starts to get up and* LILLIAN *begins to follow suit.*)

DANI

Sit down; sit down, all of you. I have some good news.

LILLY
(to MILDRED, *excitedly, as she and* BUSTER *both sit back down)*
Good news, Millie.

MILLIE

For a change. What is it? Buster finally gonna get his prostrate gland
fixed so's he don't keep all of us up at night with that constant flushin'
of his?

DANI
(looks at MILDRED *with a reproachful eye)*
Now, be nice, Aunt Millie. And I keep telling you, it's prostate gland,
not prostrate. Prostrate is when someone is lying face downward.

MILLIE

That's exactly why I call it his prostrate gland because that's what he's
always doin' up there with Lilly; lying face downward, if youse gets the
picture.

DANI

I do; I do.
(lets out a weary sigh)
However, I'm trying real hard to erase that picture you so vividly
painted in my mind. You could help a little by keeping all of, what you
consider to be clever and witty comments, to yourself.
(momentarily losing her train of thought)
Where in God's name was I now?

LILLY
(excitedly, while clapping)

Good news, good news!

DANI

All right, the good news. But before I tell you the good news, Bruce is coming over tonight and I want-

LILLY

Who's Bruce?

MILLIE

Who's Bruce? Come on, Lilly, get with it. Bruce Wigley. Dani's only been dating him for the last millennium.

DANI

That's okay; Mom just forgot.
(to LILLIAN)
Bruce, the Head Teller at the First Commercial Mercantile & Dairy Farmers Bank, where we go. You know Bruce; he's been over here tons of times, Mom.
(to MILDRED)
And, it hasn't been for the last millennium. It's only been for the last . . . the last . . . couple of . . .

MILLIE

What? Years. Try fifteen years. If I was dating a guy for the last fifteen years, it'd seem like a millennium to me, it would.

BUSTER
(to MILDRED)

There now; therein lies your problem, Mrs. Magoo. First, you said: *IF* you were dating. Now, that's a big **IF**. And second of all, I can't even possibly conceive of how lonely the poor bastard would have to be to date you for fifteen years, much less for a millennium. God help him.

MILLIE

You know, I'm just liable to reach across this table here and rip out one of your earplugs. Or, maybe both of them. How would you like that, BUSTAN?

BUSTER

Let me tell you something, Mrs. Magoo; you gotta be able to **see me** first, before you can rip out anything.

MILLIE
(*said with a schoolgirl's passion; mimicking* LILLIAN'S *voice and mannerisms*)
Oh, Wolfie,
(*a beat, then in a rage*)
BLOW IT OUT YOUR ASS!

DANI

Okay, okay, you two. Enough!
(*trying to get back on topic*)
Like I was trying to say, I called Bruce and asked him to come over tonight for some good news, but I want all of you to promise me that you'll let me tell him the good news first . . . Promise?
(*They all stare at her, dumbly.*)
Promise? . . . Do you all promise you won't say anything to Bruce?

(DANIELLE *looks around the table for an answer. Nothing. Then . . .*)

LILLY

You know, I could never figure out why they called it the First Commercial Mercantile & Dairy Farmers Bank. There ain't no dairy farmers here in New York City; haven't been for hundreds of years now. And, what's a mercantile? When have you seen one of them lately?

DANI
(*frustrated; pulling at her hair*)
PROMISE ME!

LILLY
(*frightened by* DANIELLE'S *sudden outburst*)
I promise, I promise.

BUSTER
(*raising his glass of wine and nodding towards it*)
No thanks, I already have some.

MILLIE

Cross my heart,

(*she crosses her heart*)

and hope to die.

BUSTER
We can certainly all hold hands and pray for that one.
        (MILDRED *starts to get up from the table to rip out one of*
BUSTER'S *hearing aids.*)

DANI
(*to* MILDRED)
Now, now. Aunt Millie sit down.
        (MILDRED *sits back down.*)

DANI
(*to* BUSTER)
Now, Buster, we all know that you didn't actually mean that, did you?

BUSTER
You know me like a book, Dani. I wasn't actually going to say a few,
measly prayers. I was going to do what all you good Roman Catholics
do when you want something *really* bad; I was thinking of making a
novena.
        (MILDRED *smells blood; she pushes back her chair and gets up.*)

MILLIE
Why, you old goat, you! I oughta-

DANI
(losing her patience)
ENOUGH! Everybody, just settle down.
(to MILDRED*)*
Aunt Millie, will you please sit down . . . *again.*
(MILDRED *reluctantly sits back down again.*)
Okay, now where was I . . . again?

LILLY
(excitedly, while clapping))
Good news, good news!

MILLIE
Not again. We get any more good news, I don't know if I can stand it.

DANI
I will now start all over again for the *fourth* time, if all of you will just please listen.
(DANIELLE *looks around the table. Silence.*)
Okay, as I was trying to say. The good news.
(pause)
I stopped off at the doctor's office today on the way home from work and-

LILLY
Danielle, you're not sick are you? Or worse yet, have some terrible deadly virus, do you? You could get something like that very easily clerking at that pharmacy like you do. The kind of virus that turns you black and eats your skin off from the inside out. And, it takes like years for you to be eaten alive, and you end up dying in pain and all alone in some flea-infested charity ward down in the Bowery run by some matronly, old bull dyke named Jumbo.

MILLIE
(to LILLIAN*)*
How could it be good news if she had a horrible, rotten disease like that?

DANI

No Mom, I'm fine, but where did you hear about such a deadly virus like that?

LILLY

Some sweet young girl named Esther got it on that soap opera: General Hospital.

DANI

Never mind; I'm sorry I asked.
(pause)
I stopped off at the doctor's office today on my way home from work and guess what?

MILLIE

I sure hope we're getting to the good news part.

LILLY

Me too!

DANI

Give up?
(Everyone mumbles, something or other, to the effect that they have no idea and to please get on with it.)
We're expecting.
(You could hear a pin drop in the room. Then . . .)

LILLY

Expecting what?

DANI
(with joy and enthusiasm)

We're pregnant!

MILLIE

Oh, boy. Now you've gone and done it.

DANI

Isn't that something?

MILLIE

Uh-huh. That's something all right.

LILLY

I'm pregnant!

MILLIE

Holy Moley! Now *THAT* would be something.

BUSTER
(cupping a hand over one of his ears)

What?!

LILLY

Wolfie, I'm pregnant!

BUSTER
(cupping both hands over both ears)

WHAT?!

DANI

No, Mom. When I say **we're** pregnant, I mean it in the rhetorical sense. Like collectively. Like, we're all in this together; we're all pregnant. You get it?

LILLY

You mean, I'm not pregnant?

DANI

No, not really, Mom.

BUSTER
(nervous and uptight)

Please, everyone. Let me get this straight: Who's pregnant?

MILLIE
(to BUSTER)

Don't worry, Romeo, you're off the hook. Thank God too. Somehow, I just can't imagine adding a Buster Junior to the gene pool.

LILLY
(to DANIELLE)

Then, why did you go and tell me I was pregnant and get me and Wolfie's hopes all up?

BUSTER

Speak for yourself, Lillian; my hopes weren't all up.

DANI
(to LILLIAN; frustrated)

I don't know, Mom. Poor choice of words, I guess.
(Everyone just sits there quietly, not knowing exactly what to say next. BUSTER gulps down the remainder of his glass of wine.)

BUSTER

Well, I don't know about the rest of you, but I gotta take a whiz real bad; that was a close one.
(BUSTER gets up from the table and heads into the downstairs bathroom. Everyone sits in silence, trying to fully absorb this startling information.)

LILLY

So, what does this all mean?

MILLIE

It means: Your daughter's got one in the oven, is what it all means.

LILLY
(appearing shocked)

Danielle, you mean you're . . . you're . . . knocked up?

MILLIE

Now you're gettin' it.

135

DANI

(depressed)

I thought you'd all be happy for me, like I am. This baby is very precious to me.

MILLIE

(trying to lift DANIELLE'S *spirits)*

We are, dear, we are. You just sorta took us all by . . . surprise, is all. I mean, you must admit, it is a bit of a shock, especially with you being in your early forties and all, dear. But, we're all happy; we are. Lilly, aren't we all happy for Dani?

LILLY

What's the name of this doctor?

DANI

Doctor Praetorian. Why?

LILLY

Is he any good?

DANI

Of course, he's good. Why'd you ask that?

LILLY

Well, I mean, a doctor who doesn't even know the difference between whether you or me is pregnant, can't be that good.

(a beat)

So, who's the father?

(A gigantic FLUSH from the downstairs toilet as BUSTER *emerges from the bathroom and rejoins the group at the table.)*

DANI

(shocked beyond belief)

Mother!, how can you even ask such a question?

BUSTER
(to DANIELLE*)*

What question?
*(*BUSTER *sees how upset* DANIELLE *is and how confused* LILLIAN *seems to be. He takes* LILLIAN'S *hands.)*
(to LILLIAN*)*

What question?

LILLY

I was just merely asking Danielle who the father was.

BUSTER
(to DANIELLE*)*

That doesn't seem so unreasonable, Dani.

DANI
(to BUSTER*)*

You too, Brutus?

BUSTER
(correcting her)

Buster.

BUSTER
(to LILLIAN*)*

How could she get my name wrong after all these years?

LILLY

Your hands are all wet, Wolfie.
*(*BUSTER *lets go of* LILLIAN'S *hands and wipes them on his shirt.)*

BUSTER

Sorry, dear.

MILLIE
(to DANIELLE*)*

Lilly was just futzin' around is all, Dani. Of course, we all know who the father is,

>   (*sharply to* LILLIAN)
> don't we, Lilly?

>   LILLY
>   (*totally mystified*)
> What's his name?

>   MILLIE
>   (*halfhearted laugh*)
> What a kidder that Lilly is.

>   BUSTER
>   (*chimes in*)
> I'd like to know, too.

>   MILLIE
>   (*to herself*)
> What a putz.

>   BUSTER
> I know what that means.

>   MILLIE
>   (*another feeble laugh*)
> Bruce, of course.

>   BUSTER
> Of course.

>   LILLY
> Of course.
>   (*a beat*)
> Who's Bruce?

>   DANI
>   (*indignant*)
> Mother!
>   (DANIELLE *retreats in a* huff *to the kitchen.*)

LILLY

What's the matter? All I did was ask a simple question.

MILLIE

I know, I know.

MILLIE

(MILDRED *stands up and motions everyone towards her in a small huddle at the table.*)
Look, we all gotta be especially nice to Dani now. She's gotta be goin' through a tough time and she's probably just not herself.

BUSTER

I'll say; she didn't even get my name right a while ago. I think she was trying to say Bustan, but she ended up calling me 'Brubas' or some such name.

MILLIE

Let this!,
(*pointing to* BUSTER)
be an example, for all the world to see, of what happens to a person's brain when you drink wine that has an expiration date on the bottle.
(*pause*)
Anyway, as I was saying: She's gotta be goin' through a tough time, what with her expecting-

LILLY

Expecting? Expecting who?

MILLIE

Let's not go back there, okay Lilly? We've moved on; just let me continue. Okay?
(*pause*)
She's gotta be goin' through a tough time, what with her . . .
(*mentally searching for the right word that* LILLIAN *will understand instead of 'expecting'*)
being 'knocked up' and all. Look, this has got to be a big event for Dani, especially at her age. This will probably be her one and only

child and you've already heard her say how precious this child is to her. Now, I know she's got to be a little nervous about tellin' Bruce tonight-

LILLY

Who?

MILLIE

Bruce. Bruce Wigley. Her boyfriend for the last millennium, remember him?

(LILLIAN *nods in the affirmative, but you can tell she hasn't the remotest idea who* BRUCE *is*.)

MILLIE
(*continuing*)

Anyway, Dani is so good to us, and takes such good care of us all, that the least we can do is to support her now in her time of need. So, when Bruce comes over here later tonight, let's just all disappear and let her handle this in her own way. Okay?

LILLY

Okay.

BUSTER

That's right.

MILLIE

Okay,
(*raising her voice with enthusiasm*)
'all for one and one for all!'

(LILLIAN *and* BUSTER *just stare at* MILDRED *with blank looks*.)

MILLIE
(*continuing*)

Whatever.

(MILDRED, *with the aid of her walker, fumbles her way down to the end of the table*.)

Dani, oh Dani.

DANI

(DANIELLE *comes in from the kitchen wiping tears from her eyes.*
Yes, Aunt Millie.

MILLIE

Dani, we'd all just like you to know that we're so very happy for you
and that we all support you and the new baby.

LILLY

Is it a boy or a girl, Danielle?

DANI

I really don't know yet, Mom; we're only three months along at the moment.

LILLY

Along what?

DANI

Excuse me, Mom?

LILLY

You said: 'We're only three months along.' Along what?

MILLIE

The pregnancy, Lilly. Three months along in the pregnancy, is what
she meant.

LILLY

But, she said: '*WE,*' again.

BUSTER
(perking up)

We what?

DANI

Another-

BUSTER

Another what? Baby? **TWINS!?**

DANI

Calm down, Buster. Another collective expression.
(*to* LILLIAN)
Sorry, Mom, poor choice of words . . . again.

BUSTER

Please, Dani. Don't get my heart going like that with this '**WE**' stuff.

LILLY

I hope this Doctor Pray . . . whatever his name is-

DANI

Praetorian. Doctor Praetorian.

LILLY

Pray . . . whatever. '*WE*' all just might need some praying here. I sure hope this doctor does a better job of figuring out the sex of the child then he did trying to figure out who was pregnant here.

DANI

Don't worry, Mom. The pharmacist where I work recommended him; says he's great. And, one of the other girls at the pharmacy had him as her obstetrician. I'm already impressed with him on my first visit. Do you know where the name Praetorian comes from?

LILLY

Yeah, your doctor; you just told me. What do you think, I'm stupid or something?

DANI

No, Mom, I meant the genealogy of the name; it's Latin, I think.

MILLIE

As broke as we are, we can only hope it's Pig Latin for: Will work for food.

DANI

According to Doctor Praetorian, the first Roman emperor, Augustus, in 27 B.C. established an exclusive and very elite bodyguard around himself to protect him from his enemies. They were known as the Praetorian Guard. There were about forty-five hundred of them at any given time. Their sole mission in life was to protect the emperor from any harm. Imagine, forty-five hundred troops just to guard . . . *one man*.

MILLIE

He must have pissed off a lot of people to have so many guards.

DANI

Doctor Praetorian comes from a long line of distinguished Italians-

MILLIE

A guinea, huh?

DANI

Aunt Millie, please. Try and keep your prejudices to yourself.

MILLIE

What prejudices? I merely mentioned that the guy was a spiggoty. What's that got to do with being prejudiced? You know, your generation has gone too far with this politically and culturally correct business. Seventy-six years I live in this neighborhood. The Catholics call the Jews, Hebes; the Jews call the Catholics, Fish Eaters; the Eyetalians call the Irish, Micks; the-

DANI

I get it; I get it, Aunt Millie.

BUSTER

At least she spreads her prejudices around to all the masses, races, and religions equally.

MILLIE

Alls I'm saying is: Youse people today go way overboard to be so polite to people you hate. In my day, everybody called each other the filthiest names and we all got along just fine.

DANI

Sorry, Aunt Millie. When I go to work tomorrow, I'll be sure, first thing off the bat, to call my boss, Mr. D'Aguillo, a Dago. I'm sure he'll understand that I'm just tired of being politically and culturally correct and that we all ought to go back to the good old days of ethnic name-calling.

MILLIE

I'm sure he'd understand; if he was any kinda decent, respectable, Dago boss, he would.

DANI

Anyway, Doctor Praetorian believes he can do what it took forty-five hundred men to do. He told me it was his mission in life to guard me and my baby from any harm.

MILLIE

It sounds like this Doctor Praetorian may want to do more with your body than just *guard* it.

DANI

Oh, come on now, Aunt Millie, he's a nice man.

MILLIE

Uh-huh. What's his first name?

DANI

Augustus, after the first emperor of Rome.
(*pause*)
Anyway, Gus says-

MILLIE

Ah, is it Gus now? In only one day. Getting a tad familiar, aren't we?

DANI

No; as a matter of fact, I'm not. Doctor Praetorian prefers to have all of his patients call him Gus.

MILLIE

Is he single?

DANI

I believe so, but what has that got to do with anything? I have Bruce, remember?

MILLIE

Uh-huh.

LILLY

Danielle, can me and Wolfie baby-sit for you?

DANI

We'll see, Mom, we'll see.
(*a beat*)
Anybody want anything to drink?, in celebration.

MILLIE

No thanks, Dani.

DANI

Buster?

BUSTER
(*cupping a hand over one of his ears*)
What?

DANI

Do you want anything to drink?

BUSTER

I'll take another one of those glasses of that Mad Dog 20/20 Wine, as long as you're buying.

DANI

Mom?

LILLY

Who's Bruce?

DANI

We're off that subject now, Mom. Do you want anything to drink is the current topic for discussion?

LILLY

No thank you, Danielle.

DANI

Okay then, just Buster and me. One last drink before my self-imposed six months of drought; I intend to make it a stiff one.

MILLIE

(DANIELLE *heads into the kitchen.* MILDRED *sits back down at the table. The front doorbell* RINGS. *The trio at the table stare at each other, then at the door.*)
I suppose one of us should get it.

BUSTER

Get what?

MILLIE

The door, you old goat.

LILLY

Who's at the door?

MILLIE

I don't know, Lilly, that's why I suggested that one of us should get it.

LILLY

Is it that . . . that, what's his name? That fellow friend of Danielle's?

MILLIE

Bruce Wigley? Could be, but we'll never know that until one of us gets the door, now will we?

BUSTER

Know what?

MILLIE

(The doorbell RINGS *for a second time.)*
Never mind; I'll get it myself.

LILLY

(MILDRED *gets up and gropes her way towards the front door with her walker.)*
What are you doing, Millie?

MILLIE

Trying to get to the front door, Lilly.

LILLY

Well, would you like a hand?

MILLIE

(cynically)
Geez-O Lilly. Since I know that garden of earthly delights next to you ain't gonna help me, that would be awfully sweet of you to help me here . . . before I break my neck and end up in that charity ward down in the Bowery run by that matronly, old bull dyke named Jumbo.

LILLY

(LILLIAN *gets up to help* MILDRED *answer the front door.* BUSTER *tags along and stands behind the two women. The doorbell* RINGS *again.* MILDRED *looks through the peephole in the door.)*
Who is it?

MILLIE

I don't know; I can't see them.

> LILLY

Here, let me look.

> MILLIE

(LILLIAN *looks through the peephole.*)
Who is it?

> LILLY

I don't know; I don't recognize them.

> BUSTER

Here, let me.
    (BUSTER *moves closer to the door and yells at the peephole.*)
WHO IS IT?
    (BUSTER *puts his ear to the peephole, listening for a response. The doorbell* RINGS *another time and everyone jumps back a step except* BUSTER *who doesn't hear it.*)

> LILLY

Well, who is it?

> BUSTER

I don't know; I can't hear them.

> DANI

(DANIELLE *comes out of the kitchen with a glass of red wine in one hand and a scotch and water in the other.*)
What's all the commotion in here?

> LILLY

Someone's at the door.

> DANI

Well, answer it.

> LILLY

Don't you think that's what we've *all* been trying to do?

MILLIE
(*to* LILLY, *facetiously*)
Maybe she thinks we decided, all at once, to just get up and huddle all together over by this door here, just for the hell of it.

DANI
Oh, for the love of . . . Here, let me get it.
(*After taking a healthy swig from her glass,* DANIELLE *puts both glasses on the table, goes to the peephole, and looks out.*)
Why, it's Bruce.

MILLIE
I knew it. I just knew it!

LILLY
You didn't 'just *knew it*!' I was the one who suggested that it might be . . . what's his name? That fellow friend of Danielle's?

MILLIE
Yeah, but it was me who suggested that one of us should *get* the door or else nobody was gonna find out who it was.

DANI
Ssssh!, all of you; I'll get the door. Now, remember what we all promised.

LILLY
What'd 'WE' promise? Or, is this another one of those 'collective expressions'?
DANI
(DANIELLE *conspiratorially waves them all together and in a loud whisper*)
All of you promised me that you'd let me tell Bruce the good news first.

LILLY
(*whispers back,* LOUDER)
What's the good news?

DANI

Never mind, Mom.
(*The doorbell* RINGS *for the fifth time as* DANIELLE *opens the door. In walks* BRUCE WIGLEY, *a man in his late fifties, dressed in a conservative business suit.*)

BRUCE

(BRUCE *sees this crowd amassed by the door and nervously breaks into song.*)
'Hail!, Hail!, the gang's all here, what the heck—

DANI

Right.
(*a beat*)
Okay, you guys. Let's all move away from the door and give Bruce some breathing room. As it is, he's probably wondering just what the heck we're all doing piled up against the door here anyway.

BRUCE

Me? Wondering that? Not me. I've come to expect a lot stranger behavior than that from this apartment.
(*to* DANIELLE)
So, what's the good news?

LILLY
(*to* BRUCE)

WE just had a close one.

BRUCE

A close one?

LILLY

WE, like in collectively. WE all thought I was pregnant.

BRUCE
(*stammering*)
Th . . . Thought you were preg . . . pregnant?

LILLY

Yeah, but I shouldn't have gotten my hopes up, it wasn't me. It was-

DANI

(*quickly changing the subject*)

Come on in, Bruce; just don't stand there, stammering.

(DANIELLE *leads* BRUCE *over to the love seat where he sits down.*
LILLIAN *leads* MILDRED *back to the table with* BUSTER *bringing
up the rear; all three take a seat at the table.*)

DANI

(*continuing*)

Care for a drink, Bruce?

BRUCE

Thanks, but no thanks. Too early in the week.

(DANIELLE *gets her drink off the table and sits next to* BRUCE *on
the love seat.*)

BUSTER

(*to* LILLIAN; *cupping a hand over one of his ears*)

What'd he say?

LILLY

Too early in the week for a drink.

BUSTER

(BUSTER *knocks back a slug of his wine.*)

Not for me.

BUSTER

(*continuing; to* LILLY *as he nods towards* BRUCE)

Where'd he get them rules from?

LILLY

Who?

BUSTER

Bruce.

151

LILLY

Who's Bruce?

MILLIE

Must be some kinda banker's rules; I never heard of 'em.

BUSTER
(*Everyone in the room appears a little stiff*)
So, how are things down at the bank? You aren't taking any wooden nickels are you, Bruce?
(BUSTER *begins to laugh heartily at his own feeble attempt at a joke.*)

MILLIE

Just when you think it's safe, out of nowhere, up pops Mr. Mad Dog drooling in his glass of wine.

BUSTER
(*to* MILDRED; *still laughing at his joke*)
Don't you get it? Wooden nickels. The bank. You aren't taking any wooden nickels are you, Bruce?

MILLIE
(*stonefaced*)
Yeah, I get it; it just ain't funny, is all.

BUSTER
(*to* LILLIAN; *poking her in the ribs*)
You aren't taking any wooden nickels are you, Bruce? Get it?

LILLY

No, I don't get it. Who's Bruce?

DANI
(DANIELLE *takes a sip of her drink; to* BUSTER)
How we coming with that drink, Buster?

BUSTER
(*tosses back the rest of his glass of wine*)
Don't mind if I do.

DANI

That's not what I meant, Buster.

BUSTER

What'd you mean?

MILLIE

She meant that 'WE,' like in collectively, have something to do, don't 'WE.' So Dani can be the first to tell Bruce the good news.

BUSTER

Aye-aye. Come on, Lillian, let's go upstairs to bed.
(BUSTER *gets up and takes* LILLIAN *by the hand.*)

MILLIE

Horny old fool.

BUSTER

I heard that!

MILLIE
(*to herself*)
I doubt that very seriously.
(BUSTER *leads* LILLIAN *up the stairs to their bedroom.*)

MILLIE
(*continuing; to* DANIELLE)
Look at him; salivatin' already, like the mad dog that he is.
(a beat)
Well, I better be gettin' along too.
(MILDRED *bangs up the stairs to her bedroom, walker and all.* DANIELLE *and* BRUCE *are now alone on the love seat.*)

DANI

Finally, some peace.

BRUCE

For however short a time that may be.

(*Just at that moment,* BUSTER *comes out his bedroom and walks down the hallway into the bathroom.*)

DANI

Well, I'm not going to let anything spoil our good news.

BRUCE

Ah yes, the good news.

DANI

Well, let's see, how shall I go about putting this now?

BRUCE

Well, why don't you just come right out and say it, since it's good news and all?

DANI

Why not indeed. *We're* pregnant.

(*A gigantic* FLUSH *from the upstairs toilet.* BUSTER *emerges from the bathroom, goes back down the hallway and into his bedroom.*)

BRUCE

We're . . . **WE'RE** what?

DANI

I stopped off at the doctor's office today on the way home from work and well, we're . . .

(*pause*)

Sorry, I always use 'we're' in the collective sense like, we're all in this together, you know. I guess I just want to include everyone in my happiness. Anyway, I mean, I'm pregnant. Isn't that good news?

(*Awkward silence.* BRUCE *just sits there on the love seat, his mouth agape, shocked beyond even moving.* OFFSTAGE, LILLIAN *speaks to* BUSTER *from behind their bedroom door.*)

LILLY

Your hands are all wet, Wolfie.

BUSTER

Sorry, dear.

DANI
(*to* BRUCE)

Well, isn't it?

BRUCE

Isn't it what?

DANI

Isn't it good news?

BRUCE

Isn't what good news?

DANI

Come on, Bruce, you're beginning to sound a little like Mom.

BRUCE

No kidding. I guess that's because I'm suddenly beginning to feel a little like . . . Mom. What was the question again?

DANI

Isn't that good news, about me being pregnant?

BRUCE

Good news? Well, it certainly is a surprise; I'll say that much.
(*a pause*)
Who's the father?

DANI

(DANIELLE'S *jaw drops open; she stands up and begins to anxiously pace about.*)
You know, that's the second person I heard that from today.

155

BRUCE

Who was the first? Your doctor?

DANI

No, my mother. I could kind of understand something like that coming from her, what with her condition and all, but how could *you* even think such a thing, Bruce?

BRUCE

Because I thought you were on the . . . the-

DANI

Pill.

BRUCE

Well, yes, as a matter-of-fact.

DANI

Well, guess what, Bruce? Nothing in life is one hundred percent safe, now is it?

BRUCE

Evidently not.

DANI

And, in case you're wondering, those pills don't come with a money back guarantee either.
(*a beat*)
You know, Bruce, I'm starting to get the impression that you're not all that happy about our good news here.

BRUCE

Maybe that's because it's not **OUR** good news; it's yours.

DANI

What do you mean, mine?

BRUCE

Well, I was never consulted in any capacity; and, for that matter, not so much as even asked my opinion. I didn't have anything to do with this, so how can it be our good news?

DANI

Didn't have anything to do with this? You had plenty to do with this. How do you think I got three months pregnant? I didn't do that by myself; I had some help! From guess who?
(*pause*)
You know, Bruce, it's not as if I planned this.

BRUCE

Oh, isn't it?

DANI

Do you think I deliberately arranged all this?

BRUCE

I wouldn't put it past most women who are getting . . . desperate. For the last year or two, I've heard nothing but how you're not getting any younger and how-

DANI

DESPERATE! Bruce, for God's sake, neither of us is getting any younger.

BRUCE
(BRUCE *jumps up*.)
Ah-ha! So there, you did plan all this.

DANI

No, I didn't; it just worked out this way. But, I'll tell you something: I'm glad it did work out this way because I'm beginning to see now exactly where you stand on this issue.
(*a pause as Danielle collects her thoughts*)
Okay, look Romeo. To me, this baby is the single most important thing in my whole life and I fully intend to have it, with or without

your support. As it turns out, this is truly my last chance and I'm not about to throw it away.

BRUCE

Well, I'm not that desperate and, as far and I'm concerned, it's not my last chance.

DANI

What does that mean? Are you still trying to find yourself, is that it?
(pause)
Who do you think you're gonna find inside you? There's nobody in there but you . . . just you.
(*pause*)
Look Bruce, as far as I'm concerned, you don't need to find yourself; I love you the way you are.

BRUCE

Well, I don't. I've been trying to tell you for years, Dani, I'm just not ready to commit yet.

DANI

Not ready to commit yet? Bruce, you're fifty-eight years old; when do you think you'll be ready?

BRUCE

I just don't feel the time is right.

DANI

Not right? When do you think the time will be right, Bruce? When Medicare rolls around? When you start collecting Social Security? Hey, Bruce, I hate to break your rice bowl, but you'll be eligible in four years. Is that when you intend to settle down and start raising a family?

BRUCE

Look, I just can't afford to start a family now. I'm up for a promotion at work, for one of the Assistant Manager's jobs, and I don't need anything ruining it. With that promotion, I could get into one of the more prestigious gentlemen clubs in the Wall Street area.

DANI

Like having a baby might ruin your chances of getting the Assistant Manager's job at the First Commercial Mercantile & Dairy Farmers Bank?
(*pause*)
That's a great career move for you, Bruce,
(*sarcastically*)
moving up from Head Teller to being **ONE** of the Assistant Managers. Rather late though in life, wouldn't you say, Bruce, since you've been at the bank for thirty-six years now? But, heaven forbid, me and the baby, we wouldn't want to ruin an opportunity like that for you: a chance to get into one of the more prestigious, downtown, gentlemen clubs!

BRUCE

(*Strained silence in the room.* BRUCE *is glaring at* DANIELLE.)
What do you expect from me?

DANI

(*indignantly repeating his question*)
What do I expect from you? Certainly not to man-up to anything; that's obviously not gonna happen.

BRUCE

Well? I repeat: What do you expect from me? Do you expect me to marry you, or something like that?

DANI

'OR SOMETHING LIKE THAT?!' What would be the 'something like that' choice, Bruce?
(*pause*)
Because, I think I'll take what's behind Curtain Number Two; the 'something like that' curtain, Bruce?

BRUCE

Look, I was hoping you weren't going to try to force me into something.

DANI

I'm not trying to 'force' you into anything, Bruce. But, do go on. 'I paid my money, I's gets to take my chances,' as the expression goes.

Go ahead, Bruce, open up Curtain Number Two; let's see what's back there.

BRUCE

It's just that . . . I hope you don't expect me to support-

DANI

SUPPORT?

BRUCE

Yeah, you know, pay you child support or any kind of money-

DANI

Ah, there it is! Curtain Number Two: **MONEY!**
     (cutting in deeper)
And here I thought it was going to be a beautiful boat or a vacation to Disney World. But no. It's . . . **MONEY!** That's even better, especially for a . . . *desperate* woman like me.
     (pause; trying to get her temper in check)
A girl should never be without money, isn't that right, Bruce? Especially one that's three months pregnant, working at a job paying a pittance while trying to support an elderly mother with senility who's living with her deaf, elderly boyfriend and a blind old aunt.

BRUCE

Tell me about it; all three of them together barely equal one fully functional person. But, they're your problem, not mine. And don't be trying to hang another one of your problem on me, Dani.

DANI

Another one of my problems? Since when is a precious, little, unborn baby another problem? You sound like a bad James Cagney impression, out of one of his old gangster movies, where some cop is trying to frame him up for something:
     (mimicking James Cagney)
Don't try and pin that rap on me, copper!
     (pause)

No Bruce, I don't expect nor do I want anything, either emotionally or financially, from you; not now, nor in the future. Only one condition, Bruce. You just have to promise me one thing, Bruce, and that's it.

BRUCE

Ah, here it comes; here comes the catch.

DANI

No catch, Bruce. You just have to promise me that I'll never see you around here ever again, and that from now on, ad infinitum, you will NEVER make any claims whatsoever on me or *MY* baby.

BRUCE

That's it?

DANI

That's it, Bruce.

BRUCE

(BUSTER *walks out of his bedroom in his bathrobe, slippers and flip-flops; then, down the hallway into the bathroom as,* BRUCE, *not believing his good fortune, excitedly sticks out his hand to shake on it.*)
You got a deal!

DANI

A deal? A deal over a begotten fetus.
(*pause*)
How elegantly and professionally put, especially from a man who wants, ever so much, to belong to a gentleman's club. It is truly something a gentleman, and Assistant Manager at the First Commercial Mercantile & Dairy Farmers Bank would say. In another thirty-six years, I can just see you as the Manager there.
(DANIELLE *shakes* BRUCE'S *extended hand.* BRUCE *heads towards the door; just as he's about to open it, he turns to* DANIELLE.)

BRUCE

(*a massive smile on his face; the first one of the night*)
I really do appreciate you being such a good sport about this, Dani.

161

DANI

Glad I could help, Bruce. It's always so nice to see your face light up like that.

(BRUCE *exits through the front door.* DANIELLE *sits down at the dining room table. The* LIGHTS *fade to black; a lone* SPOTLIGHT holds on DANIELLE.)

DANI
(*continuing; to herself*)

And so, it ends.
(*looking straight ahead, as if in daze*)
After a millennium, that's what I'm remembered for: 'Being a good sport.'

(DANIELLE *puts her head in her hands and we hear her softly* CRYING. *The lone* SPOTLIGHT *fades to black. A gigantic* FLUSH *from the upstairs toilet.*)

CURTAIN SLOWLY FALLS

END OF ACT I

Act 2

Deaf, Dumb And Blind
ACT II

A Saturday afternoon, six and a half months later.

As THE CURTAIN RISES, *we see* MILDRED *with her walker struggling again to get down the stairs in her apartment. She is dressed in a beautiful, expensive-looking dress and has a pretty shawl wrapped around her shoulders.*

The apartment is decorated nicely: a new, white, linen tablecloth accompanies fresh flowers on the dining room table. A large banner hangs from the second floor loft that reads: **CONGRATULATIONS AND BEST WISHES TO DANI AND GUS.**

On the dining room table is a bowl of spiked punch, assorted bottles of liquor, some platters of delicatessen food and a bottle of Mad Dog 20/20 Red Grape Wine that is half-full.

We see BUSTER *sitting in the lounger, watching TV while drinking a glass of Mad Dog 20/20. He is dressed in a tuxedo with tails. The TV is turned up to super-high.*

MILLIE
(*trying to talk over the blaring TV set*)
Lilly? Lilly! **LILLY!**
(BUSTER *looks around, unsure if he hears something or not.*)

BUSTER
Billy?
(MILDRED *makes it to the bottom of the stairs and just stands there, irritated with* BUSTER.)

MILLIE
Here we go again.
      (*shouting across the room to* BUSTER)
LILLY!
      (*shakes her head at* BUSTER *in disbelief*)
What a putz!

BUSTER

I heard that!

MILLIE

(MILDRED *walks towards* BUSTER.)
I don't know how, what with that TV set so God Almighty loud.

BUSTER

(BUSTER *gets up and turns the TV set off.*)
There, you happy now. I was right in the middle of watching ***The Dating Game*** . . . Where do they get these people? Man-oh-man, some of them say the stupidest things.

MILLIE

(*looks <u>directly</u> at* BUSTER; *with sarcasm in her voice*)
Tell me about it.
(*a beat*)
I don't know why you want to watch that show for; we got our own little *Dating Game* goin' on right here.
(MILDRED *motions with her hand towards the colossal Congratulations banner.* BUSTER *sits back down in the lounger and continues to sip at his wine.* MILDRED *anxiously stomps around the table with her walker.*)

BUSTER

Tell me this: Why is it you always come along and try and ruin my fun? I watch ***The Dating Game*** because it's fun; it takes my mind off my troubles.

MILLIE

(*This last statement lights a fire under* MILDRED.)
Troubles? Takes your MIND off your TROUBLES? What troubles you got, you old goat?
(*pause*)
If you call sittin' around in a LA-Z-BOY lounger getting soused on red wine and aggravating me, if you call that troubles, well then, yeah . . . I guess, maybe, you got some troubles then. But, the way I see it, you

ain't got no troubles at all. Come to think of it, the way I see it, you ain't got much of a *mind* left either.

BUSTER

What do you mean by that crack?

MILLIE

I mean, instead of watchin' re-runs of **The Dating Game**, turn that TV set off, every once in a while, and do something with your life.

BUSTER

Oh yeah, like what?

MILLIE

Did you ever think of getting yourself a hobby?

BUSTER

I got one.

MILLIE

Somehow, I don't think boffin' my sister, night and day, exactly qualifies as a hobby; it's more like a . . . a perversion.

BUSTER

Your sister don't seem to think so.

MILLIE

She would if she was in her right mind.

BUSTER

Yeah, well tell me this: What exactly qualifies you as an expert on perversions? According to you, the Bible is a marital aid.
(MILDRED *is seething, too angry to even speak;* BUSTER *continues, rhetorically.*)
What exactly would you know about sex?
(*pause; philosophically*)
To me, sex is like shaving. You shave today and by tomorrow, you've got to do it all over again.

MILLIE

Sort of like a daily ritual, an obligation of sorts . . . a responsibility to be fulfilled.

BUSTER

Exactly. I consider it an obligation to Lillian . . . And me? Why, I'm just fulfilling my responsibilities to her, is all.

MILLIE
(*incensed*)

Oh please; spare me.

BUSTER

Besides, I got one.

MILLIE

Got one what?

BUSTER

A hobby.

MILLIE

I know you do; I can hear you testin' it out on the bedsprings upstairs . . . night after night.
(*imitating the sounds of bedsprings*)
Boing!, boing! Like a dog in heat. Boing!, boing! You just can't hear yourself, is all.

BUSTER

Your mind's always in the gutter.
(*a beat*)
I do have a hobby though.

MILLIE

And what, pray tell, would that be?

BUSTER

Building model submarines.

MILLIE

From your days in the Silent Service.

BUSTER

I was in The Big One all right, W.W. Two.

MILLIE

Yeah well, I think that sub you were on, in 'THE BIG ONE,' dove a little too deep, once too often.

BUSTER

What else would you have me do?

MILLIE

Ever try reading a book? That is, if you still remember how.

BUSTER

At least I can still see one to read it.

MILLIE

Okay, okay; you win. You're getting me off the subject anyway. Tell me this, old man with the tin ear . . . Correction, old man with the two tin ears who hears only what he wants to hear: If you can hear me callin' you a putz from across the room with the TV blasting away, why is it you can't hear Lilly when she leaves the house . . .
(*a beat*)
because **SHE'S GONE, AGAIN . . . YOU PUTZ!**

BUSTER

Gone where?

MILLIE

(*exasperated*)

If I knew where, why in the world would I be asking you?

BUSTER

She always comes back.

MILLIE

Yeah . . . when someone goes after her.

BUSTER

Well, I saw Dani go out about ten minutes ago.

MILLIE

What makes you think she went looking for Lilly? You ask her?

BUSTER

No. I just figured that she wouldn't be going out, especially on a day like today, of all days, and especially dressed the way she was.

(At just that moment, the door opens and in comes DANIELLE; she's nine and a half months pregnant, all out of breath, and dressed in a big, white wedding gown with a flowing train attached to the back of the dress. LILLIAN, following her through the door, is wearing a beautiful, flowered dress; on her head is a floppy bucket-type hat, the brim of which is pulled down around her face; it has a big, white lily in the front.)

LILLY
(singing)

'I'll build a Stairway to Paradise, with a new step ev'ry day.'

DANI
(to LILLIAN)

Phew!; tell me about it.

LILLY
(marches over to MILDRED, singing louder)

'I'm going to get there at any price;
            (points dramatically to the sky)
Stand aside, I'm on my way!'

DANI
(to MILDRED)

Mom is right; those five flights of stairs do seem to be getting longer and longer. Only-

LILLY
(really caught up in the moment now)
'Shoes,
(points to her shoes)
Go on and carry me there!
(down on one knee now, imitating Al Jolson in voice and mannerisms)
I'll build a Stairway to Paradise
With a new step ev'ry day.'

DANI
That's nice, Mom. All you need is some blackface and you'd have that
little tune mastered.

LILLY
(sensing encouragement, sings a refrain)
'With a new step ev'ry day.'

DANI
All right, already, Mom; give it a break.
(to MILDRED)
Those stairs, they don't feel like fifty flights anymore, they feel more
like a hundred and fifty flights.

MILLIE
(to DANIELLE)
You, being nine and a half months pregnant, that wouldn't have
anything to do with it, would it? . . . Here, let me give you a hand.
(MILDRED, *encumbered by her walker, tries to help* DANIELLE
to one of the chairs at the dining room table; LILLIAN *gives whatever
assistance she can as* BUSTER *just looks on.* DANIELLE *is so big from
the pregnancy that she is having an extremely difficult time just getting
into a chair and* MILDRED *remarks on this.)*
MILLIE
(continuing)
Are you sure you're having this kid by Bruce and not by the Elephant
Man?

MILLIE
(After they all finally are seated, MILDRED *turns to* BUSTER *who is still solidly fixed in the lounger.)*
We don't need any help, but thanks anyway, Buster.

BUSTER
(points to his glass of wine)
No thanks, I got a little left.

DANI
Mom, why don't you and Buster do me a favor and go into the kitchen and get the cake for me, please, while I have a *little* word here with Aunt Millie?
(DANIELLE gives MILDRED *the evil eye as* LILLIAN *gets up from her chair.)*

LILLY
(to DANIELLE)
Sure, Danielle.
(to BUSTER)
Come on, Wolfie, let's go.

BUSTER
Where we going? To bed? That's okay with me but, it's a little early in the day for that, wouldn't you say, Lillian?

MILLIE
(to herself)
Horny old fool.

LILLY
(to BUSTER)
No Wolfie, we're going into the kitchen and finish up getting everything ready.
(BUSTER gets out of his lounger and refills his glass of wine.)

MILLIE
(*to* DANIELLE)

Tell me, if you can, why God gave man both a penis and a brain, but only enough blood to run one at a time?

BUSTER
(*to* MILDRED)

I can see now why nobody ever married you. You need to attend a few of those anger management classes.
(BUSTER *and* LILLIAN *head towards the kitchen.*)

MILLIE
(*yells after* BUSTER)

I'll tell you why I never got married. Tryin' to find a good man is like tryin' to find a stick with only one end.
(*to* DANIELLE; *nodding towards* LILLIAN)
Where was she this time?

DANI

Feeding peanuts to the parking meters, again.

LILLY
(*calls back to* DANIELLE, *just before entering the kitchen with* BUSTER)

No, no, no, Danielle. The peanuts were for the pigeons in the park.

DANI
(*to* LILLIAN)

Right Mom.
(*Alone now,* DANIELLE *looks sternly at* MILDRED.)
Aunt Millie, I thought we all agreed; as a matter of fact, it was exactly six and a half months ago when we discussed this . . . the last time that Bruce was here. We all agreed from that moment on, and into the forever future, there would be absolutely, under **NO** circumstances, for **ALL** times, no mention of Bruce in this house, ever again.

MILLIE

You're referring to that Elephant Man remark, aren't you?

DANI

For **ALL** times, no mention of Bruce.

MILLIE

It was just a joke.

DANI

Under **NO** circumstances.

MILLIE
(sheepishly)
I forgot; it won't happen again.

DANI

I certainly hope not. And, on all days . . . my wedding day.

MILLIE

Yeah, your wedding day. Boy, it was certainly a stroke of luck meeting Doctor Praetorian . . . I mean, Gus. Of all things, having your obstetrician turn into your husband. Talk about killing two birds with one stone . . . And he's such a nice man, too. Much better than that Bruce Wigley. Now there was a guy aptly named: Wigley. He sure wiggled out of any kind of commitment with you.

DANI

Aunt Millie, I thought-

MILLIE

Okay, okay but, there were a lot more issues there than met the eye: lack of commitment, failure to communicate, emotional fatigue. I'm just saying that you're a lot better off the way things worked out. Who'd have thought it? You go into the doctor's office, don't even know the doctor, you're three months pregnant, he falls in love with you, and you end up marrying him. Of all things. It's like one of those love stories out of <u>Modern Romance</u> magazine.

DANI

I know; I'm very lucky to have found Gus.

(a beat)

Gus was the one that insisted on this big enchilada with all the trimmings. I mean: the wedding gown, the priest-

MILLIE

Who is this priest, by the way?

DANI

Father Patrick O'Shea from Saint Bartholomew's Church of the Apostles in the Village here. He's one of those semiretired priests that lives in the rectory and celebrates mass occasionally. I was lucky to get him to come over here and officiate. Now, if the groom would only show up.

MILLIE

Hey, that's what you get when you marry a doctor. When's he due back here, anyway?

DANI

Actually, he didn't even have to go in today. He had an emergency delivery at Saint Vincent's Hospital. He'll be back just as soon as he can.

(LILLIAN *and* BUSTER *come out of the kitchen carrying a wedding cake.*)

LILLY
(singing)

'Happy Birthday to you,
Happy Birthday to you,
Happy Birthday dear Danielle,
Happy Birthday to you!'

(LILLIAN *and* BUSTER *set the cake down on the dining room table.*)

DANI

That's very nice, Mom, but it's not my birthday.

LILLY

It's not? Then, why the birthday cake?

DANI

It's not a birthday cake, Mom, it's a wedding cake.

LILLY

You know, I thought something was funny about that cake, what with those two people all dressed-up standing on top of it like that with no candles on it. But, I didn't want to say anything to spoil your birthday, so I told Wolfie: 'Just play along.' That's exactly what I told him. 'Just play along,' I said and 'pretend like we don't notice it's a wedding cake instead of a birthday cake.'
(*a long pause as she stares at the cake*)
But, it's a wedding cake, you say?

DANI

That's right, Mom, I'm getting married today.

LILLY
(*pretending like she knew all along*)
Oh yeah sure, to that Bruce fellow.

DANI
(*to* MILDRED)

I go with Bruce fifteen years, she can't remember his name. The day I'm getting married to another guy, **now** she remembers his name.
(DANIELLE *stands up, and using a knife like a judge's gavel, pounds the dining room table. Both* LILLIAN *and* BUSTER *sit down at the table to await her pronouncement.*)
Hear ye, hear ye all! I said it before and I'll say it again, *one last time*: Bruce and me made a deal the last time he was here. I agreed never to expect, nor want, anything from him, either emotionally or financially. I never intend to be indebted to him in any way. I don't want anything from him, including his name. He agreed that I'd never see his face around here ever again and that he'd never make any claims, whatsoever, on me or my baby. I fully intend to honor our deal.
(*sarcastically*)

After all, Bruce is a *'gentleman'* and I'm *'a good sport.'*

LILLY

I'll say you're 'a good sport'; after all, you're marrying him, aren't you?

DANI

No, Mom; I'm marrying Gus.

LILLY

Who's Gus?

DANI

The guy I'm marrying, Mom.

LILLY

I thought you were marrying Bruce?

DANI
(irritably)

GUS, MOM, GUS!; I'm marrying Gus.

LILLY

Okay, okay. No need to get so testy.
(to herself)
A person asks a simple question.
(to DANIELLE, sulking)
Bruce? Gus? I can't keep track of all these men. I'm not a mind reader you know.

DANI

Sorry, Mom.
(a beat)
Anyway, Gus has never once asked me anything about the father of my baby, not even his name; he could care less. He believes that this is truly his baby. Let every member of this household . . .
(sternly looks around the table)
do the same; put the name of Bruce to rest, once and for all.

177

MILLIE

(Dead silence falls over the room. Then, MILDRED jumps up.)
Give me an AMEN, brothers and sisters!
(Everyone breaks into hoots, howlers with Amen's galore.)

BUSTER

Don't mind if I do.
(BUSTER jumps up and pours himself another glass of wine.)
Would any of you mind if I turned the TV on?

MILLIE

Ah, come on, Buster.

BUSTER

I won't turn the sound up, I promise.

DANI

Go ahead, Buster.
(BUSTER bobs and weaves his way over to the TV and turns it on; then, plops into the lounger, all the while sipping on his wine.)

DANI

(continuing; to MILDRED)
Is it me or is Buster beginning to list towards starboard?

MILLIE

Well, being as how Buster's an old Navy man, I'd have to say: He has three sheets in the wind and the other one's flapping.

DANI

I mean, is he going to be able to give me away? He's walking around here like he's got one roller skate on.

MILLIE

Sure, he'll be able to give you away, along with the Brooklyn Bridge, the Island of Manhattan, and whatever loose change he has in his pockets. We'll just have to put him to bed tonight with a shovel is all, because he'll be pissed up to his eyebrows.

DANI

Look, I'm going to go and fix myself up; Gus should be here any minute.

MILLIE

Sure, go get yourself all gussied up.

MILLIE

(DANIELLE *goes into her downstairs bedroom. MILDRED sits back down at the dining room table with* LILLIAN.)
Lilly, why don't you have a nice glass of punch with me? I spiked it up some; just to give it a little flavoring.

LILLY

I'd be delighted; I'll pour.
(LILLIAN *pours two glasses of punch from the bowl and each takes a sip. The doorbell* RINGS.)
Who's that?

MILLIE

Be hard to tell from here, Lilly. Maybe one of us should get the door, you think?

LILLY

Maybe I should get the door.

MILLIE

Excellent idea, Lilly.
(LILLIAN *gets up, goes to the door, and looks through the peephole. The doorbell* RINGS *again.*)

MILLIE
(*continuing; to* LILLIAN)

Who is it?

LILLY

I don't know; I don't recognize him.

MILLIE

Well, what does he look like?

LILLY

He's short, with white hair, and he's all dressed in black, like Johnny Cash. He looks older than us; could be an undertaker. Did any of us die in here during the night?

MILLIE

Nah, sounds more like that Mick priest Dani finagled over here for this wingding; let him in.

(LILLIAN *opens the door and* FATHER PATRICK O'SHEA *bounces into the apartment with a spring to his step.*)

FATHER O'SHEA
(*with an Irish brogue and a bubbly personality*)
Ah!, and you must be Ms. Goodwright.

LILLY

I am.

FATHER O'SHEA
(*while shaking* LILLIAN'S *hand vigorously*)
Well then, my Best Wishes to the lovely bride.

LILLY

Who?

FATHER O'SHEA

Why you, of course, my dear.

LILLY

Bride?

FATHER O'SHEA

Yes dear, you are.

LILLY

I am?

(*to* MILDRED; *screaming with excitement*)
Did you hear that, Millie? I'm gonna be a bride. And me without a thing to wear.

MILLIE

I heard. I'm not the one that's deaf, remember?

LILLY

Who's deaf?

MILLIE

Your roommate, remember?

LILLY

Speaking of that: Are Wolfie and me getting married?

MILLIE

Yeah,
(*pause*)
when hell freezes over.
(MILDRED *gets up and starts to work her way over to the door.*)

LILLY
(*to* FATHER O'SHEA)

Who?

FATHER O'SHEA

Why you, my dear. Aren't you Ms. Goodwright?

LILLY

I am but, when I said: 'Who?,' I meant: Who are you?

FATHER O'SHEA

Oh, I'm so sorry, my dear, for not introducing myself properly; how forgetful.

LILLY

Don't worry about it; I'm quite forgetful myself these days.

FATHER O'SHEA

I'm Father Patrick O'Shea from Saint Bartholomew's Church of the Apostles.

LILLY

Well, Father Patrick O'Shea-

FATHER O'SHEA

Please, just call me Father Patty; everyone at the church does.

LILLY

Well okay, Father Patty, I'm a little confused.

FATHER O'SHEA
(trying to flatter her)
Perfectly normal, my dear. All young brides are on their wedding days.
(By now, MILDRED *has arrived at the door.)*

MILLIE
(to FATHER O'SHEA*)*
Well, given this
(nodding towards LILLIAN*)*
young bride's condition, she's probably doubly confused . . . Father. I think you've got the wrong Ms. Goodwright.

FATHER O'SHEA
(to MILDRED*)*
And, whom do I have the lovely pleasure of addressing now?

LILLY
(to FATHER O'SHEA*)*
Oh, excuse me, Father; I'm Lilly and this is my sister, Millie.
(to MILDRED*)*
Millie, this is Father Patty.

FATHER O'SHEA

Glad to meet you, Millie.

MILLIE

Likewise.

FATHER O'SHEA
(while shaking MILDRED'S *hand vigorously)*
Well then, my Best Wishes to the lovely bride.

MILLIE

You're battin' zero today, Father Patty; I'm not Ms. Goodwright either. The Ms. Goodwright you're looking for is Danielle Goodwright and she's in her bedroom right now getting all slicked up for this big shindig here.

FATHER O'SHEA

Oh dear me; my mistake.

MILLIE

That's all right. No harm, no foul, I always say. In the meantime, while we're waiting for the real bride to get ready, why don't we all go back over to the dining room table and have some punch . . . or maybe a nice glass of some Irish whiskey. I think we may have some of that lying around somewhere.

FATHER O'SHEA

Ah, a woman after me own heart.

MILLIE

Ah, you Shamrocks always were a bunch of sweet talkin' leprechauns. Where's your shillelagh?
(They all walk over to the dining room table and take a seat.)

MILLIE
(to LILLIAN)
Lilly, why don't you pour Father Patty here, a nice tall glass of that fine Irish whiskey we have, and a couple of glasses of punch for us?

LILLY

As Wolfie would say: 'Don't mind if I do.'

(LILLIAN *pours out the drinks all around.*)

MILLIE

Are you from Ireland, Father Patty?

FATHER O'SHEA

That would be a yes, my dear. I was born in Kerry County, in a town called Dingle; moved here as a lad.

MILLIE

I thought as much.

FATHER O'SHEA
(offers a toast)

'May your glass be ever full. May the roof over your head be always strong. And may you be in Heaven half an hour before the devil knows you're dead.'

LILLY

Before who knows what?
(to MILDRED*)*
I don't care if he is a priest, he is very confusing.

MILLIE

Never mind, Lilly, just have a sip of your punch there.
(They all sample their drinks.)

FATHER O'SHEA

And, where now is this fine fellow, Wolfie, I hear you speak of?

MILLIE

Ah, geez-o. For a minute there, I thought I was gonna like you.

FATHER O'SHEA

Excuse me?

MILLIE

An old Irish saying, Father Patty.

FATHER O'SHEA

Is it? Funny, I never heard that one before.

(FATHER O'SHEA *sees* BUSTER *sitting in the lounger in his tuxedo, watching TV and drinking. With his whiskey in hand,* FATHER O'SHEA *goes over to introduce himself.*)

FATHER O'SHEA
(*continuing; to* BUSTER)

Well then, Congratulations to the handsome groom.

(FATHER O'SHEA *grabs* BUSTER'S *free hand and vigorously shakes it.* BUSTER, *unaware that anyone has even come into the apartment, is startled.*)

MILLIE
(*to* herself)

This oughta be good.

BUSTER

Where in hell am I?

FATHER O'SHEA
(*chuckling*)

I can absolutely guarantee you, my son, you're surely not there.

MILLIE
(*adding*)

But, then again, . . . that would have been nice to see.
(*to* LILLIAN)

Did you finish putting out everything on the table?

LILLY

Why no, I forgot the napkins and paper plates.

MILLIE

Come on; I'll give you what help I can.

(MILDRED *and* LILLIAN *go into the kitchen.* BUSTER *gets up to greet* FATHER O'SHEA.)

FATHER O'SHEA
(while shaking BUSTER'S *hand vigorously)*
Well, I'm finally glad I guessed one right. Now, I'm batting three-thirty-three. I missed out on who the bride was in this house twice, but with you and the tails, you must be the groom for sure, or my name isn't Father Patrick O'Shea.

BUSTER
That's right.

FATHER O'SHEA
(confused as to BUSTER'S *response)*
What is?

BUSTER
You're Father Patrick O'Shea.

FATHER O'SHEA
(still very much confused)
That's right. Just call me Father Patty; everyone at the church does.

BUSTER
That's right.

FATHER O'SHEA
Let me ask you something, Wolfie? How do you hear that TV, what with it being so low?

BUSTER
(BUSTER *points with both hands to the hearing aids in each of his ears.)*
I'm just a little hard of hearing.

FATHER O'SHEA
No, what I mean is: How do you understand what's going on in a program like what you're watching there, ***The Dating Game***, without the sound?

BUSTER

I've got a good imagination.

FATHER O'SHEA

You must have.

DANI

(DANIELLE *walks out of the bedroom, sees* FATHER O'SHEA, *and walks over to introduce herself.* FATHER O'SHEA *is beside himself to see a nine and a half month pregnant woman in a white wedding dress.*)
Hi, you must be Father Patrick O'Shea from Saint Bart's.

FATHER O'SHEA
(in a mental turmoil)
Don't tell me you're . . . you're the bride?

DANI

Why yes, I'm Dani Goodwright. Is something wrong?

FATHER O'SHEA

No . . . NO! Of course not. Why?

DANI

You sounded a little taken aback just now, is all.

FATHER O'SHEA
(trying to cover up his faux pas)
Oh no. What I meant was: Don't tell me, you're the bride!
(while shaking DANI'S *hand, vigorously)*
Best Wishes . . . to the bride . . . again today, for the third time.

FATHER O'SHEA

(FATHER O'SHEA *is totally discombobulated now. He looks at* DANIELLE: *in her early forties, pregnant, and in a wedding gown. Then, he looks at* BUSTER: *in his eighties, and in a tux with tails. To* DANIELLE, *back to* BUSTER. *Thinking they are to be married, he downs the rest of his whiskey in one large gulp.*)
Love works in mysterious ways. I'm back to batting zero.

DANI

Excuse me?

FATHER O'SHEA

You know, my dear, I think I could rather do with another spot of that fine, Irish whiskey you serve here, if it's not too much trouble.

DANI

(DANIELLE *immediately grabs* FATHER O'SHEA'S *arm and leads him to the dining room table.* BUSTER *sits back down in the lounger.)*
No trouble at all, Father O'Shea.

FATHER O'SHEA

Patty. Please, call me Father Patty, everyone at . . .
(FATHER O'SHEA'S *voice trails off in mid-sentence as he continues to look at* BUSTER, *then back at* DANIELLE, *as she pours him another glass of whiskey. Then, they both take a seat at the dining room table.)*
Aren't you having anything to drink?

DANI

(as she pats her stomach)
I can't . . . or haven't you noticed?; I'm nine and a half months pregnant.

FATHER O'SHEA

Oh, I noticed all right.
(looks pointedly at BUSTER)
I'm holding myself back from being a . . . a butt-in-ski, is all.

DANI

A buttinski?

FATHER O'SHEA

It's sort of a Polish expression.

DANI

You must have a lot of will power. The average person, who sees a pregnant woman in a wedding dress, would have had tons of questions to ask by now.

FATHER O'SHEA
(raising his glass in a toast)
'May there be a generation of children on the children of your children.'
(FATHER O'SHEA *takes a drink, all the while looking at* DANIELLE *who is still squirming and struggling, because of her swollen size, to get comfortably seated in her chair.)*

DANI
Nicely said. I'm going into the hospital tomorrow to have labor induced, in case you were wondering.

FATHER O'SHEA
I wasn't wondering. Did I look like I was wondering?
(a beat)
Cutting it a wee bit close, aren't we?

DANI
It was the groom's idea.

FATHER O'SHEA
(looking at BUSTER)
What was? To cut it a wee bit close?

DANI
No, no. To have this wedding with the priest and gown, and all. He insisted we do it up all proper and legal so when the baby comes into this world, it'll be all legit on the birth certificate and all. He says: 'Children today have enough problems in life; might as well try and start out on the right foot without stigmatizing the child by being illegitimately born.'

FATHER O'SHEA
(musing to himself; voice trails off)
Does he now? Really? At his age, I wouldn't have thought—

DANI
Do you think I'm making a mistake, Father Patty?

189

FATHER O'SHEA

Oh, that's not for me to say, my dear; that's for God to . . . for God
to . . .
 (staring <u>directly</u> at BUSTER *and fumbling for words)*
I've seen some pretty strange, no, make that bizarre things in my
lifetime, but if I've learned anything, it's not to meddle in affairs of the
heart about who would make a suitable mate in life.

DANI

No, I meant making a mistake about getting married. I just wanted
to have my baby and then . . . down the road, think about getting
married. You know . . . if it all works out . . . in a couple of years.

FATHER O'SHEA

If it all works out? In a couple of years? Do you think
 (staring directly at BUSTER*)*
he'll . . . I mean, you'll both have that much time?

DANI

Sure, why not? We've got plenty of time.

FATHER O'SHEA

That's a very optimistic attitude, my child. You must have a touch of
the Irish in your blood.

DANI

I know you could fall in the shower tomorrow and crack your skull
wide open. You could walk across the street and get hit by a bus that's
headed over to Flatbush.

FATHER O'SHEA

No, I wasn't exactly thinking along those lines. I had hardening of the
arteries more in mind. Or, possibly liver failure.

DANI

Whose?

FATHER O'SHEA
(*whispering to* DANI)

Why Wolfie's, of course.

DANI

Wolfie's? You mean, Buster's arteries? What's Buster's arteries and liver got to do with all of this?

FATHER O'SHEA

Well, isn't he the man you'll be a marrying?

DANI

(DANIELLE *bursts out laughing;* FATHER O'SHEA *looks on dumfounded.*)
I'm sorry to be laughing, Father Patty, but wherever did you get that idea?

FATHER O'SHEA

Yes, wherever indeed. I just assumed, what with Wolfie, or rather Buster, in the tuxedo with tails. I mean, I shook hands with Buster earlier and congratulated him on being the groom and he seemed to acknowledge that he was.

DANI

Let me ask you this, Father: Did Buster actually say he was the groom?

FATHER O'SHEA

Well no, not exactly in so many words.

DANI

What exactly did he say when you congratulated him on being the groom?

FATHER O'SHEA

I believe he said: 'That's right' which, of course, led me to assume-
(DANIELLE *begins to laugh uproariously again.*)

DANI

Father, Buster always says: 'That's right' when he hasn't got the faintest notion what a person is talking about; he's almost stone deaf.

FATHER O'SHEA

Oh well, that would explain a lot now, wouldn't it? Yes, indeed, God Almighty, that would explain a lot now. Yes in-deed-dy!

(FATHER O'SHEA *and* DANIELLE *both start laughing at the ridiculousness of the situation.*)

DANI

Buster is my mom's boyfriend. And, as far as Buster getting married, he'd rather be in hell with his back broken. He's dressed that way because he's supposed to give me away; that was my mother's idea since my real father died almost thirty years ago. Mom's my maid of honor and Aunt Millie's my bridesmaid.

FATHER O'SHEA
(laughing)

You know, I think this calls for a wee touch of that giggle water that you serve up so well here.

(FATHER O'SHEA *holds out his empty glass and* DANIELLE *refills it once again.*)

DANI

No, the real groom is my obstetrician, Doctor Augustus Praetorian.

FATHER O'SHEA

Your obstetrician? How convenient for you. He must be a happy father.

(FATHER O'SHEA *is steadily sipping on his whiskey.*)

DANI

Oh, he is, but he's not the real father.

FATHER O'SHEA
(almost chokes on his drink)

Just when I think I've got this soap opera all figured out, up pops another knot in the rope.

(*a beat*)
My dear, your life has more twists and turns than the Pretzel Lady at the carnival.

DANI

I know, Father Patty. That's what I was trying to say before: Do you think I'm making a mistake about getting married?

FATHER O'SHEA

Well let me ask you this, Dani Goodwright: Are you in love?

DANI

Oh, he's a wonderful man. I mean, any man that would accept . . . no, not just accept but . . .
(*mentally searching for the right word*)
love another man's child as if it was his own, that is a man to be loved.

FATHER O'SHEA

I agree, but the question was: 'Are *you* in love?'

DANI

How would I know, Father?

FATHER O'SHEA

A British playwright, a Sir James Barrie, once said about love: 'If you have it, you don't need to have anything else, and if you don't, it doesn't matter much what else you have.'

DANI

Then, I have it.

FATHER O'SHEA

Well then, let me get me Bible.

FATHER O'SHEA

(*Reaches into his pocket and pulls out his Bible; just then he has a thought.*)

By the way, just as a sort of point of order, where exactly is this groom, if I may be so bold?

DANI

He should be here any minute. He had an emergency delivery at the hospital.

(DANIELLE *suddenly feels a pain in her stomach*.)
Oh . . . Oh! Ut-oh! **UT-OH!**

FATHER O'SHEA

What is it, my child? What's with the ut-oh's?

DANI

I think it may be time, Father.

FATHER O'SHEA

Oh no, please; please don't say that!

DANI

Okay, Father, I won't say it; but, not saying it isn't gonna make it not happen.

FATHER O'SHEA

(folds his hands together, as if in prayer, and looks towards Heaven)
Please. Oh please, Dear Lord! Not on my watch.

DANI

Could you help me over to the couch, Father Patty?

FATHER O'SHEA

Gladly.

DANI

(FATHER O'SHEA *helps* DANIELLE *up and they start to struggle over to the sofa.*)
You know, Father, I think maybe we should try and get some help.
(While on the way to the couch, FATHER O'SHEA *starts calling for help; his pleas getting louder and longer as he closes on the sofa.)*

FATHER O'SHEA
(flustered and in a panic)

Help. HElp. HELp! **HELP!**

(LILLIAN *and* MILDRED *come out of the kitchen;* BUSTER *stands up and heads towards the couch; they all meet in front of the sofa. Pandemonium breaks out in the living room with everyone rumbling about, talking over the next person, interjecting their own chaotic thoughts and views at breakneck speed.)*

LILLY

What in the world is going on in here?

BUSTER

What indeed? Even *I* heard all that racket!

DANI
(in pain)

Oh!, Oh!

FATHER O'SHEA

Dani seems to be about ready to have her baby.

BUSTER
(to LILLIAN*)*

What'd he say?

MILLIE

Where?

FATHER O'SHEA

Where? Right here!

LILLY
(to BUSTER*)*

Baby? What baby?

DANI

UT-OH!

FATHER O'SHEA

Now, now, my dear; I thought we'd agreed we wouldn't use that expression, ut-oh, anymore.

BUSTER

What's all this noise about?

MILLIE

She wasn't supposed to have her baby until tomorrow.

BUSTER

That's right.

LILLY

What's right? Will somebody please tell me what is going on here?

FATHER O'SHEA
(to DANI*)*
I hope you have a good H.M.O.?

BUSTER

No, we don't have cable.

FATHER O'SHEA

Sweet Jesus!, what fresh Hell is this?

(FATHER O'SHEA *finally gets* DANIELLE *settled onto the sofa where she lies down. The couch is angled in such a way on the stage that the audience only sees the back of it; therefore,* DANIELLE *is not visible to the audience when she goes into labor. Every once in a while, her hands and arms, or occasionally her head, will pop up for a moment to make inane gestures over the back of the sofa like a jack-in-the-box but, for the most part, we only hear her throughout her ordeal, moaning and groaning in pain.)*

DANI

OH!, OH!

(Everyone is gathered in front of the couch, pacing about and jabbering to themselves, as DANIELLE *writhes in pain.)*

LILLY
(*to* FATHER O'SHEA)
Do something, Father!

FATHER O'SHEA
As Prissy, that servant girl to Scarlett O'Hara in <u>Gone With the Wind</u>, once said: *'Lawdy!, we got to have a doctor. I don't know nuthin' 'bout birthin' babies!'* . . . That pretty much sums it up. I'm just a priest, not a doctor; all I know how to do is pray. And believe me, I'm praying. And how!
(FATHER O'SHEA *pops open the Bible in his hands and starts madly thumbing through it, looking for an appropriate prayer.*)

MILLIE
(*under her breathe*)
And drink.
(*to* FATHER O'SHEA)
When our butts are in a tight spot, we can all pretty much pray; wouldn't you say, Father Patty?

LILLY
(*to* MILDRED, *while nervously wringing her hands*)
Do something, Millie!

MILLIE
Like what, Lilly? I can't even see Dani on the couch, which is right in front of me.
(MILDRED *proceeds to start cleaning her glasses on her dress and squinting as if this will help a blind person see better.*)

LILLY
(*to* BUSTER)
Do something, Wolfie!

BUSTER
(BUSTER *is standing in front of the sofa; his eyes diverted to the side, so as not to see any of this.*)
Like what?

(BUSTER *puts both hands over his ears to drown out the noise then, an inspiration hits him.*)
I know, I'll call for help.

MILLIE

FINALLY!, the *'Hunk of Burnin' Love'* comes up with a good idea.
(BUSTER *heads over to the curio cabinet and dials 911 on the portable phone.*)

LILLY

Do something, Father Patty!

FATHER O'SHEA
(reading from his Bible)
'Dearly Beloved . . . We are gathered together here in the sight of God, and in the face of this company, to join this Man and this Woman in Holy Matrimony which is-'

MILLIE

Not yet, Father, the groom's still not here yet.

BUSTER

(LILLIAN *is following alongside* BUSTER, who *is aimlessly wandering around the room with the portable phone to his ear.* BUSTER *is talking loudly on phone to 911 because he can't hear.*)
Emergency! Emergency! We have an emergency here! . . . What? . . . What do you mean: 'Who is this?'
(to LILLIAN*)*
They want to know who I am.
LILLY
(to BUSTER*)*
What has that got to do with our emergency?

BUSTER
(to 911)
What has that got to do with our emergency? . . . What? . . . Never mind!
(to LILLIAN*)*
They told me to: 'Never mind.'

LILLY

(*to* BUSTER)

Never mind what? Our emergency?

BUSTER

(*to* 911)

Never mind what? Our emergency?

(*a beat; to* LILLIAN)

No, never mind my name.

(*to* 911)

What? . . . Yeah, of course, I'm still here . . . What?

(*to* LILLIAN)

First, they want to know who I am, now they want to know who I'm talking to. What's with these people?

(*to* 911)

I'm talking to you, that's who I'm talking to. Who do you think I'm talking to?!

LILLY

(*to* BUSTER)

What does that have to do with our emergency?

BUSTER

(*to* 911)

Yeah, what has that got to do with our emergency? . . . What? . . . Never mind!

(*to* LILLIAN)

They told me to never mind again.

LILLY

(*to* BUSTER)

Never mind what? Talking to them?

BUSTER

(*to* 911)

Never mind what? Talking to you? . . . What?

199

(*to* LILLIAN)

No, talking to *you*. How do they know who *you* are if they don't even know who I am?

DANI
(*loudly, from across the room*)
OH!, OOH! . . . OOOH!

BUSTER
(*to* 911)

Things are getting worse? . . . With what? . . . With our emergency here, that's with what! . . . What? . . . I can't hear you very well in here with all this noise; wait a minute while I go upstairs.

(BUSTER *heads upstairs, through the hall window and out onto the fire escape, mumbling into the phone the entire way as* LILLIAN *follows.*)

DANI

OH!, OOH! . . . OOOH!

MILLIE

Can't you do anything, Father?

FATHER O'SHEA

What can a mere priest do here?; this is a job for an exorcist!
(*buries his head back in his Bible*)

'Into this holy estate, these two persons come now to be joined. If any man can show just cause why they may not be lawfully joined together, let him now speak or else hereafter forever hold his peace.'

(FATHER O'SHEA *looks around for any objections and at just that moment, in through the door bursts a man in green hospital scrubs carrying a small, black medical bag; it is* DR. AUGUSTUS "GUS" PRAETORIAN, *a handsome man in his mid-forties, who is huffing and puffing from exhaustion.*)

FATHER O'SHEA
(*continuing*)

I knew it; I just knew it! Someone to object. What more can go wrong at this wedding?

(*to* GUS)

Go ahead; what's your problem? Up until this wedding, I thought I had heard it all; evidently, I was sadly mistaken. But, after today, I know I will definitely have heard it all. Go ahead; out with it!

GUS
(*to* FATHER O'SHEA)

I'm Gus . . . the groom . . .
(*He opens his medical bag, snaps on a pair of rubber gloves, and kneels down next to* DANIELLE, *who is stretched out on the couch.*)
and the doctor.

FATHER O'SHEA

Splendid, splendid! That's the best news I've hear all day. By God, I'll drink to that.

MILLIE

Not just yet, Father; let's get this 'coming out' party, so to speak, finished first . . . and quickly.

BUSTER
(*yelling into the street below*)

WE HAVE AN EMERGENCY HERE! HELP! **SOMEBODY PLEASE HELP US!**

GUS
(*to* DANIELLE *as her head rises up over the back of the sofa.*)

You doing okay, honey? I got back as soon as I could. I heard all the commotion, from down the street, and ran up those five flights of stairs, two at a time.

DANI

I'm glad, at least, one of us is in shape.

GUS
(GUS *gives* DANIELLE *a quick kiss; then, she lies back down on the sofa.*)

Well, hang on; here we go. The Praetorian Guard to the rescue . . . Push!

(*Because of the positioning of the couch, the audience can see* GUS'S *head but not the actual delivery of the baby.*)

FATHER O'SHEA
(*to* GUS)

Gus, 'wilt thou have this Woman to be thy wedded wife, to live together after God's ordinance in the holy estate of Matrimony?'

GUS

I will.

FATHER O'SHEA

Wait, I'm not done yet . . . 'Wilt thou,' Gus, 'love her, comfort her, honour, and keep her in sickness and in health; and, forsaking all others, keep thee only unto her, so long as ye both shall live?'
(*a very long pause*)

Now, Gus, now!

GUS

I will.

FATHER O'SHEA
(*to* DANIELLE)

Dani, 'wilt thou-'

GUS

A little faster, Father.
(*to* DANIELLE)

That's it, that's it; keep pushing!

FATHER O'SHEA

Dani, 'wilt thou' . . . do the same thing?

DANI
(DANIELLE'S *head quickly pops up.*)

I wilt!
(*Just as quickly,* DANIELLE'S *head pops back down.*)

FATHER O'SHEA
(*to* GUS *and* DANIELLE)

Okay, I'll tell you what. In the interest of time, I'm going to say the following prayers, and you both repeat them after me as we go along; that ought to speed things up a bit.

(*a beat*)

'I', and each of you now say your own name.

GUS

I, Gus.

DANI

I, Dani.

FATHER O'SHEA

Splendid, splendid; we're doing just splendid, here.

GUS

No need for a running commentary, Father; this isn't Wide World of Sport here; instead, let's just stick to the prayers and instead of a little faster, make them a LOT faster.

FATHER O'SHEA

'Take thee.' Say each other's name now.

GUS

Take thee, Dani.

DANI

Take thee, Gus.

FATHER O'SHEA

'For my wedded.' Say wife and husband respectively,

GUS

For my wedded wife.

DANI

For my wedded husband.

FATHER O'SHEA
(FATHER O'SHEA *proceeds to speed through the rest of the following prayers with Gus and Dani simultaneously repeating the words after him.*)
'To have and to hold from this day forward, for better for worse, for richer for poorer, in sickness and in health, to love and to cherish, 'til death us do part.'

BUSTER
(*yelling from the fire escape*)
HELP! HELP!
(*responding to someone in the street below*)
What? What do you mean: 'Shut the hell up.' **WE HAVE AN EMERGENCY HERE!**

FATHER O'SHEA
(*to* GUS)
Repeat after me, Gus. 'With this ring, I thee wed . . .'
(*a beat*)
Where's the ring? Gus, do you have the ring?

GUS
(*sweating bullets while working away on* DANIELLE)
Can't we just skip the ring part; my hands are kinda busy right now.

FATHER O'SHEA
Splendid idea. 'Those whom God hath joined together, let no man put asunder.'
(DANIELLE'S *head pops up once again; she is breathing loudly in and out, a mile a minute. She immediately lies back down.*)

GUS
Father, you ever hear of Sudden Death overtime in football? Well, we're there!

FATHER O'SHEA
I'll take that to mean, I better be finishing up.
(*the following words from the Father are said faster than the speed of light*)

'Forasmuch as Gus and Dani have consented together in holy wedlock, and have witnessed the same before God and this company, and thereto have given and pledged their troth, each to the other, and have declared the same by holding hands;'
(to GUS and DANI)
Are you holding hands?
(looks and realizes the predicament of the delivery; to himself)
I'd say that was holding hands, after a fashion.
(continuing; to GUS and DANI)
'I pronounce that they are Man and Wife in the name of the Father, and of the Son, and of the Holy Spirit. Amen!'
(We hear a slap on a baby's behind, then a baby screaming.)
MILLIE

AMEN!
(to FATHER O'SHEA)
Father, you are one fast talkin', Mick priest.

FATHER O'SHEA
I'll drink to that!
(FATHER O'SHEA goes over and pours himself a stiff drink of whiskey, then tosses it back.)

GUS
I need a blanket.

MILLIE
(MILDRED takes off the shawl around her shoulders and hands it to GUS.)
Here.

GUS
(to FATHER O'SHEA)
Father, I don't know, but if you ever leave the priesthood, I'd say you'd be pretty good at calling horse races.

MILLIE
(with tongue-in-cheek)
And to think they call the Kentucky Derby: 'the greatest two minutes in sports.'

GUS
(*to* DANIELLE)

She's a girl.

DANI

(ĐANIELLE *rises up from the sofa and holds the baby, which is wrapped in* MILDRED'S *shawl, up in the air, as she looks at her, jubilantly.*)

No, she's . . . *PRECIOUS!*

(*The front door bangs open and two, out of breath, New York City police officers rush into the room with their guns drawn.*)

Police Officer #1

Okay, where's the emergency?

GUS AND FATHER O'SHEA
(*simultaneously*)

WHAT?

Police Officer #2

We got reports, from all over the neighborhood, that some crazy, old man was yelling 'Emergency' from the fire escape and it sounded like someone was bein' murdered in this apartment!

BUSTER
(*yelling from the fire escape while choking back tears of frustration*)

WE HAVE AN EMERGENCY HERE! HELP! SOMEBODY PLEASE HELP US!

(*All the heads in the room slowly turn to the upstairs fire escape where* BUSTER *and* LILLIAN *are standing.*)

CURTAIN FALLS

END OF ACT II

Act 3

Deaf, Dumb And Blind
ACT III

A Sunday afternoon, one year later to the day.

As THE CURTAIN RISES, we see MILDRED with her walker struggling yet again to get down the stairs in her apartment. She is in a pleasant-looking dress.

The apartment is nicely decorated with a festive tablecloth, colorful balloons all around, and both unopened and opened birthday presents for a small girl on the dining room table and floor. A big banner hangs from the second floor loft that reads: **HAPPY BIRTHDAY, PRECIOUS**.

On the table, we see a bowl of spiked punch, assorted bottles of liquor, some platters of delicatessen food and a bottle of Mad Dog 20/20 that is half-full.

MILLIE

(in a panic; an urgent tone to her voice)

Lilly? Lilly?

(We see BUSTER, sitting in a chair next to the dining room table, dressed in a hideous mixed-matched ensemble to wit: a pair of loud plaid shorts, white shoes, a white nautical Captain's hat, and wearing a t-shirt that reads: 'Grandpa.' He is rocking a cradle while singing a song to PRECIOUS who is inside, sleeping.

Throughout this act, PRECIOUS is not actually seen; she's either in her cradle or else wrapped in a pink blanket.

BUSTER is singing, off-key, and at the top of his lungs into the microphone of a karaoke machine. He is singing a song without any defined melody; a song that he is making up as he goes along.)

BUSTER

(singing)

'I've had my fair share of grog in Gibraltar,
Been shanghaied in Singapore,
Been made to walk the plank in Port Moresby,
The rest of the world it bores me,

It's a sailor's life for me, me little buckaroo matey.'

MILLIE

Lilly? Lilly! **LILLY!**

BUSTER
(BUSTER *looks around, unsure if he hears something* or not, then continues singing.)
'Yo!, ho!, ho!, and a bottle of rum, ye wee little lassie,
I'm the son of a salty buccaneer,
And as I sip on my gin,
I'm beginnin' to grin,
It's a sailor's life for me, me little buckaroo matey.'

MILLIE
(as she gets to the bottom of the stairs)
Here we go again.
(shouting towards BUSTER)
LILLY!
(BUSTER *stops singing, puts down the microphone, and takes a swallow from his glass of wine;* MILLIE *continues.*)
I thought you were watchin' her.

BUSTER
Well, you thought wrong . . . again. How can I be watching her when I'm already watching baby Precious here.

MILLIE
(MILDRED *walks over to the table and stands next to* BUSTER.)
Look at you. All dressed up there like Liberace's stunt double.
(a beat)
You can't watch two people at once? Like a seventy-nine year old, senile woman and a one year old baby. But then again, I guess that'd be too tough an assignment for the son of a salty buccaneer who's walked the plank in Port Moresby . . .' me little buckaroo, matey.'

BUSTER

(Exasperated, BUSTER *turns to MILDRED.)*
Well, you did it again.

MILLIE

I did it again? I did what again?

BUSTER

Ruined all my fun; you're always doing it. If it's not when I'm watching **The Dating Game** on TV, it's when I'm singing me sailor songs to baby Precious here.

MILLIE

You call what you were doing there, singing? Well, it sounded like some poor old dog being castrated, in an alley, with a beer bottle, to me.

BUSTER

Yeah well, this old dog here doesn't think so, and neither does Precious.
(BUSTER *peeks into the cradle at* PRECIOUS *and smiles.)*
Just look how she's sleeping like a log.

MILLIE

I don't know how, what with all that racket; she must be on drugs . . . and at her age too. Don't you at least know some kind of a lullaby for a baby?

BUSTER

(A bit of a cry comes out of the cradle from PRECIOUS.)*
Now, there you've gone and done it!
(BUSTER *puts his finger in his glass of wine, then reaches into the cradle and puts some of the wine on his finger onto Precious's gums; all the while,* MILDRED *is hunched over the cradle watching these proceedings.)*

MILLIE

I saw that! You are druggin' that baby!

211

BUSTER

It's just an
(in baby talk)
itsy-bitsy, teensy-weensy bit of wine
(back to regular voice)
on her gums, is all.

MILLIE
(mimicking his baby talk)
An itsy-bitsy, teensy-weensy bit of wine.
(back to regular voice)
And, how would you know? You only being an expert on shavin'.

BUSTER

I'd guess you ought to know better than me about drinking and all, you being the expert on perversion that you are.

MILLIE
(MILDRED looks at BUSTER'S 'Grandpa' t-shirt.)
Grandpa.
(derisive laugh)
Grandpa, my ass! Grandpa, the drug pusher, is more like it.
(pause)
You are a Mad Dog all right. That stuff you're drinkin' there is fortified wine; it's thirty-six proof. It's got like eighteen percent alcohol in it. You're gonna turn that poor child into an alky, just like yourself. Why don't you just put that rotgut in her bottle and force-feed it down her throat as you sing *Ninety-Nine Bottles of Beer on the Wall* through that karaoke machine there?

BUSTER

I'd like to force feed something down your throat, and it wouldn't be no rotgut, as you call it.

MILLIE

Yeah, what would it be then?

BUSTER

How about we start with some one hundred percent, straight arsenic, though I'd doubt that'd get the job done.

MILLIE

You know, if I wasn't afraid of wakin' the baby, I'd seriously consider murder. I know the police would let me off, scot-free; they'd consider it a case of justifiable homicide.

BUSTER
(MILDRED *makes a threatening step towards* BUSTER *as if to physically strangle him with her hands.*)
Beware Macduff!
(BUSTER *rises to meet the challenge; however, when he stands up, he steps on a baby doll, one of those talking doll toys.*)
PRINCESS
(*the doll; talking*)
Hi! My name is Princess.

MILLIE
(MILDRED *looks at* BUSTER *with contempt.*)
Sit down, Princess. I'm not gonna hurt ya.
(*a beat*)
That'd be just like you to hit a defenseless, blind woman.

BUSTER

Yeah, the blind wearing glasses; you're about as defenseless as a four-eyed rattlesnake.
(MILDRED *backs off and* BUSTER *sits back down; the two just glare at each other.*)

BUSTER
(*rhetorically*)
What have you got against *Ninety-Nine Bottles of Beer on the Wall*? That's a chartbusting, golden oldie.

MILLIE
(A stillness, like that of eternal night, creeps over the room then . . .)
Well?

BUSTER
Well what?

MILLIE
Who's watchin' Lilly?

BUSTER
I saw Gus go out after her.
(At just that moment, in through the front door comes LILLIAN *in shorts, sneakers, and wearing a t-shirt that reads: 'Grandma,' followed by* GUS *in a smart-looking shirt and a pair of dress slacks.)*
See, there they are; what were you so worried about?
(BUSTER *picks up a Mother Goose mobile from a box on the table and starts trying to put it together.)*

MILLIE
Lilly, come on over here and have a seat; tell me all about your day.

LILLY
(MILDRED *sits down at the table;* LILLIAN *walks over and sits down in a chair next to her.)*
What do you want to know?

MILLIE
Well, let's start with: Where've you been?

LILLY
I went for a walk in the park, is all.

MILLIE
Oh, the park again.

LILLY

But, I forgot my peanuts to feed the pigeons. That's all I was doing until Bruce here showed up and brought me home. You people treat me as if I was some kind of shut-in.

MILLIE

(*to* GUS; *teasing him by deliberately calling him by the wrong name*)
Is that true, **Bruce**? She was just going for a walk in the park?

GUS

(GUS *walks over to the table and teases* MILDRED *right back by addressing her by the wrong name*)
Pretty close, Mabel; she was talking to the parking meters and wanting change back.

LILLY
(*to* MILDRED)

Who's Mabel?

MILLIE

No one, dear; it's just Gus's quick wit there. You remember Gus, don't you, Lilly?; he's the one that married your daughter, Dani.

LILLY

Oh course . . . Gus?; I knew that.
(*to* GUS)
And, by the way, Gus: Where is Danielle?

GUS

She'll be home soon. Until then, we all have to take care of baby Precious.
(*to* BUSTER)
How is Precious doing there, Buster?

BUSTER

Fine, just fine, Gus.

MILLIE

Yeah fine, if you call being lit to the gunnels for hours on end, fine.

GUS

(*to* MILDRED)

What are you talking about?

MILLIE

(*to* BUSTER)

Go ahead, Mad Dog, tell him about your new drinkin' buddy there in the cradle.

GUS

What?

BUSTER

Nothing; it's nothing, Gus. You know Millie; she makes a mountain out of a molehill, she does.

MILLIE

(*to* BUSTER)

Some molehill. Go ahead and tell Gus about your new miracle cure for babies who like to wake up, when you prefer them to be sleepin'. Tell him how you can fix it so they catnap for days on end, if you want 'em to.

BUSTER

(*to* MILDRED)

Oh shush up, you old blind bat, will you?

MILLIE

Why you-

GUS

All right, all right. No name-calling; just tell me what happened here.

BUSTER

The baby was crying a little and I just put an itsy-bitsy, teensy-weensy bit of wine on her gums, to quiet her a little, is all.

MILLIE

Listen to him.
(in baby talk)
An itsy-bitsy, teensy-weensy bit of wine.
(back to regular voice)
He's Precious's drug connection is what he is; a fine example.
(pause)
Well, I guess it's like that proverb says: 'If you can't be a good example, be a horrible warning.'
(a beat)
We can only hope that baby Precious will grow up to see what not to grow up and be like.

GUS
(to BUSTER*)*
Buster, now you know you can't be doing that; you have to shape up. Do you think that's possible?

BUSTER

I'll try harder, Gus. I sure don't want to have to ship out.

GUS

Good.
(to MILDRED*)*
And Millie, why don't you cut Buster some slack? He's going to try harder. Don't you think it's possible for him to shape up?

MILLIE

I guess. Anything's possible this day and age. They can grow teeth in a petri dish nowadays.

MILLIE
(PRECIOUS *starts to cry.*)
Ah, she's wakin' up; must be needin' her afternoon eye-opener.
(to BUSTER*)*
Hey, Buster. Heat up some of that Dago red you got there; nothing like a nice hot toddy after a leisurely nap while getting ready for the cocktail hour.

GUS

(GUS *reaches into the cradle and picks up* PRECIOUS *who has a pink blanket wrapped around her; he begins to rock her in his arms. Just then, the doorbell RINGS. GUS looks around for someone to get the door, as he is currently busy.*)
Lilly, will you get the door for me?; my hands are kind of full.

LILLY

Okay.
(LILLIAN *walks over to the door and looks through the peephole.*)

GUS

Well, who is it?

LILLY

An undertaker.

GUS

Who?

LILLY

That same small guy who was here last year; the one in the black suit with white hair, who talks funny.

GUS

Oh, you mean Father O'Shea; I'm expecting him. I figured we couldn't have a birthday party for Precious, and most especially not her first one, without having Father Patty here to help us celebrate; let him in.

FATHER O'SHEA

(LILLIAN *opens the front door and* FATHER O'SHEA *steps inside and bows.*)
Mrs. Goodwright, what a pleasure to see you again.

LILLY

Oh, now I remember you; you're that confusing priest that drinks.

FATHER O'SHEA
(MILDRED *laughs as* LILLIAN *walks* FATHER O'SHEA *over to the dining room table; to* MILDRED)
I can understand what she means by the drinking part, it's the confusing part I don't quite understand.

MILLIE
She means your accent is confusing.

FATHER O'SHEA
Oh.
(*nods towards* BUSTER)
Buster.

BUSTER
That's right.

GUS
Good afternoon, Father Patty; glad you could make it.

FATHER O'SHEA
Wouldn't have missed it for the world. I must say last year's wedding/ birth combo was definitely the most unusual one I ever presided over. Come to think of it, it's the only one I ever presided over.

GUS
Well, have a seat, Father, while I get the baby some . . .
(*looks pointedly at* BUSTER)
milk.
(*to* LILLIAN)
Lilly, please get the good Father a glass of Irish whiskey.

LILLY
Again?

GUS
Yes, again.

(GUS *goes out into the kitchen with the baby.* FATHER O'SHEA *and* LILLIAN *take a seat at the table with* MILDRED. *Lillian pours* FATHER O'SHEA *a whiskey, then a glass of punch for herself and one for* MILDRED.)

FATHER O'SHEA
(*to* BUSTER)
Won't you be having any punch, Buster?

BUSTER
No thanks.
(*raising his glass of wine and nodding towards it*)
I'll go home with the gal that brought me to the party.

FATHER O'SHEA
Loyalty!, that's important in a man today.
(*a beat*)
Not interested in a bit of blended whiskey either, I take it?

BUSTER
Nope. Used to drink that stuff in the Navy; made me harder than Chinese algebra and grew hair on my teeth. Don't need that at my age; I'm hard enough already.
(*giggles; to* LILLIAN)
Ain't that right, Lillian?

MILLIE
Oh brother! With all the things in the world one has to worry about like nuclear proliferation and anal leakage, I need this like I need a wood tick in my eye.
(BUSTER, *with the Mother Goose mobile gift, gets up, moves over, and sits in the lounger to better assemble the mobile.*)

FATHER O'SHEA
(*somewhat embarrassed; offers a toast*)
Well then,
(*nervously coughs*)
'Here's to you and yours

220

And to mine and yours.
And if mine and ours
Ever come across you and yours,
I hope you and yours will do
As much for mine and ours
As mine and ours have done
For you and yours!'

LILLY
(*to* MILDRED)

Now tell me that ain't confusing?

MILLIE

I know; he sounds like an Irish Jesse Jackson.

FATHER O'SHEA
(*to* LILLIAN)

Now I know why you think I'm confusing and you know something, Lilly, you're right. But, that's the way the Irish are. You know what Sigmund Freud once said about the Irish, don't you?

LILLY

That they were confusing?

FATHER O'SHEA

No, but that would have been a good guess.

LILLY

Does this Freud guy work at the pharmacy with Danielle?

FATHER O'SHEA

Ah, no. He was the Father of-

MILLIE

Let's just get to the quote there, Father Patty.

FATHER O'SHEA

Roger that. What Freud said about the Irish was: 'This is one race of people for whom psychoanalysis is of no use whatsoever.'

MILLIE

A man who evidently knew what he was talkin' about . . . Now, a drink to Precious.

BUSTER
(raising his glass of wine)

No thanks; I'm still good.

FATHER O'SHEA

Here!, here!

BUSTER
(not one to be left out of whatever everyone else is toasting to)

Aye!, aye!
(They all clink their glasses together and have a taste.)

LILLY
(to MILDRED)

Whose father was he?

MILLIE

Not ours.
(GUS enters from the kitchen and takes a seat at the dining room table; he is feeding PRECIOUS, still wrapped in her blanket, some milk from a bottle.)

LILLY
(to GUS)

When are we going to have some cake, Bruce?

MILLIE
(to LILLIAN)

His name is Gus, Lilly.

LILLY

When are we going to have some cake, Gus? I'm hungry. I can't wait any longer for Danielle to get home.

GUS

Well, how about right now, Lilly? Why don't you go and get it from the kitchen?

LILLY
(while clapping her hands)

Oh goodie!

MILLIE

And take the boy wonder with you; the genius, Mr. Goodwrench, over there in the lounger, who can't even seem to put together that Mother Goose mobile he's been workin' on for the last half hour. In another half hour, Precious will be mature enough, both physically and . . .
(looking directly at BUSTER)
mentally, to put it together herself.
(pause)
Probably, along with what's left of Buster's brain.

LILLY
(LILLIAN *gets up and heads towards the kitchen; to* BUSTER)
Come on, Wolfie, let's go.

BUSTER

Where we going? To bed?

MILLIE
(to herself)
Horny old fool. Still has the desire, like an old fire horse that hears the sound of the alarm broadcasting a four-alarm blaze, but can't seem to get out of the stall to run to the fire.
(looks pitifully at BUSTER)
I just hope, if I ever end up like that, someone will be compassionate enough, to take pity on me, and put a gun to my head.

LILLY

No, Wolfie, we're going to the kitchen to get the birthday cake.

BUSTER

(BUSTER *gets up from the lounger and, just before entering the kitchen with* LILLIAN, *turns to* MILDRED)

I heard that!

MILLIE

(to herself)

I doubt that very seriously.

FATHER O'SHEA

(FATHER O'SHEA *smiles at* PRECIOUS; *to* GUS)

One year old; that's hard to imagine. Time goes so fast, and so much changes in a year.

GUS

(sadly)

I know; I know. You're preaching to the choir here, Father Patty.

(a beat; trying to lighten up the subject)

Speaking of changes, take a look here at some of Precious's baby pictures.

FATHER O'SHEA

(GUS *slides over a photo album and* FATHER O'SHEA *begins to thumb through it; to himself*)

What a beautiful baby.

(a toast to everyone at the table)

Here, here! To Precious!

MILLIE

I've got a toast.

(MILDRED *stands and raises her glass.*)

To Precious, the love of all our lives; may the love never end.

FATHER O'SHEA
(stands)
And, it never will. I think it was your American author, Richard Bach, who once said: 'Real love stories never have endings.'

GUS
(GUS *stands with* PRECIOUS.)
As Buster would say: 'Aye-aye!'

EVERYONE
(They all clank their glasses together and have a short nip. BUSTER and LILLIAN, both wearing conical party hats on their heads, enter from the kitchen carrying a birthday cake with one lit candle on it. EVERYONE joins in singing.)
'Happy Birthday to you,
Happy Birthday to you,
Happy Birthday dear Precious,
Happy Birthday to you.'
(BUSTER *and* LILLIAN *set the cake down on the table, then pick up noisemakers and blow on them while* GUS, MILDRED, *and* FATHER O'SHEA *put on party hats.)*

LILLY
If all of you don't mind, I'd like to make a birthday wish on behalf of Precious, then blow out her candle this year since she's not old enough yet.

GUS
Of course.

MILLIE
Sure.

LILLY
(LILLIAN *goes over to* GUS *and peeks into the blanket containing* PRECIOUS *and quickly sings to* PRECIOUS)
'Happy Birthday to you,

Squashed tomatoes and stew,
You look like a monkey,
And you live in a zoo.'
  (Everyone laughs and blows on noisemakers. LILLIAN *leans over the cake, closes her eyes, makes a wish, and then blows out the candle.)*

                    MILLIE
What'd you wish for, Lilly?

                    LILLY
I can't tell you, Millie. I can't tell anyone; otherwise, it won't come true.

                    GUS
Oops!

                    LILLY
What oops?

                    GUS
It feels like Precious just had a little accident. I'll be right back after I change her. Excuse me, everyone, for just a minute.
  (GUS heads into DANIELLE'S *bedroom.)*

                    MILLIE
                (to LILLIAN)
You know what we forgot?

                    LILLY
The napkins and paper plates.

                    MILLIE
Would you mind-

                    LILLY
I'll get them.
                (to BUSTER)
Wolfie.

                    226

BUSTER

(BUSTER *is hopping up and down with an urgent need to relieve himself.*)

In a minute, I gotta go see a man about a horse right now.

(BUSTER *scurries into the downstairs bathroom as the doorbell* RINGS.)

MILLIE

Geez-O. If it ain't one thing, it's another.

LILLY

Why? What's it now?

MILLIE

The doorbell; it's the doorbell now.

LILLY

Oh.

MILLIE

I'll tell you what; I'll finish getting the napkins and plates, you get the door.

LILLY

You sure you'll be okay?

FATHER O'SHEA

I'll help her, Lilly.

MILLIE

(to LILLIAN; mimicking her voice)

I'm not 'some kind of shut-in,' you know.

(back to regular voice)

Besides, I'd rather get the napkins and plates; how would I even know who's at the door?

LILLY

How will I?

MILLIE

Well, just look through the peephole; at least you'll be able to see 'em.

LILLY

Oh.

MILLIE
(*to* FATHER O'SHEA)

Come on, Father.

LILLY
(MILDRED *and* FATHER O'SHEA *head into the kitchen. LILLIAN goes over and looks through the peephole of the door; to herself*)
Oh, I know him.

BRUCE
(LILLIAN *opens the front door and in walks* BRUCE.)
Hello, Lilly. Long time no see.

LILLY
(*fumbling for his name*)

Hello . . . er . . .

BRUCE

Bruce.

LILLY

Bruce. Of course. I knew that.

BRUCE

I was just in the neighborhood and thought I'd stop by and say hello to Dani.

LILLY

She's not here right now.

BRUCE

Do you know when she'll be back?

LILLY

Soon. She'll be home soon. At least, that's what everyone keeps saying.

BRUCE

Oh. Soon, huh.

(Not knowing exactly how to explain himself, he gropes around for a conversation starter.)

I just wanted to tell her that . . . that I've had plenty of time to think things over . . . since . . . since I was last here. And, I also wanted to tell her that . . . well, that . . . I didn't get that promotion at work, the one for the Assistant Manager's job. Needless to say, I didn't get into any of the more prestigious gentlemen clubs over in the Wall Street area either. So,

(pause)

So, I'm ready. I'm ready to commit now.

(GUS *comes out of the bedroom with* PRECIOUS, *who is wrapped in her pink blanket. He sees* LILLIAN *at the door, talking to* BRUCE, *and walks over to them.)*

LILLY

(*to* GUS)

This here is a fella named Bruce. And he's ready to be committed.

GUS

Excuse me?

BRUCE

(*to* GUS)

I'm Bruce Wigley. A friend of Dani's.

GUS

(*to* BRUCE)

Oh, so this is the real Bruce. Lilly has mistakenly called me by that name on several occasions.

GUS

(to LILLIAN)

Lilly, where's Millie?

229

LILLY

In the kitchen, getting the napkins and paper plates . . . I think.

GUS

Why don't you do me a big favor and go check on her, please; see how she's doing.

LILLY

Okay.

GUS

(*to* BRUCE *as* LILLIAN *heads into the kitchen*)

I'm Gus, Dani's husband.

BRUCE

(BRUCE *is visibly shaken as this is the first he's heard that* DANIELLE *has a husband.* GUS *holds out his hand; they shake hands.*)

Oh?

GUS

We were married one year ago today, as a matter of fact.

(GUS *opens the blanket so that* BRUCE *can see* PRECIOUS'S *face.*)

And, this is Precious.

BRUCE

(BRUCE *looks at* PRECIOUS *in the blanket, smiles, then wipes a tear from his eye.*)

I can see that she's aptly named; she is Precious.

GUS

Dani named her.

BRUCE

(BRUCE *looks around the apartment, realizing what he has lost, then looks back at* GUS.)

You are a lucky man.

(*a pause*)

Yes . . . a lucky man indeed.

GUS

I know. How well I do know.
(GUS *looks around the same apartment, smiling.*)
A guy'd have to be deaf, dumb, and blind
(*nodding towards* PRECIOUS *and the apartment*)
not to realize what he's got here.

BRUCE

Indeed he would.
(BRUCE *looks at* PRECIOUS *for what he knows will be his last time.*)
Well, I better be going now. Tell Dani I'm sorry I missed her and not to worry, I'll honor our deal in the future.

GUS
(*looking at* BRUCE *somewhat perplexed*)
I thought you knew?

BRUCE

Knew? Knew what?

GUS

Dani passed away.
(*a long pause*)
A couple of days after childbirth. She lost a lot of blood . . . then, there was the infection.
(GUS *sees that* BRUCE *is totally shocked by the news and had no idea.*)
I'm sorry; you said you were a friend of Dani's. I just thought you knew.

BRUCE

No, I didn't know. We hadn't seen each other for a while. But, then again, that's the story of my life. What's that trite, little expression everyone uses? "A day late and a dollar short."

GUS

But, how true though. It seems life is what passes you by as you're making plans for the future. You turn around one day and suddenly

231

realize the moment is no longer, having slipped by without your even knowing it.

BRUCE
(sadly)
That's me, all right; always thinking I had plenty of chances in life.
(a beat; a bit puzzled)
But, Lilly. Lilly said: "She'll be home soon."

GUS
I know. She has a tendency to get confused about things and we just tell her that . . . that Dani will be home soon. That way, it's much easier on the rest of us. We don't have to constantly open that wound and go through the pain all over again.

BRUCE
I'm very sorry about Dani.

GUS
Not possibly as sorry as I am. I was her doctor. But, more than that, I was her Praetorian Guard; I was supposed to guard her from any harm. Instead, I let her down.

BRUCE
I'm sure you did your best.

GUS
Maybe, but it wasn't good enough. I've vowed to do much better with Precious.

BRUCE
And, I'm sure you will.
(BRUCE *extends his hand; they shake again.*)
Well, good-bye and good luck. I know you won't need the luck part; you already are a lucky man.
(somewhat awkwardly)
I just said that, didn't I?

GUS

(PRECIOUS *starts to cry.*)
Excuse me, I've got to put her in the crib; time for a little nap.

BRUCE

Sure. I'll let myself out.
(BRUCE *heads towards the front door while GUS sits in a chair at the dining room table and rocks* PRECIOUS *back and forth in the cradle next to him. The* LIGHTS *fade to black; a* SPOTLIGHT *holds on* BRUCE *at the front door. Another* SPOTLIGHT *holds on* GUS.)

GUS

(talking soothingly to PRECIOUS; *trying to put her to sleep)*
Your mommy would be soooo very proud of you . . . You are so very precious, just like your mom.
(to himself)
The cycle of life remains unbroken.
(BRUCE *takes one, last look at* GUS *rocking the cradle, wipes another tear from his eye, then exits. The* SPOTLIGHT, *holding on* BRUCE, *fades to black. The entire set is black except for the one* SPOTLIGHT *still holding on* GUS.)

GUS

(continuing, all choked-up; to PRECIOUS)*
Your mom was like a beautiful sunset; she was for the whole world to enjoy . . . She's really not gone, you know. She'll be with us forever; real love stories never have endings.
(GUS *gets up and walks out of the* SPOTLIGHT *into the darkness of the stage. The* SPOTLIGHT *continues to focus on the cradle, rocking back and forth.* LILLIAN *steps out of the darkness and into the* SPOTLIGHT.)

LILLY

(whispers to PRECIOUS)*
I know it'll be okay if I told you my wish.
(looks around to make sure no one else is listening)
I wished Danielle would come home soon, so we'll all be together again.

(LILLIAN *steps out of the* SPOTLIGHT *back into the darkness of the stage. The cradle rocks back and forth.* MILDRED *steps out of the darkness and into the* SPOTLIGHT.)

MILLIE
(*to* PRECIOUS)

I made a secret wish too, you little puddin'head.
(*pause*)
I wished I could see you smile, just once.

(MILDRED *starts to leave then turns around with an afterthought.*)
Happy Birthday, Precious. We're all gonna have a great life together, you'll see.

(MILDRED *kisses the fingertips of her right hand, then touches them to* PRECIOUS'S *head in the cradle.*)
(*in a whisper*)
You're '*me little buckaroo matey*' too.

(MILDRED *backs out of the* SPOTLIGHT *into the shadows of the stage. The cradle continues to rock back and forth. We hear: a gigantic* FLUSH *from the downstairs toilet.* BUSTER *steps out of the darkness and takes a seat in the chair next to the table. He begins to rock the cradle as he softly sings.*)

BUSTER
(*singing slowly and softly, like a sad lullaby*)

Ninety-Nine Bottles of Beer on the Wall,
Ninety-nine bottles of beer,
Take one down, pass it around,
Ninety-eight bottles of beer on the wall.
(*a pause; sings softer and slower as* PRECIOUS *falls asleep*)
Ninety-eight bottles of beer on the wall,
Ninety-eight bottles of beer . . .

(*The lone* SPOTLIGHT *fades to black.*)

CURTAIN SLOWLY FALLS

THE END

On Moments And Second Chances

"Sometimes second chances don't come around that often in life;
sometimes, they never come around.
But, if one does, be smart enough to use it."

D'Artagnan Bloodhawke

*****

"What is life? That's simple. It's a series of moments—some good,
some bad—all strung together and we have no other choice but to
live through them, as they're meted out—moment to moment—
until they run out. And, when the sands in the hourglass run out,
if you end up anywhere near to the person you thought you'd be,
when you were growing up, then you've done fairly well in life.
Some of us are more fortunate, in that, we get to live more moments
than others do; make sure you take advantage of every one."

D'Artagnan Bloodhawke

*****

To all my friends, loved ones, and readers:

Thanks for the moments and I wish all of you the best that life and love has to offer; may happiness follow you—wherever you may go—now and into the future. I will think of you fondly for the rest of my moments.

From moment to moment,

The Duke of D'Ar
Author's Website: www.DarBloodhawke.com

"I write to amuse myself; I write that I can dream and within myself imagine humankind ("A comedy to those who think, a tragedy to those who feel." - Horace Walpole) inhabited with diverse characters of varied strengths and unusual infirmities; I write to acknowledge to myself—and only myself—my own self-worth."

D'Artagnan Bloodhawke

******

"Dishonest people conceal their faults from
themselves as well as others,
honest people know and confess them."
(Quote by Christian Nevell Bovee
February 22, 1820-January 18, 1904
Epigrammatic New York writer.)

*****

"The more sins you confess, the more books you will sell."
(Quote by Ninon de Lenclos
10 November 1620-17 October 1705
French author, courtesan, and patron of the arts.)

*****

A Confession

I'd like to take the time to make a confession now, since you've already bought my book and can't take it back.

For those of you who have finished my book and have enjoyed it, maybe you're wondering how you can get a copy of Volume One of this book. Well, there is no Volume One; I just made that up to make you think that I've done this before.

Well, okay. Since I'm confessing all, don't look for the unabridged copy of this book either; there is none. This is it: the abridged copy, the unabridged copy, or whatever other copy you may be looking for; this is all there is. You've got the whole enchilada here.

Oh, and one last piece of information, some food for thought for you readers out there: While you're doing all this looking and wondering, don't be that confident that I even exist, much less believe what you read about me in my bio.

Well, good-bye and good luck in life and as Porky Pig used to say: "Th-th-th-that's all folks!" (For now.)

D'Artagnan Bloodhawke
Author's Website: www.DarBloodhawke.com

About The Author

Mr. *D'Artagnan Bloodhawke* is a Yaghan, born of royal blood, and claims the title of 37th Duke of D'Ar. His family tree can be traced back from the ninth century to the Archipelago of Tierra del Fuego; specifically, the island of Cape Horn—which overlooks the Strait of Magellan—where Duke Bloodhawke still resides to this day on his royal Dukedom with his older Yaghan sister, Katscan.

Duke Bloodhawke is a citizen of the world, equally dividing his time (50%) between summer stays at his dukedom on Cape Horn, living a pastoral lifestyle, herding livestock; and, on his winter estate (62% of his time)—which is on one of the floating islands in Lake Titicaca, in southern Peru—where his express and sole purpose is to escape taxes; and finally (another 73% of his time), traveling extensively to rural havens with his pet snake, Oscar, and enjoying the local activities such as: snow skiing down the Left Bank in Paris dressed in a bunny suit; actually participating (as one of the combatants) in the world renowned chicken fights in Barcelona while imbibing copious amounts of his favorite libation, Wild Turkey Bourbon; and swimming nude (with only orange, rubber, swim flippers on) in the Oceanario de Lisboa Aquarium.

Among the Duke's varied accomplishments, the top five that he is most proud of, are:

1) being born
2) being able to breathe
3) simultaneously understanding and speaking English (his only language, to date)
4) running-in-place to Rossini's William Tell Overture

5) and placing twenty-seventh, out of twenty-seven contestants, in the "Bumfuck, Egypt Camel-Turd Tossing Contest."

And lastly, Mr. Bloodhawke is a philanthropist, right up there with the likes of Carnegie, Mellon and the Rockefeller's; his favorite charity being himself, which he contributes to quite frequently.